i know
it's
over

i know
it's
over

c. k. kelly martin

random house 🏠 new york

Visit us on the Web! www.randomhouse.com/teens

Educators and librarians, for a variety of teaching tools, visit us at www.randomhouse.com/teachers

Library of Congress Cataloging-in-Publication Data
Martin, C. K. Kelly.
I know it's over / by C. K. Kelly Martin.
p.   cm.
Summary: Sixteen-year-old Nick, still trying to come to terms with his parents' divorce, experiences exhilaration and despair in his relationship with girlfriend Sasha especially when, after instigating a trial separation, she announces that she is pregnant.
ISBN 978-0-375-84566-6 (trade)—ISBN 978-0-375-94566-3 (lib. bdg.)
[1. Love—Fiction. 2. Pregnancy—Fiction. 3. Interpersonal relations—Fiction.
4. Sex—Fiction. 5. Emotional problems—Fiction. 6. Divorce—Fiction.
7. High schools—Fiction. 8. Schools—Fiction. 9. Canada—Fiction.]
I. Title. II. Title: I know it is over.
PZ7.M3644Ikn 2008
[Fic]—dc22
2007029180

Printed in the United States of America

10 9 8 7 6 5 4 3 2 1

First Edition

race on

i know
it's
over

one

THe FIrST TIMe Sasha lay spread across my bed, I felt like the world had changed. She was wearing cutoff jean shorts and a plain white T-shirt, not the tiny, cropped kind lots of girls wear— Sasha never wears that kind of stuff. "So it has to be my rules," she repeated, propping her head up and peering steadily into my eyes. I stared at her long, tan legs and thought: Don't screw this up now, Nick.

"Your rules," I agreed, and I didn't screw it up, not then anyway. We went on like that for nearly five months, stretching her rules, rewriting them together, until she told me we were getting too serious, that I was too much of a distraction and she had her whole future to think about.

"I want to worry about school," she said, crossing her arms and frowning like only Sasha can—like the world was coming to an end. "Not about trying to get on the pill."

Now I know she was wrong about the world, though—either

wrong or early—because I can live without Sasha. The past month has proven that. But I don't know how to deal with what she's telling me now.

"Say something," she says urgently, grabbing my arm and squeezing hard. "Don't do this to me, Nick."

I glance up the driveway towards my house, at the icicle lights everyone but my mom continually forgets to switch on, and wrench my arm away. Dad will be here to pick me up in less than an hour. Christmas at his place with Bridgette—that was my big problem until thirty seconds ago.

"Nick," Sasha repeats. Snow is falling on her hair and she's wearing the leather gloves her mom bought her at the end of October. She still looks beautiful to me, or at least I know she would if I could feel anything.

I run a hand through my snow-crowned hair and say, "This has to be a mistake." It's what everybody says and now I know why.

"Don't you think I checked?" Her hands close into fists. "You think I'd come over here to tell you if I didn't know for sure?"

"I don't know what you'd do, Sasha." I squint in her direction. The sky is filled with white as bright as sunshine. "I don't know you anymore, remember?"

Sasha laughs like she hates me. She turns in the direction of the road and stands there, motionless. She's prepared to wait, to become some kind of ice princess at the edge of my lawn. Not a nice fairy tale—the pregnant ex-girlfriend—but then I guess most of them aren't. Not in the beginning anyway. I glance at the dark hair spilling down the back of Sasha's coat and shiver. My heart stopped beating at the beginning of this conversation.

"So what do you want me to say?" I snap, taking a step back. Sasha laughs again, shakes her head, and stares down my street. What has she done to deserve this, that's what she's thinking, no doubt. There's snow on her lashes, her cheeks are red from the cold, and suddenly I feel like a complete asshole.

"Does anyone else know?"

"Lindsay was there when I took the test." She swivels to watch me from the corner of her eyes. It's not safe to look at me yet. She doesn't know who I'll be.

"What about your parents?"

Sasha doesn't laugh this time. Her parents aren't a joke to either of us. We spent five months arranging meetings behind their backs and coaching Lindsay and Sasha's other friends on alibis. We never even came close to getting caught. Or so I thought.

So what happened? Okay, I know what happened, but it barely qualified as a mistake. And it was once, that's all. I reach out and touch Sasha's arm—she doesn't pull away. She's more mature than I am maybe, at the very least she's had more time to think. "We should've gone—" I begin, but Sasha's way ahead of me.

"I know we should've." Her cheeks hollow out as the cold steals the word from her lips. "I wish we did. It's too late now." Our eyes lock. Freeze. Dart away. "Shit!" Sasha exclaims, her eyes on the road.

Mom is motoring up the street towards us, waving, with her extreme happy face fixed firmly in place. If there's one thing I can't deal with now, it's that lame happy holiday face. The real thing is bad enough, but Mom's imitation sucks any real life out of the holidays and reminds me of a time when they used to mean something besides trying too hard. Or maybe back then I was too impressed by stuff like company Christmas parties where the boss would dress up as a skinny Santa Claus and dole out cheap board games and action figure knockoffs. I mean, I know it wasn't perfect. I remember the arguments as well as anyone, but I also remember the four of us driving around looking at Christmas lights for weeks beforehand and my parents taking turns bringing my sister, Holland, and me shopping for each other's presents. Some of that was real. I can feel the difference.

"Sasha, I have to go," I say. "My dad's picking me up soon."

Sasha shoots me an incredulous glare. "This is important."

"Yeah, I know." I take a step back as Mom pulls into the drive. "I'll call you when I get there, okay?"

Sasha doesn't wait for my mom to get out of the car. She storms off, kicking up snow and folding her arms in front of her. I know that's a shitty thing to do—just let her go like that—but I can't help it. Well, I could, but I don't want to have to try. I keep thinking maybe she's wrong about the whole thing. Those tests can't be a hundred percent accurate—nothing is.

Mom opens the car door, ducks down in front of the passenger seat, and emerges with a collection of bags. "Nicholas, give me a hand," she says, handing me half her stash. That stupid stale smile is stretched across her face so tight she's practically mummified. "Get the door, please," she sings, all nursery rhyme–like. I'm glad I'm not going to be here for Christmas, if you want to know the truth. All the pretending gives me a massive headache, but whenever Holland or I decide to stop, Mom withdraws into a catatonic state.

I pull my keys out of my pocket, unlock the door, drop the bags down by the wall, and prepare to sprint upstairs before Mom can question me about Sasha's former presence on our lawn. Holland zooms around the corner towards me, her rainbow-colored hair back in a ponytail and her legs drowning in baggy pants, before I can make my escape. "There's a message from Babette on the machine," she mutters. "They're going to be *a little later than expected due to the inclement weather*." I laugh in spite of everything. If you

4

knew Bridgette, that's exactly how she sounds, like she was born in a country club.

"Lights," Holland says abruptly. She rushes past me to flick on the icicle lights, nearly colliding with Mom in the doorway.

"Just once I'd like to come home and find the Christmas lights already on," Mom complains. "It's Christmas Eve, for heaven's sake." She turns towards me, her lips on the verge of a new sentence: "Nicholas—"

"It's not even dark yet," I cut in, doing my best to distract her. "It's too snowy to really get dark."

Mom nods and hands her bags to Holland. "What are these?" Holland asks. *Thank you, Holland.* I kick off my shoes and rush upstairs to start packing, Holland's voice wafting up through the vent under my desk. Sometimes I wonder what Mom would do without Holland and me. Maybe she'd be that sleepwalker person all the time if she never had to pretend.

I start emptying my closet into my backpack. Way too many clothes—I need a bigger backpack. I'll have to carry Dad's present. He'll be disappointed that there's only one; he's hinted often enough about buying Bridgette something too. I told him he was lucky I was coming in the first place. Look at Holland, she hasn't spoken to him since she found out about Bridgette—or Babette, as she prefers to call her—last March.

Bridgette's not really the Babette type, though; for one thing she's too old, and for another she's got too much class. Too much class for her own good actually; she's plenty stuck-up. Still, Holland has a point. She always does. Holland's fourteen and a half going on thirty, or so she likes to think. She'd never get herself into Sasha's situation.

Shit, my hands are shaking. I drop the backpack on my bed and fan the fingers on my right hand out in front of me. I look like some kind of freak who talks to his multiple selves on the street. I don't know if I can go through with this. How could this happen to me?

I sit down in front of my bed and try to calm down. I can't think about anything, not right now. No, that's wrong. I need to think about something else entirely, something distracting. But that makes me think of Sasha too. I was just beginning to deal with the fact that I was an unwanted distraction. Do you know what it feels like to be an unwanted distraction? It was worse than never having been with Sasha. I'd sit there in law class, staring at the back of her head and thinking about all the things I would've changed about us. Things could've been right, I think. We just needed another chance. But I guess now I'll never know for sure.

There's a rapid-fire knock at my door and before I know it, Holland's bursting into my room. She wrinkles her nose and looks down at me with wide eyes. "What're you doing?" she asks. "You look like you're praying."

"Right," I say sarcastically. "I'm a closet fanatic."

"Okay, I don't want to know," Holland grumbles. "Mom sent me up to ask if you want anything to eat before you go."

"No," I say, scowling. "Get out of here." Holland studies the pile of clothes half stuffed into my backpack and furrows her eyebrows. "Are you deaf, Holland?"

She gawks back at me like I'm certifiable. "You know it's only a day and a half, Nick. You don't need all that stuff." She tries her X-ray vision out on me, but I guess it doesn't work because she says, "You are coming back, aren't you?"

"Of course I'm coming back. You think I'd stay there with Dad and Bridgette?"

"What's with all the clothes, then?" she asks suspiciously.

"Nothing." I shake my head at her like the idea is ridiculous. It is too. I'd never leave Mom and Holland behind. The guilt would tear me up. Anyway, Dad wouldn't want me with him and Bridgette all the time. They're practically living together these days and I would spoil the romantic atmosphere. Nothing like a sixteen-year-old with a pregnant ex-girlfriend to provide a reality check. How would I even tell them?

"My mind was on other things," I add. "That's all." I don't tell Holland what other things and she doesn't ask.

"Okay," she says. I guess she sounds relieved. "So no food, right?"

"I'm not hungry." I want to add that I wouldn't go anywhere like that, not without telling them first and probably not at all, but I don't. It seems like I can't say any of the right things today.

I jump up, shaking hands and all, as Holland closes the door behind her. She's right about the clothes. I don't need a bigger backpack after all. I scoop a bunch of shirts into my arms, fling them into the open closet, and collapse onto the bed. Where's Sasha now, I wonder. Will she tell her parents? I'm not ready for that. I'm not even ready to know myself.

I switch the stereo on, notch up the volume, and lie facedown on the pillow, listening to Beanie Sigel. The same thing happened to one of my so-called friends last year. Actually, the guy's pretty much an asshole. He talked his girlfriend into having an abortion. He told her it was better because no one would ever have to know and they could just keep going the way they were. I don't know what she wanted to do, but she did it and they didn't keep going either. He broke up with her two months later and then everyone knew.

I lie there thinking about that and about last summer and the months before I became a distraction and Sasha realized she had to get serious about her future. "I don't want us to get too heavy," Sasha said at the time. "Do you know what I mean?"

Sure, Sasha. But it so happens that I can't control my feelings. I still can't figure out how she did it, how she could pull the plug on us so fast that it made my head spin. We could've worked this out last month. I would've helped her if she'd given me a chance. But none of that matters now. What's done is done.

I force myself out of bed and fix my hair in the mirror. I don't want any questions, any weird looks. I have to be extra normal—the uneventful son. "Everything's fine," I'll say, and save the bad news for a phone conversation. Of course Mom won't be any easier. Will she pretend it's okay or stare through me like I've disappeared?

My hands aren't shaking anymore. I sit on the end of my bed, my backpack slung over one shoulder, and wait. The music helps a little but not enough, and finally it's time to go downstairs. If I stall too long, Mom will show up here anyway, wrap her arms around me like she's drowning, and wish me a merry Christmas. I know she doesn't want me to go. She wishes I could be like Holland—solidly on her side—but I can't.

"He broke Mom's heart," Holland said to me when they first split up two years ago. "How can you even look at him?"

But what he did has nothing to do with me. I don't want to be anyone else's conscience. "Don't drag me into it!" I shouted at her. "You're not the moral authority of this family." We said a lot of worse stuff after that and spent a long time not talking to each other. Holland doesn't talk about my father at all anymore, just Bridgette.

My phone rings at the bottom of the stairs. I wrestle it out of my backpack as Mom sidles up to me and hands me three packages wrapped in candy cane paper, each one topped with a different-colored bow. I let the phone ring, plant a quick kiss on Mom's cheek, and balance the presents under my left arm.

"Thanks," I say. "Do you want me to open them now?" My presents for her and Holland are already under the tree, waiting for Christmas morning, but Mom's always had a thing about watching people open their gifts.

"You can open them with your father," she says. "Stick them at the top of the pile." That's a jab at Dad's money, which, yes, he does have plenty of.

"Really? We can leave them till I get home if you want—open them together."

"No, no." She purses her lips as she glances through the open French doors at the Christmas tree. "It's not the same if it's not on the day."

This is news to me, but I don't have the energy for head games. "Okay, then," I tell her. Outside, a car honks. Last chance, I think. Last chance to come clean and tell her what's happened. "That's Dad," I say. "I better go."

Mom shouts for Holland to come in and say goodbye to me. Holland shuffles into the entranceway, leans against the wall, and waves. "Good luck," she calls as I step into the freezing air. She has no idea how much I need it.

Now, you'd think my dad would be a modern guy, what with the mid-life divorce and new girlfriend, but he's not. He has all the old expectations, and as soon as I get into the car, he says, "What has Holland done to her hair? I could barely recognize her."

"That's the style now," Bridgette coos in an aloe vera voice. "Body piercings and tattoos."

"It's not a big deal," I say with a scowl. I hate when Bridgette tries to sound helpful, like she has a clue about what's going on. If I want to know what fork to use, I ask Bridgette; that's about all she's good for. Sometimes I wonder what the old man could've been thinking, running off with Bridgette. Was *this* what he was missing his whole life—a decent plate setting?

"So how are you, Nicholas?" Dad asks, wisely dropping the subject.

Here's where things get tricky. My concentration isn't too good right now. Then again, my dad isn't the most perceptive guy in the world. What does he know about normal teenage behavior?

"I'm all right," I tell him. "Pretty tired. Busy day at work. I might have a nap on the way." The busy part is true enough: crowds of last-minute parents crammed into Sports 2 Go looking for in-line skates, snowboards, and team jerseys. I can never sleep in the car, though, not since I was about seven years old.

I slouch down in the backseat, letting my head flop to the side. It was Sasha who called me before. I know without looking. Why doesn't she understand that I can't talk to her now? I will call her back . . . later. She's bound to call Holland and get Dad's number if I don't.

Sasha's dad was never a big fan of mine. He wasn't loud about it, but he didn't hide it either. He'd come in and stand by the TV at nine-thirty, announcing that it was time "for Nick to return to his place of residence." It could've been funny if he'd said it in the right way, but he never did; he said it like I'd been holed up in his living room for the past seven years, living off his groceries and puking behind his couch.

I ran into him at the beach once, back in August, when Sasha was giving sailing lessons. I'd planned to hang out with her that day, in between lessons. The beach was swarming with kids baking in the sun. A bunch of them in dripping swimsuits were crowded around Sasha on the pier, waiting for her to dismiss class. They scurried off towards shore when she said goodbye, and I weaved through them, calling her name.

"Nick, my dad's here," Sasha warned, looking swiftly over my shoulder.

And there he was, striding towards us in a golf shirt and cotton pants. "Sasha, did you put on sunscreen?" he asked, handing her a tall paper cup filled with water.

"*Yes*, I put on sunscreen, Dad." She said that with a wad of impatience, but smiled as she raised the water to her mouth.

"And you're here too." Her father bunched his eyebrows as he scrutinized me. He always spoke to me in that same pinched nasal voice. "Does that mean we won't have the pleasure of your presence at dinner this evening?"

Let's get things straight, I avoided Sasha's family and house as much as possible, but this was a girl with a nine-thirty curfew who was under strict instructions not to enter my house without an appointment personally confirmed by my mother.

"Dad, stop being such a pain," Sasha lectured. Apparently she could get away with saying that kind of thing every so often as long as she played by the rules.

"So sensitive." Her father sighed, his thin lips drooping into a frown. "Don't be late for dinner." He turned and strode towards the parking lot, not looking back.

"*So sensitive*," I repeated sarcastically, once he was out of earshot. "What's his problem?"

"You know what his problem is." Sasha beamed at me like she used to, like I'd done something amazing. "Us. There's only one thing we can do to make him happy." *Break up.* Wasn't going to happen anytime soon. I can tell you, his attitude was really starting to piss me off, though. The rules were bad enough.

My towel was hanging around my shoulders, waiting to hit the sand, and I knew I should let it all go, but I couldn't. "I get that he doesn't trust me, but he doesn't have to be a total dick about it," I said.

Sasha sipped her water. "Not everybody is like your parents, Nick. Some people can't even have boyfriends at sixteen. You probably just don't know them."

No, I don't know them. I just know Sasha and how much she'd hate to disappoint her father. Will he want to protect her from this too, or will it change the way he feels about her? I don't want to be the one that changes her life like that.

I burrow into the seat, listening to Dad and Bridgette discuss Christmas dinner. Her parents are going to be there, apparently, and some old uncle of Dad's. Too many people. I don't think I have a performance like that left in me.

"Shit." I clench my fists. Bridgette and Dad glimpse back at me, my first clue I've said it out loud. My backpack is ringing again. It won't quit. It rings and rings and rings. She's redialing and redialing and she won't stop. I dig into my backpack, grab my cell, and press it to my ear.

"So you finally decided to pick up," Sasha says in a low voice.

"I'm in my dad's car. I told you I'd call you when I got there."

"You weren't very convincing. Do you know what it's like sitting here waiting for you to call me back, Nick? Every second is . . ." Her voice breaks on the last word. She swallows, pauses, and begins again, stronger: "Don't make me call you back again."

"I can turn off my phone," I threaten, and for a moment that makes me feel good. I'm not completely powerless; I can still hurt her.

"You'd do that?" Sasha asks, her voice sinking. I imagine her lying on my bed like she did that first day, only this time she's shriveling in front of me. What happened to her rules?

"No, I wouldn't," I tell her, but it's too late—Sasha's hung up. Whatever power I have can only be used in bad ways. Nothing good will happen anymore.

Bridgette and Dad are polite enough to pretend that nothing's happened. They resume their conversation, their voices more animated this time, but I can't do it. I can't pretend. "Dad, we have to stop," I say.

"We have *quite a distance* to go," Bridgette declares, flashing me her own special brand of irritation. "We're already behind schedule."

I'm still holding the silent phone in my hand. It won't ring again, not tonight, but I can't fake it a minute longer.

"Dad, we have to stop somewhere," I plead. "Now."

Dad looks over his shoulder at me, frowning. "What is it, Nick?"

"There." I point to the Burger King up ahead.

"What is it?" he demands. He veers into the fast-food parking lot and that's it—I throw my backpack over my shoulder and head for the door. I rush through Burger King, past the two waiting cashiers, and charge into the washroom, where I punch Sasha's phone number into my cell and pace the littered floor.

You'd think she'd be waiting for my call. You'd think she'd snap the phone up right away. But no, not Sasha. She knows I'm bad news. "Hello," a voice says at last. "Hello?" Her father's voice. If he doesn't hate me already, he will very soon. I'll always be the one who ruined everything for Sasha. He won't understand that she's the one too—the one who ruined everything for me.

"Can I talk to Sasha?" My voice doesn't even sound normal. I sound like a 911 call, but what difference does it make?

There's silence on the other end of the phone for a long time, then a click as though someone's hung up. The line doesn't go dead, though; Sasha's been on the line, listening to me, for some time.

"Sasha," I say. "Talk to me."

"What for?" she asks, sounding light-years away. "You have nothing to say, Nick. All this time I've been sitting here waiting for you to call and the problem didn't go away once. I'm still pregnant." She laughs and falls silent. "You see. You still have nothing to say."

"Sasha," I begin. My stomach is churning and my mind is in knots. I'm not somebody's father. This isn't how it's supposed to work. I have a part-time job in a sports store and another year and a half of high school. I don't know how to make anybody happy. I remember Sasha's father that day on the beach, bringing her water. His rules were in my way. That's how stupid I am.

The door bangs open behind me and I swing around, the phone still glued to my ear. I'm not hanging up on Sasha this time—not for anyone.

Dad stares over at me like I'm a complete stranger, the guy behind you in line at the ATM. "Nicholas, what are you doing here?" he asks, unnaturally calm. "Why don't we get back in the car?" He must've decided that I'm on drugs. He's read some article, or Bridgette has, and this is the way you're supposed to approach the whacked-out addict. No sudden movements.

"Go on," Sasha says bitterly. *"Why don't you call me back later?"*

"No." I clutch the phone harder and lower my backpack to the floor. "I'm not hanging up."

"Nicholas, what's going on here?" Dad repeats.

"We have to go back." I'm shaking on the inside, speaking through a fog. "I have to see Sasha."

On the other end of the phone, Sasha sighs. "Okay," she says slowly. "Okay, come." And I know she knows. Yes, I finally got it.

14

"She's pregnant," I say, looking him in the eye. "I have to see her now."

Dad's face falls. His eyes pop open and he rocks back and forth on his heels, speechless. This is a book he hasn't read. I know how he feels—I haven't read it either. "Dad, please," I say. *"Please."* This is the best I can do. I don't know what comes next.

Dad's lips bite the air, forming an unspoken word. The lines in his forehead deepen as he takes a stranger's step towards me. His right hand reaches down for my backpack. He lifts it up, slings it over his shoulder, and nods into the space between us.

two

THere are THree types of girls at my school: girls with high-pitched laughs that act like they're trying to get with you, even when they aren't; girls who act like they don't give a shit whether you're in the room or not; and finally, the rarest kind, girls without an act—girls who smile when they feel like it and stand next to your locker when they have something to say or when you want them to listen. That last kind is the rarest but most important. If they say something nice, you feel it; if they tell you that you're an asshole, you wonder if it's true.

I didn't think Sasha Jasinski was that kind of girl. For one thing, we barely spoke. We'd nod vaguely in each other's direction when we passed in the hall. That was about it. Sometimes I'd watch her scribble down notes in English class. She was okay to look at if you stared hard enough. No makeup or anything, but nice lips, dark eyes, and a killer body. Her concentration face, the corners of her mouth dipping and eyebrows drawn tightly together, made her look angry. I wondered if that's how she looked when she was actually pissed off. Not like I thought about her all the time; I just noticed certain things about her. For example, Ms. Raines, our English teacher, was deeply impressed with her. She'd cross her arms, her head sloping in Sasha's direction, and nod in agreement as Sasha made these intelligent observations on Shakespearean themes or whatever we happened to be discussing at that particular moment.

Anyway, I thought Sasha was a type-two girl if I ever saw one, but that didn't stop me checking her out from time to time. It didn't make me right either. See, she was as far from being a type two as any girl I've ever met.

The whole thing with us started back in June. Everyone was in a good mood because the sun had finally come out to stay, everyone except Mom. Not that I blame her. She'd obviously bought into the "till death do us part" deal. I mean, there she was with a vegetable garden, a cushy part-time job at the library, and a reasonable facsimile of the perfect family. Then Dad blew it for her by escaping to this swanky condo in Toronto. No wonder she was pissed. But the fact is, life is like that. Things start to suck when you least expect it. Like now Mom has this crappy admin job and half her waking life is ruled by Mrs. Scofield, bitch of the century.

Sometimes I can sit there and listen sympathetically to Mom's complaints. I understand that it sucks and that it helps to have someone else say it out loud for you, but then again, how many times can I say it? The drill gets a bit much, especially when nothing ever changes and whatever I say doesn't make the slightest bit of difference.

That's why I went to the mall with Nathan that night in June, although it's on the bottom of my list of appealing places to visit. My job at Sports 2 Go means I'm there enough as it is, and sometimes the fact that the mall seems like the only place to go makes me determined to stay home. But everything is situation specific, I guess, and in that particular situation—Mom itching to recap the latest evidence of Mrs. Scofield's ever-expanding ego, and Nathan sounding bored out of his skull and begging me to meet him at Courtland Place—the mall genuinely seemed like the best option.

But I had second thoughts as soon as I got to the food court. Nathan wasn't alone. He and Sasha were standing by the railing, looking down at the ground floor and talking like they'd known each other forever, which knowing Nathan was highly possible. Think of that person in your high school that gets along with everyone—whether they're a skater, a jock, or the most painful nerd in the world. Nathan's that person—the guy that's everybody's friend. He's been that guy as long as I can remember.

"Hey," I called, walking towards him and Sasha.

"Hey, Nick," Nathan replied, not offering an introduction because he knew as well as anyone that the entire population of Courtland Secondary was already known to each other—at least by name.

"Hi," Sasha said, abandoning her standard Nick Severson non-greeting. She was wearing loose cargo pants and a reasonably tight T-shirt and the minute I noticed that, she folded her arms in front of her chest as though she'd noticed too.

"So what're you doing?" Nathan asked Sasha. "You coming with us?"

"I better call Lindsay and see what's up," she said, reaching into her side pocket and pulling out her cell phone.

"Catch up with us later if she's not showing," Nathan offered. The two of us pushed off in the general direction of food. "She was supposed to meet Lindsay here, but she never showed," he explained.

"Yeah, I figured that out," I told him. I didn't mention that I wasn't in the mood for another person. Nathan is the kind of guy I could say that to, but it was too late, his offer was already out there. That makes me sound antisocial, right? Most of the time that's not true. Ask Keelor, my best friend in the universe. He'd tell you I was up for anything. Partying with Vix and the girls. No problem. Dodge math class, smoke a joint in the park, and laugh at joggers. Okay. Midnight hockey followed by endless amounts of beer, spilled in sleeping bags that'll have to be washed out the next morning. Maybe a girl next to me in the sleeping bag. Maybe not. It's all okay, most of the time. But every now and then I just want to keep things low-key. Have a quiet conversation or whatever.

Nathan and I split up in front of Taco Life and I headed towards DQ, in the mood for something's flesh. My order was in the middle of being assembled by some cranky Korean guy, who was probably a lawyer or something like that in his home country, when someone sidled up next to me and crowded my space. Why do people do that? Do they have some kind of mental retardation when it comes to personal distance?

I squinted over to check for signs of mental deficiency and was surprised to find the complete opposite. Sasha was standing beside me, looking equally uncomfortable with the proximity. "Where's Nathan?" she asked.

My eyes scoured the food court and landed on Nathan's red T-shirt in front of Gino's Pizza. "Over there." I tilted my head in his direction and glanced back at the Korean guy, who was happy enough to take my money, even though he couldn't spare a smile. See what I mean? There are times when I shouldn't be around people.

"Hey, I ordered fries—not onion rings," I told him, pointing to my full tray.

"Yes." He shook his head in aggravated agreement. "I remember. There is a new girl today. I am sorry. I will get your fries." He disappeared back to the grill to rip into the girl, leaving Sasha and me to our world of awkward distances.

"So," Sasha said. *So?* I leaned against the scrap of counter not occupied by my order and raised my eyebrows at her. A piece of her hair fell forward a bit and I swear, I almost reached out to slide it back behind her ear, just like that, as though it was the most natural thing in the world. "Well," she added. *Well* and *so.* Must be my turn to jump in and expand the conversation. But no, she managed another sentence and saved me the effort. "I'll grab us all a seat."

Off she went to complete her mission. Me, I waited for like five minutes while my order got straightened out and then the guy let me keep the onion rings too. By the time I got to the table, Nathan and Sasha were deep in conversation.

". . . call my dad," Sasha was saying. "I can never think of anything to do at the mall. That's Lindsay's department."

"Like him." Nathan pointed at me as I sat down next to him.

I made a face that demonstrated how right he was.

"So what're you doing here, then?" Sasha asked. Her long brown hair was tucked back behind her ears again, and her eyes, so dark they're practically black, were stuck on mine.

I raised my eyebrows again and motioned, with exaggerated weariness, towards Nathan.

"I guess it's unavoidable," Sasha said, smiling. "Everybody ends up here sometime."

"Twice a week at least," I told her. "I work downstairs at Sports 2 Go."

She nodded. "I haven't been in there in ages. What's it like?"

It's okay actually. The guys there are good to joke around with.

We all help each other out with the customers—make sure to throw some at whoever's lagging behind in sales that day. I always have sales to spare anyway. Practically every girl that walks through the door approaches me. Seriously. I look a lot like my dad, which is a good thing, apparently. He's got salt-and-pepper hair, but it used to be pitch-black like mine. I also have his green eyes and a lot of other stuff—his weird super-pointy elbows and his cat allergy.

I told some of that to Sasha—the work stuff—and then the three of us moved on to Nathan's job, which involves lots of chopping vegetables and rushing waiters. According to Nathan, the new waiter, some French guy named Xavier, was a real prick, acting like he was above the kitchen staff and spending more time on break than he did serving. The way Nathan complained made it sound more funny than irritating, though, unlike my mom.

"What about you?" I asked Sasha. "You working?"

Sasha eyed my onion rings hopefully. "Mind if I have some?" *Nope.* She thanked me and reached across to grab some from my tray. "Um—no, not really," she said, getting back to my question. "I babysit for some people around my neighborhood, but my parents won't let me have a real job during school. I'm teaching sailing at the lake this summer, though."

"Cool," I said. "Have you been doing that long?"

"Long as I can remember—my dad taught me." She shook her head and let out a groan. "I can't wait to start. The babysitting is such a drag. There's this one family: twin girls and an older brother. The girls are okay, but the boy . . ." She bit into another onion ring. "He's completely over-active, so he's not supposed to have any sugar. Then one night I came downstairs after putting the girls to bed and he was in the basement with a half-empty box of Cocoa Puffs, playing with his dad's saw." Nathan and I traded looks as we laughed. "Yeah," Sasha continued. "Then this other time I came down and he'd pulled the ladder out of the garage and was up on the roof."

"The roof," Nathan echoed. "That's wild."

"Yeah," Sasha said. "I don't think he means anything by it. I think his parents are just too restrictive, you know?"

"Like somebody not letting their kid have a part-time job," I offered, then wondered if Sasha would take it the wrong way and think I was putting her down, which I wasn't.

"Right." Her lips jumped up into a smile, like a signal to keep going.

"So what happens to people like that—aside from the roof climbing?" I flashed a grin back, wondering if I'd been wrong about her. Maybe she wasn't one hundred percent serious all the time. Maybe she wasn't one of those people who believed they had to play out their high school label. Sometimes I get so sick of that shit, you know what I'm saying? You don't have to talk to me because our friends are tight and you don't have to avoid me because they're not. But I know that's a hypocritical thing to think because I do it just as bad as anyone.

"I don't know." Sasha put her concentration face on. "They probably get on the honor roll, get a scholarship for a good school, and end up with a PhD—something like that."

"Yeah, probably," I agreed. "Sounds boring, though, doesn't it?" Don't get me wrong, I have okay grades. I'll get into university, without a doubt. There has to be more to life, though. I'm thinking one day I'll visit the pyramids, go on safari, get stoned in Amsterdam, and hook up with a French girl with a sexy name like Anaïs or Solange, some cool girl who walks around with a guitar on her back.

"You have a better idea?" Sasha pressed her hair back behind her ears although it hadn't come loose again. "Forget I said that," she added. "I don't want to know."

"Hey, now I'm offended," I said lightly.

"No, you're not," she countered, still smiling, and she was right. At that moment she could've said anything and not offended me, as long as she kept smiling in my direction.

Nathan grabbed the table and chuckled. "Looks like your dirty mind is showing, Nick."

Sasha wiped her fingers on her napkin. "Everybody's got a dirty mind," she said indifferently.

Tell me more. Was that my line? Instead, I leaned across the table and said, "I meant to tell you before—I really liked your story." Ms. Raines, English teacher extraordinaire, was always saying that she wanted to keep us thinking for ourselves, not just force-feed us Shakespeare. That led to a lot of creative assignments. The particular one I was talking about was supposed to be about home. No other instructions. Just a story about home. Ms. Raines read a few of them to the class after she'd marked them and Sasha's was the best of the bunch.

"Thanks," Sasha said, sounding surprised. "I liked yours better. It was so . . . I don't know . . . so natural."

Normally English isn't one of my better subjects. Obviously, I speak the language, but I'm not into picking stories apart for the sake of it and I don't give a shit about metaphors or whatever. In fact, I don't even read outside of class. Math and art come a lot easier. Somehow that story turned out all right, though. The guy in it, Terry, had quit university and was on the train home, feeling completely relieved—even though he'd pissed his parents off—because he'd finally made the decision. I thought Ms. Raines would like something like that. I didn't think I would, but I was wrong.

I meant it about Sasha's story being better, though. Way more

23

profound. Like something you'd read on an exam and afterwards there'd be questions about character motivation. Basically it was about this family immigrating to Toronto and having a tough time settling in. None of them could speak English, for one thing, and they had no idea how to get on the subway or anything.

"Mine was trying too hard," Sasha said. "Yours sounded like it really happened." She made me feel like pulling my story out and reading it over. She also made me wish we were somewhere else, somewhere I could test the vibes between us. I guess that meant she was right about dirty minds.

We didn't get into it any further that day, though. Sasha announced that she was going to call her dad to come get her and Nathan and I sat there arguing about where to go next. There are only three places in the mall that don't bore me: sports stores, entertainment/electronics stores, and the place we were sitting just then. Nathan, on the other hand, could spend an hour in the bookstore or trying on watches and holding his wrist up to me for approval.

I don't want to make him sound like a stupid stereotype or whatever. He wasn't obsessed with clothes or anything, he just enjoyed whatever he happened to be doing at any given moment in time—even if it meant eating bad fast food at Courtland Place with two people who usually ignored each other. Nathan and I had known each other since we were eleven and had played on the same hockey team for the last three years. Me, him, and Keelor, that's how it was. You play the game with someone for long enough and you know exactly what they'll do next on the ice. That's the way it was with the three of us up until this year when Nathan surprised us by packing it in. Said he didn't love the game the way he used to.

Keelor, the Courtland Cougars team captain, took it kind of

personally. To tell the truth, so did I, but I figured Nathan had other things on his mind. See, I'd noticed some things about him by then. He'd never come out and said anything, but I'd caught him giving other guys *the look*. It was always lightning-fast, but I'd seen it often enough to know it meant something. I suspected that Keelor had caught on too. So there were three of us walking around not talking about that because sometimes it's just easier not to, I guess.

The only other thing I remember about that day was Sasha leaving. Her dad called back and let her know he was out in the parking lot. "So I'll see you guys at school," she said, getting up and staring down at Nathan and me.

"See ya," I said, forcing myself not to look at her T-shirt again.

I watched her drop her cell phone into her pocket, turn, and walk away. At the time I figured we probably wouldn't really talk again anytime soon. I thought it was one of those moments in life when you get a glimpse at a possibility just as it disappears. It was too bad, I guess, but I can't say it actually bothered me much. I barely knew Sasha Jasinski, and nice-looking girls in tight T-shirts were everywhere in June.

*

three

THE LAST WEEK of school was too hot to think. I felt restless in my skin. Like summer had started without me. We were all impatient that week. Keelor, Gavin, and the rest of the guys lingered in the hallways, bouncing off the walls and each other, talking in the kind of loud voices that sound annoying when you hear them coming from someone else. Part of that was a pre-party rush. Dani was having one of her infamous sleepovers on Saturday, which meant no climbing through windows after dark. Her mom, unlike the rest of our parents, had the enlightened viewpoint that unisex sleepovers were nothing to be afraid of and that we were all, in fact, a lot more innocent than we looked.

I was more innocent than I wanted to be, that was for sure, even after countless unauthorized coed sleepovers at Gavin's, Keelor's, or Vix's. The first of those parties had begun as a casual midnight hockey game over at the arena. Victoria had come up with the inspired after-hours visitation idea—giving you some understanding of how she got her nickname, Vixen. She was after Keelor mostly, but she liked to party in general, if you know what I mean. Anyway, it was a good idea, as long as no one got caught. All we needed was someone's basement (or similarly private space) and a string of alibis. Like when one of the guys was having the party, the girls would say they were sleeping at Dani's, Vix's, or whoever's and would slip into the guy's house undetected after the rest of the family had fallen asleep. Vix's sister caught us at her house one night, but Vix had more than enough dirt on her sister's extracurricular activities to keep us all out of trouble.

So the upcoming party was on all our minds, that and general thoughts of summer freedom. I'd have enough hours at work to keep me in cash, huge amounts of unregulated time, and if I was lucky, maybe I'd even have Dani. We'd definitely been getting closer lately. We nearly always ended up huddled together in a sleeping bag at parties, and the last time I'd even convinced her to take off all her clothes. She'd made me keep my boxers on so we wouldn't go too far, but she was warm and trembling next to me and I knew that part of her wanted to do it too.

I did my best to work on that part, but she complained about everybody being there, although Keelor's sleeping bag was the only one I could see from our spot behind the couch and he was busy with Vix.

"They're probably all doing it too," I told her.

"No, they're not," she said, still letting me touch her. "They would've told me."

"Eljeunia and Gavin," I whispered. We could both hear them and it wasn't the first time.

"They could be doing anything," she said, and I knew then I'd lost. But you don't just give up, do you? Not when this completely hot girl with long blond hair is naked in your sleeping bag, her skin warm under your hands.

"Okay, how about something else, then?" I said softly.

Dani stopped breathing next to me. She knew exactly what I meant, and for a second I thought she was seriously considering it. Then she pinched my arm and whispered: "Do you ever give up?"

At least she didn't sound mad. That was something, right? "You like me," I said. "I know you do. Otherwise you wouldn't be here."

"Yeah, but the answer's still *no,* Nick."

Answers can change over time. My parents are a prime example—first *yes,* then *I don't know,* and finally, *never in a million years.* Nothing is ever final. People try to nail things down—make vows and sign contracts—but in the end they can't be regulated. So I had hope when it came to Dani. She called my house every week, always sounding really happy to talk to me, and she acted different when I was around, hyper-interested in everything about me. Sometimes I thought I'd get further with Dani if I invited someone else into my sleeping bag for a change, but I wasn't sure I could do that to her after she'd put in so much time with me.

That was the kind of thinking that had me jumpy that last week of school. There were other things in the back of my head, sure. Dad's girlfriend was becoming an unwanted presence in my life—answering his cell when they were in the car together, signing her name on my birthday card, and inviting me to come down and see them more often. Holland had the easy way with her high road. She didn't have to suffer the bullshit. There were enough people I was obliged to be nice to without adding Bridgette to the list.

Mostly I was thinking about good summer times and that party, though. And if that wasn't enough to wind me up, there were Keelor's words out in the hall. "Hey, man." He lowered his voice as I neared. "There's something I gotta tell you later." His lips arched up into a closed-mouth grin. "You'll love it."

"Tell me," I insisted.

"Later." He nodded at the surrounding gang. "This is for your ears only."

Our very own Vix made an appearance at that moment— cutting through the gathered group like she was strutting a cat-walk. You had to hand it to her, she really knew how to play it. Every last one of us was hot for her.

Keelor, always the boldest, stepped forward and tapped her miniskirted ass. "Looking good, Vix, baby. You got twenty minutes for me?"

We all erupted into laughter, instantly twice as boisterous. "Twenty minutes," Gavin said, smiling with his teeth. "Since when is that, Keelor? Trying to break your record?"

Keelor laughed as hard as anyone, and Vix, spotting one of her friends at the other end of the hall, smiled and disappeared into the crowd, catcalls trailing behind her.

Just then Sasha swung out from somewhere behind us. Nor-mally I wouldn't have said anything to her, but we'd had that con-versation at the mall only days before and I figured that warranted something a little extra.

"Hey, Sasha," I said, expecting a similar response or at least the traditional nod.

She spun to look at me, then continued to pass as though she'd thought better of it. A new low for the two of us. I didn't get it. I was positive she'd heard. Keelor scrunched up his face, offended on my behalf, and confirmed it. "She heard you, man. What a bitch."

Exactly. I felt my face getting hot. My throat was tightening the way it did before a fight. I'm not a violent person, but if you slewfoot me on the ice, you're asking for trouble. This felt just like that, like someone had kicked my skates out from under me, sending me down fast and hard.

I rushed down the hall after her and cut her off in front of Ms. Raines's English class before I had time to think. She must've been a full six inches shorter than me. My head bent down towards hers, my jaw square with my shoulders. "Sasha," I said irritably. "What? You don't say hi?"

"I didn't see you," she said, crossing her arms and clutching her notebook in front of her.

"No, you *did* see me," I corrected. She seemed angrier than I was and I had no idea why. I looked into her angry face and noted that it wasn't identical to her concentration face after all, not quite. She was pouting at me like a kid, like Holland used to when I'd been ignoring her. There was this force field of bad vibes between us, running all the way up to the ceiling.

"Okay, I did see," she said flatly. "You were all being such assholes I didn't feel like saying hello, okay?"

"What? You mean with Vix?" What else could she mean? I was stunned. What was the big deal?

"Victoria, yeah, I mean her. You're standing there laughing your ass off at Keelor being a moron and then you turn around and say hi to me like the whole thing was nothing." She glared at me like I was toilet paper, or something worse, stuck to the bottom of her shoe.

"It *was* nothing." I frowned. "If she's not offended, why should you be? We're all friends. You know that, right?" Shit. I didn't need that kind of bullshit from this girl.

"I'm just sick of it happening all the time around here."

She looked genuinely worn out, and I forgot to defend myself. "Is someone messing with you or something?"

"No." She shook her head. "Forget it, okay?" Embarrassment crept into her face as she stared past me at the open English room door.

I wanted to escape then too. I couldn't decide whether to move aside and follow her into English class or what. In the end I said the only thing that came into my head: "You going to English?"

"Yeah," she said. "You?"

"Uh-huh." We were still standing by the door, people filtering into class around us.

Sasha unfolded her arms and held her notebook down by her side. "Look, it's not just you guys specifically. It's everyone, you know? All the time. Making these comments or grabbing at girls and all that."

I guess I knew what she was talking about. A lot of guys around school were like that. I considered explaining just how close Keelor and Victoria were, but I didn't. I hated that she made me feel like defending my friends and myself, and I had a sneaking suspicion that the information wouldn't make much difference anyway. "So what did you want?" I asked. "Me to come running after you to apologize or was I never supposed to talk to you again?"

"I don't know." Sasha bit her lip and stared at my chest. "It's not like I planned this. I just . . . didn't like it." She looked lost standing there, her shield down and her eyes avoiding mine. Me, I could've stood there pawing the ground in front of her, trying to figure out whether I felt angry or guilty, but the bell pealed through the hall, jolting me into action.

"Class," I said simply, pointing over my shoulder. I made for the doorway, resentment pumping through me as I slid into my seat. People shouldn't be allowed to say things like that when they don't know you. Act all disappointed like you were being a prick when you were only kidding around. People have no right.

I was so sick of people being disappointed, you have no idea. Mom was disappointed when Dad left. Holland was disappointed when I wouldn't blow him off. Dad was disappointed that Holland wouldn't talk to him anymore and that I couldn't spend more time with him over the summer. There was an ocean of disappointment flowing cold between the four of us. Sometimes I felt like it made me numb, or maybe that's what getting older was like. Maybe pure excitement, pure happiness, and pure fear were just for kids. Maybe I was jaded.

I spied Sasha's head swiveling to glance back at me from her seat near the front of the class. She did it quick like she didn't want me to see, but I felt an invisible connection all through English— like that force field from the hall had followed us into the room and wedged itself between us. I felt it the way you feel someone following you, and I knew I was right.

I had a decision to make when the bell sounded again, and I made it fast. Sasha was on her feet already, racing towards the door. I bolted after her, determined not to lose her in the crowd. I didn't call her name; I didn't need to. She stopped about ten feet ahead of me and waited for me to catch up.

"Hi," she said. The word landed with a thud.

"Hi," I repeated. "Is that you actually talking to me?"

"You're making this awkward." Her serious brown eyes were peering into mine this time, which was a start.

"You started it." The words rolled off my tongue the way they did when a pretty girl came into Sports 2 Go. But that wasn't the right tactic to take with Sasha. Her eyes stared straight through me. *Bullshit,* they said. *You're so full of it, Nick. Who do you think you're talking to?* It was hard to say anything else with her performing that little invisibility trick on me. I was silent for a few seconds, looking for an angle, anticipating responses, and reviewing the past hour in my head. *What was I doing here? How did this happen?* "Look," I began slowly, "I guess I know what you're saying, okay? But I'm not really like that. I don't even know why I'm telling you this. So . . ." I sized up the hallway, planning my escape route. "Okay. I'm gonna go. I'll see you around."

I started to swing around, to disappear for real, but Sasha grabbed my arm. Gently like. She had little girl hands, hands that could never really stop anyone from disappearing. "Wait," she said.

I stopped, my body half turned towards the hall. I glanced down into her eyes and I could see that she hadn't planned that either, that she had no idea what to say next. She let go of my arm, trying to make the movement seem casual. "So what're you doing this summer?" she asked. "Are you going away or anything?"

I almost laughed. It was so weird, me running after her down the hall and her grabbing for my arm and trying to act like it was normal. I stole a look at Sasha's tiny hands. Her nails were cut real short, neat and functional. She wasn't trying to impress anybody with those nails, that was for sure. Dani painted her nails all the time, her toes too. She had this super-sexy belly-button ring that her mom had agreed to last summer.

"Working, you know." I shrugged, swallowing my laughter. I could feel it jiggling around underneath my skin, aching to break the air, but I wouldn't let it. I knew Sasha would hate it if I laughed at her just then, that she'd be angry and disappointed all over again. "Hanging out. No big plans." Dad had been on my back about planning weekends at his place, but Sports 2 Go was the perfect excuse. I couldn't commute from his place to Courtland in a hurry. The car trip was nearly two hours, and seeing as I'd just turned sixteen last month, I wasn't eligible for a full license for another seven months. "How about you?"

"Not much," Sasha replied. "Just what I was telling you before."

Right, the sailing. I couldn't think of a single thing to say about that. There was a big black hole surrounding our conversation. I shouldn't have chased after her in the first place. There was probably a reason we never talked. *Nothing. To. Say.* The whole thing was making me feel uptight, and that was the last thing I needed—the ruination of my pre-summer vibes. "You and Nathan should drop by the lake sometime," she continued. "I can get you into the beach for free."

"What about Keelor?"

Sasha shot me an impatient look: *Can we stop backsliding on this, Nick?* "I think not," she said, sounding like Ms. Raines, the voice of maturity and intellect.

"I'm just kidding." I smiled to prove it. "Yeah, I'll tell Nate. And you know where I am if you're looking for me." The truth was that I couldn't get a read on Sasha. Telling me I was a total dick wasn't the best way to get me to visit her at the lake. I touched Sasha's shoulder, determined to leave this time and feeling all the better for it. "Have a good summer, okay?"

"Yeah, you too." She jammed her nine-year-old-girl hands into her pockets and nodded at me.

"Yeah," I repeated, and sailed down the hallway, already recovering. Complications were not on my summer program. I wanted the complete opposite of that, to drift from one event to the next with no apologies or explanations. Pure. Unplanned. Perfect. Nobody talking me into anything or feeding me guilt trips. I wanted things easy for my sixteenth summer.

I swung by Keelor's locker on the way to Media Arts, ears ripe for whatever had put that dirty grin on his mouth. *Everybody's got a dirty mind,* that's what Sasha said at the mall. So what's wrong with thinking out loud? *Shut up,* I said to myself. *Who gives a shit what she thinks?*

"Yo." Keelor nudged my shoulder. "Wondered if I'd find you here. You disappeared in a hurry." We stopped in front of his closed locker, ready for business.

"So what's for my ears only?" I asked, shrugging off the last hour.

"Oh, man, lucky you." Keelor smiled gleefully as he hugged the news to himself. "You'll love this, man, but you can't know, okay? Act surprised when she does it."

"Keelor, what?" My voice strained like a rubber band pulled taut. I hadn't guessed this was about me; that cranked the suspense up two notches.

"Right." Keelor composed himself as best he could, which wasn't saying much. "So you want to know what I heard." He lowered his voice and slanted his head towards mine. "This comes from Vix, so it's reliable." He paused, the two of us listening for a silent drumroll. "Word is Dani's going to give you something special at the party tomorrow."

My jaw dropped. I clamped my mouth shut and gripped my notebook. "Shut up," I said incredulously. "If this is a joke . . ."

"No joke." Keelor was grinning at me with an almost-fatherly pride. *My best friend, about to receive his first blow job.* Few moments are quite so emotional. "You think I'd joke about something like that?"

"Why would she say that?" I wondered aloud. My body was humming underneath its skin, waiting.

"She wanted technical advice, from the sound of it." Keelor's hand clapped my shoulder. "You didn't hear this from me, right? Just sit back and let it happen." Keelor laughed and leaned against his locker. "You look like you're in shock, man." His eyebrows knit together. "Shit, I hope she doesn't change her mind now. That'd really be a drag."

"Yeah." I didn't say it so much as breathe it. *Yeah.* This is exactly what I meant about drifting. Things happen on their own sometimes, without a push from anybody. Answers change and then change again. Maybe this time I'd be on the right side of that. Maybe the perfect summer would start at that party: Dani in her belly-button ring, her long blond hair fanned behind her back, doing what I'd been waiting for. I leaned against the locker next to Keelor's and beamed at him, feeling like mid-July sun, about sixty-two degrees from numb.

four

Dani and I started spending some more time together after the party, nothing official—a few solo visits to her place and one trip to the movies. You could say it was partly pleasure and partly obligation. The balance seemed all right with the both of us. She wasn't the kind of person to start laying down rules as soon as things got sexual. The only thing she had to know was that I wasn't fooling around with anyone else. Hanging out with her every now and then was a good idea too. I didn't want her thinking I was abusing our friendship.

Before you start getting the wrong idea, I better make it clear that we never slept together. Other sexual activities went on, but we never did the deed. Sometimes I wondered if I really wanted to. I was a little worried that the rules would change, close in on me until we were practically engaged. I didn't want Dani becoming friends with Holland and my mom, picking out clothes for me, and calling me to complain about her summer job. I'd probably have been more excited about the idea of sleeping together if there was a guarantee against that scenario. That went along with my other worry, which was that right afterwards I'd want to do someone else, one of the long-legged girls with windblown hair that came into Sports 2 Go looking for cross-trainers. I hadn't made up my mind about that, but I didn't want to go messing it up with Dani if that turned out to be the case. Remaining relatively unattached seemed like the answer to everything.

"You don't want the girlfriend," Nathan said over the phone one night. "You just want the sex." It sounded like an accusation, but Nathan wasn't usually judgmental.

"I don't know what I want," I told him. "Maybe I'm not in a hurry to find out."

"Oh, please," Nathan said. "Of course you're in a hurry. You're just like Keelor. The two of you are natural predators."

Coming from Nathan, that wasn't a compliment. The three of us were old friends. Emphasis on the word *old*. They only saw each other in my presence now. I was the glue holding us together, or pretending to anyway. I don't know why we continued with the charade, unless it was for my sake. I was pretty sentimental about the three of us; we'd celebrated so many wins together and complained about careless plays that cost us, but we weren't just about hockey. I could count on them and they could count on me.

Keelor was great during my parents' split—a constant distraction, never letting me sit around to mope about Dad's sudden departure. At one point Mom had even asked me to stop spending so much time at Keelor's because "we need to take a little time to adjust to this as a family." She'd really pissed me off with that. Why couldn't she realize that what I was doing was helping me? Her words certainly didn't help. All they meant was the three of us sitting around realizing we were alone. I spent a lot of time on the phone and IMing Nathan, complaining about those words. He was easier to talk to than Keelor.

The three of us had our ups and downs, like anybody. Nathan had been having a rough time since he'd quit hockey. His dad was this former goalie, barrel of a guy who had no time for other guys that didn't play sports. You can guess how he took it when Nathan gave up hockey, although sometimes I wonder if his dad's attitude was the real reason he packed it in. Sometimes you do things to piss people off, even if you don't want to, even if it hurts you. If you figure it hurts them more, it feels worth it.

Most of that is beside the point, which is that I wasn't a "natural predator." I'll admit I was horny, but if I was really a predator, I'd have done it with Dani and not given it a second thought. Me, I had plenty of second thoughts. Third ones even.

"That's what you think?" I said. "Basically I'm an asshole."

"*Now you're offended.* I never said that, Nick. You're obviously just not ready for a one-on-one relationship, that's all I'm saying."

"And you're saying it like it's a bad thing." The least judgmental person I knew was judging me; of course I was offended.

"You know Keelor would've taken that comment as a compliment."

"Didn't sound like one," I snapped. "Maybe you're getting confused about who you're talking to. Maybe you want to call Keelor and catch up. It's been a while, hasn't it?"

"You know it has." Nathan sighed into the phone. "Look, maybe I'm just jealous."

"What're you talking about?"

"Well . . ." Nathan paused on the other end of the phone, masses of laughter spluttering out from his bedroom TV. "You have all this choice. You could be with Dani or you could be with one of these girls you're always meeting. It's not hard to find someone, is it? All you have to do is walk out the door and bingo, there's someone ready to'be your next girlfriend."

"I don't have a girlfriend," I cut in, completely missing the point.

"Yeah, well, whatever. You could if you wanted. You could practically have anybody, Nick."

"You could meet someone." My stomach did one of those roller-coaster dips, anticipating his reply. "Everybody likes you."

"Not the people I really like," he said. "I can't even tell them how I feel." More laughter erupted from Nathan's TV, filling the silence. He's trying to figure out if he can tell me, I thought, and I don't have a clue what to say.

"Okay," I said gravely, as though we'd decided something in that moment of silence. "Okay." *Let's get this over with.*

"That French guy I told you about at work, Xavier," he continued. "Yesterday I overheard him talking to one of the waitresses, and you know what he was saying?"

"What?" My throat dropped deeper into my stomach.

"He was saying, 'That young faggot from the kitchen keeps following me around, looking lovesick.' But I'm not, Nick." Nathan's voice chafed through the phone line. "I'm not following him around. The truth is I hate his guts. He's full of himself because he's good-looking. And that must be how he knows—he must see me staring at him, because I have been." Nathan whispered those last words. "I fucking hate him, but I can't help it."

Okay, I thought. So there it is. Out loud for the first time. "It's okay, Nate." My words lined up shoulder to shoulder, firm and steady. "Everybody has their own weird situations, right?" Like Sasha and me miscommunicating in the school hall.

"Yeah, but this is *really* weird, Nick." He sounded scared. I would be too. This was no small thing he was confessing.

"It's as weird as you let it be." I wasn't used to being on this side of the conversation with Nathan, and I didn't want to let him down. "He doesn't know anything for sure, right? You didn't say anything to him?"

"No, but he's right. I'm attracted to him."

"It doesn't matter," I insisted. "He doesn't know for sure."

"But it's not just him. It's everyone. It's . . . can I ever like anybody and show it or . . ." Nathan's voice hollowed into nothing, then began again, so soft that I had to strain to hear. "Do I have to be this neutral, sexless thing all my life?"

Silence stretched out uncomfortably between us. I hadn't thought about it like that, the way other people's restrictions could limit you. Then Nathan, sounding so close he could've been standing right next to me, said, "Did you know?"

"I wasn't sure."

"I was, but I didn't know what to do about it," he said wearily.

"So what're you gonna do now?"

Nathan laughed. "Maybe I'll try the news out on Keelor as a test run for my dad. What do you think?"

"I think Keelor might've guessed too."

"Good," Nathan declared. "That should make it easier."

I never mentioned Sasha or the lake to Nathan. I didn't forget, but I figured no further action was required on my part. Surely Sasha would run into Nathan and ask him herself eventually. Maybe he'd drop by and tell her everything, the way he'd told me, or maybe he'd keep it between the three of us awhile longer. He didn't seem to have decided on a course of action yet. He spent a lot of time at this gay and lesbian teen message board, reading about other people's issues. He told me about a different one every time we talked: the Pakistani guy whose thirteen-year-old sister came to visit him every week although his family had disowned him, an eighteen-year-old girl who was having threesomes because she had more fun with the other girls than with her boyfriend, a fourteen-year-old who'd made out with his best friend when they were drunk and was too scared to talk it out with him.

Keelor confided that the whole thing was freaking him out, that it was "a tough weight for Nathan to be dragging around, but I don't know what to say to him." Personally I didn't think it mattered so much what we said as long as we were listening. I admit some of the details were too much for me, and Nathan appeared to sense that and censor himself, like the time he started describing Xavier—how his gypsy looks and the strong Quebec accent that rolled around in the back of his throat gave Nathan the impression of "sexual ferocity."

"You said he was an asshole," I reminded him.

"He is," he admitted, then abruptly changed the subject.

Nathan's revelation was only the second surprise of the summer (Dani's change of heart being the first). I had some summer day shifts at Sports 2 Go, filling in for people on vacation. The days were lazier than the nights. There was time to restock the shelves and take extended breaks (whenever Brian, the manager, wasn't around). That probably sounds like a good thing, but in actuality it was pretty boring. Too many hours to make stupid chitchat with customers and listen to Grayson lay out the details of his latest sexual adventure. Sometimes you think you like someone only because you haven't spent enough time around him or her to learn otherwise.

Grayson was giving me the lowdown for the second time that week, oozing with overconfidence and eyeing the female customers like half the world was his to conquer. Sasha would hate this guy, I thought, nodding and frowning at him at the same time. I don't act like this. I hadn't even told anyone, aside from Keelor and Nathan, about Dani and me.

"You never tell me anything, man," Grayson said, as though he was reading my mind. "You're getting something somewhere, aren't you?" His nose twitched. "Don't let me monopolize the conversation."

"I keep things quiet," I said, matter-of-fact-like. "That's just how it is."

"Yeah, you like to be all mysterious and shit, huh? That's okay, though. It's all good."

Mysterious and shit. Yeah, that's me. I was really starting to hate Grayson. I scanned the store, searching for customers in need of mystery, etc. My eyes locked onto a female form stepping into the store. She looked in my direction and made a beeline for Grayson and me. *Sasha Jasinski,* looking tanned and relaxed in jeans and sun-lightened hair. Grayson oozed silently beside me, his presence growing more repellent as she neared.

I strode towards Sasha, smiling like she'd made my day. There were tiny yellow flowers painted onto her jeans and her feet were bare in her running shoes. She smelled like sunshine and watermelon. "Hi," I said, the two of us stopping in front of Sports 2 Go's collection of baseball hats. "How're you?"

"Good." She ran her fingers swiftly through her hair. "So how's your summer going?"

"Interesting," I said truthfully. "How's the sailing?"

"Wet." She smiled at me, enjoying her own joke. "You should come by sometime."

"You'll get me into the beach for free," I recited.

"Yeah, that's the idea." She slid her hands idly into her back pockets, watching me. "Are you guys busy?" She tilted her head to indicate the store. Grayson was ringing up a sale and one of the other guys was pointing a customer towards the punching bags. "Can you take a break? Get some ice cream or something?"

"Yeah, I guess." I hadn't entirely figured her out yet, but I thought I was starting to. She really wanted me to come to the lake. We wouldn't be having this conversation if she didn't.

I told Grayson that I was taking a break and wandered out into the mall with Sasha. "So, climb any roofs lately?" I asked, sauntering along next to her. I felt safe teasing her now that I suspected I had the upper hand.

"Not lately," she replied, stepping up to the Baskin-Robbins counter. "What flavor do you want, Nick?" She slid a ten-dollar bill across the counter.

"Uh." I peered through the glass and ordered the same thing I always order: chocolate fudge.

"Really sweet," she noted, ordering a scoop of pistachio almond for herself. "Do you have a sweet tooth?"

"Yeah, I guess." I felt her eyes on me, processing the answer as though it revealed something crucial. *Yeah, I'm a sweet tooth person and mysterious and shit.* "So I wasn't going to come to the lake," I said straight out. "I didn't think you really wanted me to." That sounds like I was being honest, but I wanted something from her; I wanted to pull her strings and watch her jump. Not very nice, but that's how it was.

"You think I was hard on you," she said, watching the girl behind the counter dig for our ice cream. "I just hate that kind of stuff. And I guess I kind of freaked." Sasha's eyes flicked towards mine, then darted away again. "I wasn't planning on asking you to the lake, but I did want you to come."

The girl behind the counter handed us our cones and we walked quietly through the mall together. Sasha snuck a look at me as we neared Sports 2 Go. "So I guess this was a bad idea," she said in an edgy voice. I turned towards her and watched her bite gingerly into her cone. I wasn't making this easy on her and now her eyes were nervous. "I saw you in the store and I really wanted to talk to you. I don't usually do things like this." A smudge of pistachio hung under her lip and she dabbed at it with her napkin. "This is probably crazy. I mean, you're with Dani, aren't you?"

She was digging herself deeper into the hole, looking more anxious by the second, and I suddenly realized that I wasn't enjoying it anymore, that I was actually beginning to feel bad for her. I shook my head and watched her thin fingers pinch the napkin.

"I'm not with Dani," I said. "We're just friends."

"Oh, but you probably don't even . . . think like that . . . you're probably . . ." She stared straight ahead. "God, I'm babbling. When you see me again, can you do me a favor and not mention this? In fact, don't even mention it now, okay? I don't know what I was thinking. You ever do something without thinking and want to take it back?"

I reached out and grazed her hand. "It's okay, Sasha." I scanned the dip in her top, not low enough to show off the valley between her breasts but low enough for me to imagine it. I thought about laying her back, pulling her V-neck down and kissing that spot. Would she taste like watermelon too? My chest tightened and I opened my mouth and forced air into my lungs.

"Thanks," she said lightly. "I guess I should let you get back to work." She stopped walking and held her ice cream out in front of her like she was tired of it.

"No, I mean it's okay," I repeated. "I've been thinking about you." It felt like the truth and I guess for the most part it was. I hadn't thought about her much since school had ended, but I'd watched her in class plenty of times. Maybe I'd even wondered what she was really like and wanted to find out. The ground between us was shifting and it was hard to say exactly what it was like before. "Look, I have to go, but we should talk about this. When're you at the lake?"

Sasha and I smiled at each other, on the verge of nervous laughter. "Tomorrow afternoon."

"Okay, so I'll see you then," I told her. "Maybe I'll bring Nathan." It occurred to me, seconds too late, that including Nathan wasn't the best idea if we wanted to talk. I guess I wasn't thinking clearly. My chest still hurt. I couldn't stop thinking about how it would feel to pull her V-neck down and expose that spot.

She bobbed her head like she'd forgotten all about Nathan. We both took a step back, then Sasha called out: "But what about Dani? I heard you two—"

"I told you—I'm not with Dani."

Sasha hesitated, her eyelashes fluttering. "Okay, I'll see you tomorrow."

I swung around and began walking in the direction of Sports 2 Go. The chocolate fudge tasted sickly sweet in my mouth. I tossed it into the nearest garbage and resisted the impulse to turn around and watch Sasha go. I pictured her in my head, striding off with her thin fingers wrapped around the unwanted pistachio. She was smiling to herself but still not sure about me. I'm not sure about you either, I thought. And by the time I gave in she was gone.

five

I DrOPPeD BY Dani's house after work that night. She shut her bedroom door behind us, grabbed my ass, and ground her pelvis against mine. Downstairs, her uncle was painting the hall and we could hear him lecturing Dani's mother in a sharp voice: "Voting is a social responsibility. It's plain lazy to opt out."

We switched Dani's TV on and fooled around quietly on top of her bed. I pulled her top off and kissed her breasts, thinking about Sasha. That wasn't what I'd planned; I thought messing around with Dani would push Sasha out of my head. Things never turn out how you plan, ever notice that? Mom was considering going back to school before Dad left. She wanted to get a degree in sociology, to expand her mind. Now she spent most of her energy trying to avoid the toxic fallout from Ms. Scofield's constant power struggles. After he left, Dad said the last thing on his mind was another relationship. Enter Bridgette.

Keeping plans to a minimum was obviously your best bet. So

why was I going to the lake tomorrow? Because Sasha liked my story? Because she made me feel like an asshole that day in June? I didn't have an answer, just an uneasy feeling that gnawed at the inside of my ribs and told me to call Nathan and ask him to come with me.

Millside Lake was man-made and surrounded by neighborhoods filled with upper-middle-class suburbanites who, thanks to their plastic surgeons and fitness trainers, grew younger every year. The majority of the lake was off-limits to swimmers; you had to pay to get wet. Nathan and I joined the line as soon we got there. "I feel like a third wheel," he said. "Wouldn't this be better without me?"

A group of gawky preteen girls were standing outside the cordoned-off area of the beach, pretending not to molest us with their eyes. "Just look at what you're missing," I said sarcastically, motioning in their direction. A freckly girl with red hair and chunks of flesh bulging out in all the wrong places gave me the finger. Her friends laughed and continued pretending not to look.

"You shouldn't piss them off," Nathan whispered. "This is your future girlfriend pool."

"And you think you have problems," I kidded back. Nathan and I made goofy faces at the girls, sending them into giggle fits.

Sasha had warned the cashier we were coming, and he stamped our hands and said Sasha would catch up with us when she finished the lesson. Nathan and I staked out a place on the beach and unrolled our towels. I felt self-conscious pulling my T-shirt off and then embarrassed about feeling that. I faked a smile, hoping he hadn't caught that moment's hesitation.

"Nick, you're not going to get weird on me, are you?" he asked, shoulders tensing. "I don't want this to change anything. I mean, I know it sort of does, but I'm still me and this doesn't have anything to do with us."

"I know," I said quickly.

"I mean, I know you're straight and that's cool. It's not like I'm going to try to convert you or something. You know that, right?"

"This conversation is making me nervous," I admitted. "I thought you were supposed to be calming me down."

"I didn't know you needed calming down." Nathan flipped over onto his stomach and let a handful of sand sift through his fingers. "You know she likes you. I could tell that day at the mall."

I shaded my eyes with my hand and squinted at him. "How could you tell?"

"Oh, you know, being gay makes me more sensitive to women's feelings," he said jokingly.

"Too bad that isn't any use to you." I turned over next to him. "So it's good knowing that you're not going to jump me or anything."

"Yeah, I thought you'd want to know." He was kidding around, trying to make me feel comfortable. "You're gorgeous and all, but I like older guys."

"Shut up," I said. Then: "Do you mean that about older guys?"

"Yeah, I think so. Look at people our age. Nobody has a clue what they want or what they're doing and if they do, they join the yearbook club or speech team and miss all the cool parties because they're too focused on achieving something and won't let themselves do anything else because they're terrified of becoming a drug addict or getting AIDS or never getting a good job. This is not a good time."

"You're not having a good time."

"No!" he protested, driving both hands into the sand. "Are you?"

"I don't know; sometimes I think I am," I said honestly. "Other times I feel like I'm just killing time until something better happens."

"See, that's exactly what I'm talking about," he said, wide eyes shooting over to mine.

"But you always seem like you're having a good time."

"Yeah, I know, I'm Mr. Positivity." He nodded. "This is just rough lately. Too many big life questions coming at me and I feel like I'm on the outside of all the good stuff happening. Like even now on this beach, it's not like I can walk around checking out guys. Somebody would break my nose. I'd be on the news."

"That sucks. I guess everyone's got different crap to deal with." I told Nathan about the day in the hallway, the whole thing with Keelor and Vix and then Sasha rushing by me like I was invisible and me making her tell me why.

Nathan turned over and propped himself up with his elbows. "I'll tell you right now that girl won't put up with any shit from you. This little arrangement you have with Dani—that's not going to happen with Sasha."

"I know."

"So do you know what you're doing?" That wasn't an accusing question; it was a checking-in sort of question. I could hear the difference in his voice. He cocked his head and grinned at me. "Everything happens to you, doesn't it?"

We went for a swim while we were waiting for Sasha, then bought a couple sodas from the snack counter and plodded back to our towels. A few minutes later I spotted her heading towards us in a high-cut one-piece swimsuit. It was strange to see her like that, even if it was a one-piece, and I was glad we weren't alone.

"Good to see you guys," she said, plopping herself down on Nathan's towel. "No trouble getting in?"

Nope, no trouble. I stared down at her legs and noticed they were completely smooth, like her underarms and everything else I could see. Her hair was damp and she gathered it together with her right hand and snapped a rubber band around it. "You've already been swimming," she observed, motioning to our wet hair.

"It's a hot day," I said. Her toes were as fine and tiny as her hands. I wanted to fold my fingers around her ankle, just to touch her somewhere safe.

"Humid, yeah," she agreed.

The three of us sat there watching the water. I was beginning to wonder if we'd sit there giving a weather report all day when Nathan launched into safe subject matter—updates on people from school and his upcoming Arizona vacation. Then, just when I was beginning to feel comfortable, he announced that he was going to take another dip and padded down to the lake.

"Nathan's great," Sasha said, staring at his back as he waded into the water. "Have you guys been friends a long time?"

"Forever. Me, him, and Keelor."

I didn't explain about the recent fallout between the two of them. I didn't feel like explaining much of anything. That was one thing about Dani—you never had to explain anything to her; she took things as they came. I asked Sasha how the sailing lesson went and listened to her describe the kids in her class. It was funny to imagine Sasha being someone's teacher. I couldn't remember the last time I taught someone anything really useful. I taught Holland how to tie her shoes, but that was years ago. My parents tried for months, then my mother decided they were putting too much pressure on her and that she'd come back and ask them when she was ready. But Holland never did ask them, she asked me, and we practiced it together until she could tie her shoes as well as I could. Holland was really weird about learning things when she was a little kid. It was like she thought she had to be perfect all the time.

Dad once said that was the difference between us—that Holland repeated something until she could do it perfectly and I assumed whatever I was doing was perfect from the start. He was angry with me when he said that. Keelor and I had taken out his mother's car and dented it trying to put it back in the garage. Mom told Dad he shouldn't say things like that because he'd give me a complex. "You criticize his confidence and glory in your own arrogance," she said. That was when I was fourteen, before he left.

"What're you thinking?" Sasha asked, lying down on Nathan's towel. "You look a million miles away. You look like that a lot, you know that?"

"I didn't know that," I said. "Maybe I have ADD or something."

Sasha turned on her side and stared at me. "Are you wondering why you showed up?"

"Of course not. It's just kinda weird being here with you asking me these questions when I hardly know you." I took a sip of warm soda and blinked at her. "I guess I'm trying to figure you out."

"So what do you want to know?" she asked.

"Just like that? Twenty questions?"

"Well, maybe not." She tried to smile, but it only part-worked. "You're making me nervous. Is that what you want?"

"You make me nervous too." Surprise cut into my voice. "Did you know I was watching you in English?" Her honesty made me daring. She looked amazing lying there on Nathan's towel, her suit clinging to her body like a sleek second skin.

"Were you really?" she said quickly.

"Yeah." I reached over and stroked her arm. It was flecked with freckles and golden from the sun. "I don't know what you want from me. What happens now that I'm here?"

Sasha laughed and looked down at her arm. "I have no idea."

"I thought you always knew what you were doing. You had all the answers in English class."

"Not really," she said. "I just like to discuss things. There're lots of classes where you don't have the chance. Math is rules. Science is fact."

"You don't like science?"

"No, I do. It's just different." She explained that her dad was a doctor and that she'd inherited his scientific brain. She said she wanted to get into forensics because there were definite answers waiting to be uncovered, but at the same time there was this other side of her personality that liked ambiguity and that's where English class came in. "I like stories that don't tell you everything, that leave you room to think. Dreams are a bit like that. You never know exactly what they mean. Like last night I had a dream that my brother had an eagle and there was a storm coming and I knew it had something to do with the bird. I was so scared. I was sitting in my room waiting for this storm to hit and nobody else in my family was even worried. It was weird. Do you remember what you dreamt last night?"

"I don't usually remember," I said. In this case I actually did remember, but the information wasn't suitable for her ears. I told her about a dream I'd had last week instead. I was skating on the biggest natural outdoor rink you can imagine, but when it was time to go home, I couldn't remember where I lived. The harder I tried to remember, the more panicked I got.

Sasha was quiet. She rolled onto her chest and said, "I wonder why it's always easier to remember the bad dreams."

"There's probably more of them," I guessed.

"I hope that's not true. Couldn't it be because they're distressing?"

"I guess it could be that. This is very philosophical for a day at the beach."

"Don't you think about stuff like that?" she asked.

"Sure." I shrugged. "It just doesn't usually come up in conversation."

Nathan returned around about then, his hair dripping and the back of his shoulders a painful shade of pink. "You're starting to fry," Sasha warned. He collapsed onto his towel next to Sasha, cold drops landing on her legs.

"Ahh!" she yelped, flipping onto her back. "Nice and cool!"

Nathan held his body over hers and shook his head vigorously, like a wet dog. Tiny drops of water landed on her swimsuit, her arms, and her shoulder blades. Sasha laughed and punched him on the shoulder. It was kind of erotic to watch and sent my brain spinning in wild directions. I'd have been jealous if I didn't know the truth about Nathan. In fact, I'd probably have been mad at him.

"I'm going in," I announced, already on my feet. I walked down to the water, waded in up to my waist, then threw myself in and swam out to the raft. That's probably where Nathan had gotten his burn, sitting on the diving raft to give me and Sasha a chance to talk. I hoisted myself onto the wooden raft and dove back into the lake. I was like a dolphin in the water; I could swim forever without getting tired, and for a while I did just that, launching myself repeatedly into the water and swimming effortlessly back to the raft. When my head was finally clear, I swam back to shore and joined Nathan and Sasha on the beach.

"We thought you were never coming back," Nathan joked.

"I was getting hot," I said. One hundred percent true.

Nathan nodded. "I have to get going. That shift at the restaurant, you know?"

No, I didn't know, but I got the picture. He was leaving us to our own devices. I wondered if Sasha had mentioned anything about me during my absence, something that had made him dream up a fictitious shift.

It was blistering on the beach by then and Sasha and I changed out of our suits and left soon after Nathan had gone. We walked around the lake, sweating in our clothes and downing gulps of bottled water from the snack counter. "There're trees on the hill up ahead," I said, pointing. "Let's sit down."

We climbed up the hill and secured a shaded bench. Sasha's face was flushed. Her nose was nearly as pink as Nathan's shoulders. "Do you have sunscreen with you?" I asked. "Looks like you should put some more on your face."

She fished some out of her straw bag and applied it carefully to her face and arms. "You're burning too," she said, holding up the lotion. "Can I?"

"Yeah." I closed my eyes and let her smooth the lotion across my face. I felt her dip in closer, like she was studying me, and then her lips were brushing against mine, feather soft. I licked her lips and slid my tongue into her mouth, really gentle and slow. Something told me I had to be careful with her, that I'd be sorry if I wasn't.

Her tongue skimmed against mine. We kissed for a while, my right hand on the back of her head and my left on her knee. Then she drew back and smiled.

"That was a surprise," I said.

"A good one, I hope."

"Yeah." I smiled and pulled her back towards me. I kissed her mouth and her neck and said, "You smell like the sun."

"You do too." She tilted her head pensively. I was about to ask her what she was thinking when she dropped her gaze and said, "I better go. My dad's picking me up at the beach at six-thirty. Do you want a ride home?"

"Okay." I was disappointed that we didn't have more time and I wasn't in a hurry to meet Sasha's dad. We walked slowly back to the beach together and stopped at the edge of the parking lot. "Give me your number," I said suddenly. "I'll call you."

"I don't have a pen." Sasha surveyed the parking lot, her eyes honing in on a silver Dodge Durango. The man in the driver's seat stared back at her. Sasha blinked and turned towards me. "Will you remember it?"

She recited her phone number and I repeated it, stamping the number into my head as we headed for her father's SUV, not really friends yet, not really anything, just two people who happened to kiss by a lake in July.

six

MOM WAS EATING a Greek salad in the kitchen, the *Globe and Mail* spread across the table and her legs resting on the chair across from her. She glanced up at me as I walked through the doorway. "Nicholas." She put down her fork and folded up the paper. "I thought you were out with Nathan for the night. There's salad and bread in the fridge."

"Maybe later." I explained that I'd come from the beach and was still too warm to be hungry.

"You got a lot of sun," she said, examining my face. "You should be careful with that. You have your father's coloring. He was always quick to burn." She had this way of talking about Dad that made him sound like a distant, rarely seen relation, which in some ways he was. "Dani called here looking for you not ten minutes ago." Mom picked up her fork and stabbed at a fat black olive. "You should invite her over sometime. I'd like to get to know your girlfriends."

"She's not my girlfriend," I said, drumming my fingers on the counter like it was no big deal. "We're just friends." Seemed like I was saying that a lot lately.

Mom frowned and popped the olive into her mouth. We'd spent tons of summer evenings eating cold salads and sliced meats for dinner since Dad left. Mom said that she could never stomach heavy meals in the warm weather. "You never tell me what's going on anymore," she complained. "You were such an open little boy. Now it's like pulling teeth to get any information from you."

"There's nothing to tell." *Open little boy.* Was I supposed to climb into her lap, hug her neck, and tell her everything that had happened on the playground today? Some things change in ten years, Mom.

"There's never anything to tell," she said. "Do you talk to your father about these things?"

"What things?" I asked, raising my voice a notch. "Can we not do this?"

"This?" Mom dropped her fork into the middle of her salad and glared at me.

"There's no problem here," I continued. "You're on my back for no reason."

"All right." She sighed, holding both palms up. "Fine, Nicholas."

"Good." I stepped quickly away from the counter. "I'll get something to eat later."

"Fine," she said again.

I went into the living room, flopped onto the couch, and grabbed the remote. Holland was sitting in one of the armchairs, earphones on and a book in her hands. She was one of the smartest people I knew and never hid it the way a lot of people do. I hoped high school wouldn't ruin that about her and turn her into one of those girls who was constantly checking out guys to make sure they were checking her out or worse, someone who thought they were better than everyone else and wouldn't let anyone with an IQ under 130 near them.

I'd assumed Sasha was like that, but she hadn't acted that way on the beach. It'd felt so amazing just to kiss her; it made me imagine how the rest of it would feel.

"Did Mom tell you Dani called?" Holland asked, looking up from her book.

"Yeah," I said impatiently. *Could I go five minutes without anyone mentioning Dani?*

"*Whatever,*" she shot back. "No need to jump down my throat."

"I'm not. It's just that Mom was giving me the third degree about her in the kitchen."

"Oh, right." Holland narrowed her eyes. "What did you tell her?"

"Nothing to tell," I insisted.

"Liar."

My lips snapped up into a smile. "Probably nothing, okay?"

"Probably nothing is the not the same as nothing, Nick."

"You're right," I said, getting down to the serious business of flicking channels. "It's still none of your business, Holland."

Dani's mom had the air conditioner switched to freezing. Thanks to Dani's uncle, her bedroom walls were newly pristine, a clean eggshell color with no lumps in sight. Their flawless appearance made the house seem even colder and I pulled Dani under the blankets with me, wondering if a little adjustment to the air conditioning at home would fix Mom's appetite and put some meat on the table.

Dani didn't ask me what I'd dreamt last night. She didn't seem interested in talking and I wasn't either. I thought everything could go on just as it had been and then I wouldn't have to worry about being careful with anyone. I thought that for about an hour and then guilt bit into me and kept biting. Maybe I should've felt guilty about kissing Sasha while I was with Dani, but that's not the way it was. I couldn't stop thinking about Sasha's smooth skin and the way she'd yelped when Nathan hovered over her. Sasha would never have kissed me if she knew about Dani. She'd think I was out for whatever I could get.

"Let's go downstairs and watch a movie or something," I suggested, sitting up in bed. "We can't stay in your room all the time." *Was I actually making an excuse to get out of bed with Dani?* Infinitely crazy. I really wanted to get out of bed, though. I was thinking stupid things, trying to figure out how I could lose the sexual stuff and keep the friendship. People do it all the time, right? Not a big deal. It's not like Dani and I were an actual couple.

"We can lie here and watch a DVD on my laptop if you want. It's nice just being naked together, don't you think?" Dani said.

Yeah, but . . .

"I think maybe we shouldn't be doing this," I began, and once I'd said that much, I couldn't stop. "It doesn't feel completely right. You should probably be with someone who wants to be in a real relationship with you." Dani sat up next to me, pulling the sheet up with her like we were in a PG movie. "I mean, I do like you. I like you a lot, but I think we're better as friends and this is going to fuck that up, don't you think?"

Dani's cheeks reddened as she stared at me. I thought she might cry and I wished that we could fast-forward through the part where I feel like a prick, but then she let the sheet fall and started pulling on her clothes. "There's someone else, right? Do I know her?" She sounded calmer than she looked and when she whirled back towards me, the redness was gone.

"I'm not even sure there's someone else."

"Does she have a name?" Dani persisted.

I reached down and gathered my boxers and T-shirt from the floor. "Don't get mad; there's nothing going between us . . ."

Dani put her hands on her hips and watched me put my clothes on, her question gaining momentum in the silence.

"It's Sasha Jasinski," I confessed, stepping into my jeans. "But we're not together or anything."

Dani's left hand dropped to her side as she grimaced. "You're making a big mistake. She's not your type. You'll be bored in two days."

"That's not a very nice thing to say." Stupid coming from me, I know. I pulled up my fly and clamped my mouth shut.

Dani scowled at me. "Just help me make the bed, Nick. Then you're free to go."

So I did. I helped her tuck in the sheets, then walked out of Dani's house and into the humidity, still in shock. Part of me was kicking myself. The other part was worried Sasha wouldn't be interested in me, although the evidence suggested otherwise. On top of that I was starving and dinner would probably be on the minimalist side again.

I walked all the way home, feelings jumbled up inside me like a can of stew. The house was deserted when I got there and the first thing I did was stick a pizza in the microwave. I ate it in front of the TV with a can of ice-cold Coke, trying not to think about the implications of what I'd just done and the second thing I did, I picked up the phone and called Sasha Jasinski.

seven

sasHa's parents HaD endless rules when it came to guys. They made lies a necessity from the start. We spent the odd night at their house for dinner or watching TV in the room off the kitchen and even fewer nights at my house, my mom happily presiding over the events. The rest of the time we were at the mall, the movies, the beach, or up in my room for the afternoon with the door shut (alibis courtesy of Lindsay and Yasmin) and Holland swearing not to rat us out. Not much happened up there anyway. Sasha made it clear that there were a lot of things she wasn't ready for. I told her I was okay with that and in some ways I was. I didn't want to rush her.

Of course it wasn't as simple as that. I really wanted her. I thought about her all the time. Sometimes I imagined us doing the stuff Dani and I had done. Other times I found myself speed-dialing Sasha's cell phone to tell her the stupidest things. Like once I called just because a song reminded me of "Unsent," Sasha's favorite Alanis Morissette song. Another time we watched *CSI* together over the phone, talking through the commercials, and at the end of the show Sasha said, "I have to babysit Saturday. You want to come by?"

"I don't know," I said dryly. "What's the rule book say on that?"

"Same thing it always says," she replied, "but the Wilkinsons won't be back until after midnight." Two and a half hours after Sasha's curfew. I liked the sound of that but was surprised she'd offered; she wasn't wild about breaking her folks' rules. "I've been thinking about the end of summer," she continued. "Between hockey, school, and everything else we probably won't have much time together."

"Probably," I agreed, not liking the thought of that. Keelor had been giving me shit for not spending more time on the ice lately. I'd only made two late-night hockey games so far that summer and my stickhandling had definitely gotten rusty. Weekly practices and a busy game schedule would take care of that in the fall, but usually I made more of an effort year-round.

"I'm thinking I'm going to miss you," she said.

I smiled into the phone. "We'll make time, right?"

For sure. There probably wouldn't be time for *CSI* over the phone, but there'd definitely be time for her. I didn't think I could go a week without spending time alone with Sasha. You spend months barely acknowledging someone's existence and then BOOM, you're emotionally addicted to her. Science would probably blame it on chemicals, genetics, or something equally logical, but it didn't feel like anything logical.

Sometimes I'd catch Sasha kissing me with her eyes open. It was a weird feeling, someone watching you from that close, and it'd usually make me laugh and have to stop.

"You're doing it again," I'd say.

One time she'd put her hands on either side of my face and replied, "I like the way you look when you're kissing—when I see your face, it's like I know how you feel."

I knew what she meant. I looked at her all the time too. The way she stared back at me made me feel like she was really seeing me. Because most people don't actually see you. People aren't very good at that generally. Most people can only recognize certain parts of someone else, not the whole picture. Maybe you're lucky if one other person can really see you. Maybe you're not meant to be able to see everybody; maybe that would be even more confusing. I don't really have a clue how that works except that I thought Sasha could see me and that I could see her.

So of course I'd spend Saturday night with her. I didn't feel bad about sneaking around like she did. Parents shouldn't force you lie to them. I get that lots of parents have a no-bedroom rule when it comes to the opposite sex. I get that nobody wants their kid driving around under the influence. A nine-thirty curfew, on the other hand, is total insanity. When I worked nights, I didn't even get home until nine-thirty.

I hung around with Keelor on Saturday afternoon. He'd hooked up with this girl named Karyn a few days after Dani's party and was no longer engaging in Vix-related activities. That put us in a similar position, but I knew that he didn't understand what I saw in Sasha. We'd spent all of one evening with him and Karyn during the last month, a polite but strained evening that made it obvious Keelor and Sasha weren't interested in getting to know each other any better than they already did.

When I'd asked Sasha about it later, she said, "He was in my math class last year, okay? I know what he's like. All those stupid sexual jokes. Everything is about sex with him. It's like he has no other way of relating to girls. He was totally like that with Karyn."

"He's not like that with you, though," I pointed out.

"He would be if I let him."

"You know, sometimes you take things too seriously," I told her. "She obviously likes him. What makes you think you can decide what's okay between other people?" I didn't tear down her incredibly boring friends. Never mind that Lindsay was obsessed with everything that was happening between Sasha and me because she had no life outside the educational system or that Yasmin believed dropping twenty pounds would solve all her problems when her attitude was the real issue.

"I'm not deciding for other people," Sasha said. "I know you've been friends a long time. I'm not saying you shouldn't be or anything. I'm just saying I don't like him. That's all."

"Well, I do, so maybe you could lay off him," I said defensively. It didn't matter whether she was right or not—only that she was bad-mouthing him.

Sasha got all serious on me, saying I shouldn't have asked if I didn't want the truth. I told her she'd never given Keelor a chance and the conversation circled around with no good place to go. It bothered me that she and Keelor hadn't hit it off, but I can't say that it surprised me; after all, I was their only common denominator. So we argued about it, yeah, but that didn't change either of our feelings and we got smart about it quick.

The solution was limited social crossover between Sasha and most of my friends and a little creativity when it came to scheduling, which was how I came to be over at Keelor's on Saturday afternoon. I brought my in-line skates and Keelor and I bladed over to Gavin's and played video games until his mom called the three of us up to the kitchen to stuff us with homemade lasagna. Gavin always seemed a little embarrassed by his mom. She would've made a perfect 1950s housewife—forever cooking, cleaning, decorating, and fussing over Gavin and his dad, with no career to distract her. Gavin's dad was a throwback too. He said things like "pardon me" and "that's the darnedest thing." He'd probably have a heart attack if he saw the photos stored on Gavin's computer. I have to say both his parents were nice, though. The worst thing you could say about them was that they tried too hard. His dad insisted on driving Keelor and me home later that night and even ended up taking me over to the Wilkinsons after he overheard me mentioning my plans to Keelor. I thanked him, saying that my girlfriend got nervous when she had to babysit late.

"It's a scary world out there," he agreed.

It was almost ten o'clock when we pulled into the driveway. I watched Gavin's dad reverse and then tapped softly on the door, scared I'd wake the kids. Sasha opened the door and smiled at me. "The coast is clear," she said, taking my hand. "Come in." I followed her down the hall and into the TV room. Some British detective show was on and Sasha grabbed the remote and turned the volume down.

We sat on the couch, the two of us occupying one seat. "So what'd you do today?" Sasha asked, throwing one of her legs over mine and burying her head in the crook of my neck.

I told her about Gavin and Keelor and she hummed in response. "What'd you do?" I asked, squeezing her thigh. My hands traced slowly over her top and she hummed into my ear, licking at it and making me crazy. I slid her under me, our bodies extended along the length of the couch, and slipped my hands under her top. Her *clothes-on* rule killed me at times. The fact that my hands could touch what I couldn't see made the experience frustratingly secretive. Touching her like that turned me on more than sharing a bed with Dani.

We did what we always did, we moved against each other until

I came. Sasha's hands stroked my back under my T-shirt. She bit her lip and continued pushing up against me. "You can't get off like that, can you?" I asked, stroking her hair. We'd never talked about it, but I could tell.

She turned her head so that her expression was half hidden. "It feels good. But no."

"So." I put my hand between her legs. "What about like this?"

She closed her eyes and let me do it, still pushing against me. I would've done anything she asked me to. It was only her rules that stopped me from making further suggestions. I had this little conversation about it in my head, wondering what was okay to say, as I touched her. You'd think doing something like that would use up all your focus, but it doesn't always. At that point I was thinking about how I wanted her to enjoy what we were doing as much as I did.

In the end I dropped my mouth close to her ear and said, "Is this how you do it when you're alone?" We'd never talked about that either. Maybe I was assuming too much, but how else was I supposed to know?

"Not exactly." A shy smile skipped across her lips. She reached down and unzipped her pants. I got hard again watching her do it. "Don't take anything off, okay?"

I nodded and slipped my hand down into her underwear. They felt like plain cotton and I thought I'd come again before she did if I didn't start concentrating. "You can show me how you like it," I whispered.

Sasha slipped her hand over mine and showed me and I concentrated. Or tried to. I concentrated as best I could considering both our hands were jammed down her pants.

Then all of a sudden this little kid was standing next to the couch in his pajamas, drinking the whole scenario in. "Elijah!"

Sasha cried. She zipped up her pants and leapt up from the couch in one swift motion. "What is it?"

The roof-climbing kid. I should've known he'd be a problem and he was. He bent over and threw up on the floor. Not a little. I mean, every single thing this kid had eaten for dinner was on that living room carpet—mounds of macaroni noodles swimming in orange goo and sprinkled with the remnants of an undeterminable green vegetable.

Some of the vomit was on his pajama top too and the kid stared down at it and the puddle in front of him, his eyes glassy from the effort of it all. "It's okay," Sasha soothed, taking his hand. "Let's get you into some new pajamas." She guided him out of the room and I stared over at that same British detective program continuing to unfold on the muted screen, my brain processing everything that had just happened.

The vomit puddle definitely put a spin on the situation. I cleaned myself up first. Then I went into the kitchen and rummaged around in the cupboards, searching for paper towels. A few minutes later I was busy blotting at Elijah's vomit, which smelled almost as rank as Keelor's hockey bag. I squirted stain remover onto the Wilkinsons' beige carpet and visualized the impeccable walls in Dani's house. Sometimes I still couldn't believe I'd broken it off with Dani to attach myself to Sasha Jasinski. Not that I regretted it, more that it surprised me that I didn't.

Sasha stepped back into the room about twenty minutes later, a blanket and pillow in her arms and Elijah two steps behind her. The kid was in fresh pajamas and his hair was sticking out in thirteen different directions—like mine when I rolled out of bed in the morning. "Hey, thanks," Sasha said, studying the damp spot on the carpet. "You can hardly see it."

She set the pillow and blanket down next to me on the couch

and put her hand on Elijah's shoulder. "He doesn't want to be in his room. I told him he could lie down here for a while." I nodded and vacated the couch. Elijah sat down, his bony knees pressed together, and stared straight ahead with hazy eyes. "My brother's clingy like that when he gets sick too," Sasha continued. "He doesn't like to be alone." Sasha's brother was seven and a half and crazy about her. He would never think of picking up a saw without permission. He and Sasha were about as far from problem children as you could get.

I sat down in an armchair and eyed Elijah. "So what do you want to watch?"

Sasha covered him with the blanket as he lay back. Then I heard the kid speak for the first time. "*Spider-Man 3*," he said clearly, pointing to the entertainment unit.

"That's a good movie," I said as Sasha slid the DVD into the machine. She sat in the other armchair and smiled over at me. I smiled back, although I was more restless than happy. The kid's eyes were glued to *Spider-Man 3* and I thought he was probably having a better night than I was by that point. I kept hoping he'd make a fast recovery or that Sasha would tell him it was time to go back to bed.

Instead the movie played on. About halfway through I gave up and said, "I better go. It's almost midnight." Elijah mumbled a goodbye in my direction. I said goodbye back and felt a bit sorry that I'd met the pale imitation instead of the Cocoa-Puffs-crunching, roof-climbing kid.

Sasha walked me to the door and flung her arms around my waist. "I missed you tonight," she said wistfully. "I really wanted to be alone for a while."

"I wanted to finish what we were doing." Saying it made the feeling stronger, and I leaned down and kissed her hard.

"Me too," she said, after we'd inched apart. Her cheeks were flushed and she glanced guiltily at the door. "You make me crazy sometimes, you know that?" She pulled me back down towards her and kissed me again. She threw her whole body into it, pressing up against me like she couldn't get enough. She tugged at my hair and licked my neck. She made *me* crazy, kissing me like that when we both knew I had to go.

"I make you crazy?" I repeated, breathing heavy. "I'm not the one holding everything back."

"How am I supposed to feel when you say something like that?" she said, pulling away. "It sets the whole relationship up wrong. Like we're on opposite sides."

"Hey, it's not like that. I'm just saying you could trust me a little." I pinched the hem of her top between my fingers. "I don't even know what you look like under this. Has anyone ever found out?"

Sasha furrowed her eyebrows like I'd just proven her point. "Why do you have to push it?"

"This is coming out wrong. I'm not trying to get you to do it." *But we could be closer in other ways.* I didn't say that last part. I dangled my hands at my sides and slowly exhaled. "It's just . . . things were going really well earlier. I really like you. I guess that makes it hard for me to slow things down in my head."

"You know how it is, Nick," she insisted. "I really like you too, but I told you from the beginning—I'm not ready for all the heavy stuff yet. Why can't we just hang out and enjoy whatever we're doing without any pressure?"

"We can," I said, and meant it. I knew I'd get home, replay the whole night in my head, and be completely pissed off with myself for opening my mouth in the first place. "You're right. I don't want there to be any pressure between us." I kissed her on the forehead, innocent as could be. "Hey, what about the kid? Will he tell his parents?"

"I'll tell him not to," she assured me. "He's okay. I think we're safe."

"Good. The last thing I need is to get in trouble for something I didn't even finish."

Sasha's lips spread into a smile. She smacked her mouth against mine, then opened the front door. I grabbed my in-line skates and stepped outside thinking how things were never this confusing with Dani. *Pure. Unplanned. Perfect.* All hope of that had disappeared at the beginning of July. I bladed home, warm summer wind at my back, and let the good and bad feelings pile up on top of each other until I didn't know what I was feeling, only that I couldn't stop and that I wasn't sure I'd want to, even if I could.

eight

Sasha was right about fall. There was barely enough time for us. I had two hockey games a week, practice, shifts at Sports 2 Go, and a steadily increasing amount of homework. Sasha and I were in the same law class and she handed her homework over for me to copy at least once a week. At first I didn't like doing it, not as a general thing but specifically because it was hers and I wasn't into the idea of using my girlfriend. After a while it became almost a necessity, like the lying. Besides, I usually lent my math homework to Keelor, which balanced the whole arrangement in my head.

Holland had started at Courtland Secondary that September and sometimes I checked up on her in the hall. She was hanging around with a bunch of smart arty kids mostly—kids that'd probably devoured the Lord of the Rings trilogy in grade school and now wrote angst-filled poetry for their blogs. Holland refused to give me the Web address for hers. She said anonymity was the whole point, allowing her to say whatever she wanted. "So what're you hiding?" I asked jokingly.

She stuck out her tongue at me and said, "You'll never know."

I figured it was nothing to worry about. She was a good kid. She could've been part of Sasha's family if it weren't for the rainbow-colored hair Mom had agreed to at the end of August.

One night, after a subdued Grayson-free shift at Sports 2 Go, I asked Holland what she thought of high school. "It's the same old thing with a few new faces," she said with a shrug. "Hannant is really good. You ever have him for history?"

"Nope." That was the word around school, though, and it definitely wasn't based on his looks. He was one of those guys who had a single thick eyebrow slashed across his face and furry, paw-like hands. "Raines is good too. Not by the book all the time, you know? Like she's really into what she's doing."

"Yeah, I heard that," Holland said. "Diego said she was the best teacher he had last year and that she had a book of poetry published a few years ago."

"You know Diego?" The only Diego at Courtland Secondary was in twelfth grade. He had a heavy Italian accent and was the star of the school soccer team. We had a couple mutual friends and ran into each other at parties.

"Small school," Holland said. "You know how it is—everybody knows everybody." Yeah, and everybody definitely knew Diego. He was one of those guys all the girls wet their pants over. Last thing I heard he was acutely serious with some girl in Quebec, which seemed to make him all the more attractive to the female side of the student body.

"Yeah, I guess."

"Anyway, high school is just a stopover," Holland added. "It has nothing to do with what's really happening."

"Let's hope not," I said grimly.

Holland cocked her head and gave me a funny look. "These are the best years of your life," she said in an auditorium voice. Then the phone rang and she snapped it up and repeated it into the phone before pressing the receiver to her ear. "For you," she said quickly, passing me the cordless.

"Nicholas, was that your sister?" Dad's voice boomed.

"She's a freak," I confirmed.

Dad chuckled dryly into the phone. He never knew what to say when it came to Holland, not since she'd decided to ignore his existence. "How's the hockey going?" he asked. "Keeping your head up?"

"You bet."

"Good, good," he said, an unmistakable spring in his voice. "I thought I'd come up and catch a game sometime. It seems like the only way to work myself into your busy schedule."

"Really?" I asked doubtfully. "When?" Dad always made a big deal of trying to get me down to Toronto to visit him, but sitting around his condo, watching the sports network and wondering what everyone in Courtland was doing, got old fast. I'd spent thirty-six hours there in the middle of August, three and a half of which were spent in a French restaurant listening to Bridgette rave about the production of *Giselle* she'd seen two days earlier. Even Dad had looked bored.

"Well, what's your game schedule look like?" Dad asked. I filled him in on the details and he said he'd come to my next home game. "I'd like to meet your girlfriend too," he added. "Why don't you ask her to come along?"

I didn't have a lot of enthusiasm for that idea. I still felt weird about having Sasha around Mom and Holland. Don't get me wrong, the three of them liked each other well enough; I was the problem. I'd never minded my friends and family mixing, but it was different with Sasha. She made me feel sort of exposed. In a way it was what I wanted, but I didn't want to feel that with everyone. You had to protect yourself a little.

Sasha got all excited about meeting my dad, even though I'd already explained what he was like. "He'll probably ask a lot of questions," I warned. "Don't feel like you have to answer everything. It's just his way of trying to get a handle on you."

"Why does he need a handle on me?" Sasha asked.

"I don't know. To try and figure out why we're together, maybe." He was always trying to figure something out. I remember this fight he and Mom had when I was about eleven. We were on our way to Niagara Falls and disembodied eighties synth music was on the car radio. I hadn't been listening to what my parents were saying, but then Mom's voice spiked up: "It's only ever your analysis of circumstances that matters, isn't it? How do you keep from getting lost in your own bullshit?"

Dad had groaned noisily, rolling his eyes as if to say, "It's not my fault that your mother's emotionally unstable. I am clearly the voice of reason."

"Don't worry about it," Sasha said, grinning at me. "We'll be evasive. Drive him crazy."

I laughed, but I knew Sasha wouldn't be like that on the day, that she'd probably answer just about any question he asked.

In fact, the questions started in the car with Dad projecting all his charm into the backseat. "Are you a hockey fan, Sasha?"

"Not much," she admitted. "I like watching Nick play, though. He's a great skater."

"He should be. He's been skating since he could walk." Dad looked over at me approvingly. "Same thing with swimming."

I mentioned Sasha's interest in sailing and Dad launched into a full-blown Q&A that continued until we got to the arena. Nervous energy danced under my skin as I swung into the dressing room. Partly it was the upcoming game, which always made me a little edgy, even when we were playing a sloppy team like the Garrytown Braves. Mostly it was the thought of Dad and Sasha's eyes on me and Sasha's willingness to please. The potential free flow of information made me more uncomfortable than it should and I threw my hockey bag down on the floor and tried to clear my head of everything but the game.

Keelor was halfway through taping his stick, the first step in his pregame ritual. He raised his chin and said, "How's the old man?"

"Same as always," I confirmed. Keelor's parents had been great about chauffeuring the two of us to and from games since Dad's departure. Mom didn't come close to pulling her weight in that department.

"Yeah?" Keelor said. "You're lucky he's not in the picture more often. Mine grounded me for life this morning."

"What for?"

"The grass in my desk." Keelor rolled his eyes. "Can you believe that? They went through my fucking desk. How's that for trust?" I shook my head and unzipped my bag as Keelor continued. "They said I've been acting erratic lately." He snickered. "Do I seem erratic to you?"

"Where'd they get that idea?" I asked. There were probably only three or four people I knew who didn't seem erratic.

"That time with Karyn in the living room," he reminded me. "And Bekker called my house about the geo classes I missed. Man, what a joke." Geography was the one class you could normally skip without fear of retribution. Mrs. Bekker was this uncoordinated, walking disaster area of a woman with a bizarre mash-up accent that translated words into unintelligible sounds like: *highgraascoppik coeefishint.*

"That's rough, man. You should tell them you and Karyn are finished. It might help."

"Oh, I told them," he said forcefully. "Didn't make any difference. I don't even think they believed me." It was the truth too. Funny how the people that have known you the longest can't recognize the truth when they hear it. Maybe that meant I didn't have anything to worry about with Sasha and Dad after all.

My head emptied out the moment I stepped onto the ice. Cold air rushed into my lungs and I forgot everything. Just us and the puck and the wide-awake feeling under my skin that said something real good was going to happen. Sometimes the game goes better when you're feeling good and sure enough, I got an assist twelve minutes into the first period, feeding the puck to Keelor in the upper slot. He took a snap shot and scored the first goal in what ended up being a hat trick. The Braves drove him into the boards all night, but Keelor didn't stop. He kept going to the net and so did I. I was just behind the goal line when I caught the Garrytown goalie napping and banked a shot in off his shoulder.

Back in the dressing room, Gavin, Keelor, and the rest of the team walked around slapping each other on the back, congratulating each other on the 4–1 win and talking about how the Braves couldn't get it together out there on the ice.

"Nick, was that your dad out there?" Gavin called from across the room.

"He's having a get-to-know-you session with Sasha," Keelor confirmed. An elbow pad sailed through the air between us as Gavin groaned sympathetically. I lobbed the pad back in the general direction it'd come from and began unlacing my skates, in a hurry to get the rest of the night over with. At least Bridgette hadn't made the trip. I didn't think I could endure another ballet lecture, not politely anyway.

And polite I was, listening to Dad and Sasha chat about science, politics, and the depletion of the ozone layer. I dove in and out of the conversation while checking out the Toronto Maple Leafs game on the monitor across the restaurant. "Do you ever think of giving it up?" Dad said, suddenly focused on me. "Hockey seems to keep you very busy. You want to keep your grades up for university, you know."

"I know that." This was the part of the evening where he began to demonstrate fatherly concern for my well-being. *Got it, Dad. Could we move on to the next act?* "I'd give up my job before I'd give up hockey."

"So why not do that?" he asked.

I focused a level gaze in his direction. "Because I need the money." Mom's job and the child support payments covered the basics, but since when did the basics get you anywhere?

Dad raised his eyebrows at me before shifting his gaze to Sasha. "Do you have a part-time job too?"

"I do a lot of babysitting," Sasha piped up, "but the pay is lousy."

"And there's the sick kids and power saws," I reminded her.

"Right," Sasha said, eyes dancing. I asked her how our young friend Elijah was lately and for a few seconds it felt as though it was just the two of sitting there in that wooden booth, letting the conversation wander effortlessly back and forth between us. I actually missed her when Dad's voice joined in again.

All in all, the evening wasn't too bad. Things never go wrong at the moment you expect them to. When you're completely relaxed, oblivious to any potential dangers, that's when bad things happen.

Someone should flick you in the head and tell you to keep your head up when they see you walking around like that.

Sasha's parents insisted on having Dad in for coffee when we dropped her off. Mrs. Jasinski had a good look at him, like she was trying to memorize his features for a police description. "You two look so much alike," she commented. "You must hear that all the time." *Uh-huh.* Then Mr. Jasinski asked about Dad's job as a city planner, which provided plenty of fuel for conversation.

"They seem like a nice family," Dad said in the car later. *Yup.* "And Sasha is a bright girl." *Uh-huh.* "Nicholas." That last word hung in the air as Dad fixed his stare on me. "Is everything okay with the two of you?" *Sure it was.* "What I mean is—you're being careful, aren't you?"

Being careful? My head snapped up before I could stop it. That was a conversation I didn't want to have for so many reasons. For one thing, it was none of his business what happened between me and my girlfriend. For another, the topic was premature and I didn't want him to know that either. The fact that we weren't sleeping together was as much personal information as if we had been.

"Everything's fine, Dad," I said. "You don't have to do this."

"I'm sure I don't," he continued, eyes back on the road. "But I still think I should. Just because we don't see each other all the time doesn't mean that I don't want to be involved in your life. You can always talk to me. I hope you know that."

"Thanks," I said abruptly. That was a good thing to hear, but I didn't want to go there. Nathan was the only person getting any information on the subject and I didn't even tell him much. Mostly it was just Sasha and me working things out as we went along and the new rules, clothes optional, were working out just fine.

"So just let me get it out then, okay?" Dad's voice was weirdly conscientious, like he was afraid he'd mess up his lines. "A lot of young people have sex without considering the consequences, but there are a lot of things to worry about—diseases and pregnancy—and you need to act responsibly, for both your sakes. You have to take care of the girl you're with. Even if she says she's on the pill or having her period. Got it?" I nodded like my life depended on it, embarrassment scratching at the inside of my stomach. "You don't want to find yourself in a complicated situation until you're ready to deal with it. So condoms all the time, right?"

"I hear you," I said in a low voice. A tangled weed was growing inside me; its pointed leaves tickled the lining of my stomach. I glanced out the car window and noticed, with a shallow breath of relief, that we were two blocks from my house.

"Okay." Dad nodded. "Good."

Neither of us said anything until we pulled into the driveway. I thanked Dad for coming to the game and grabbed my hockey bag from the trunk. "I miss watching you play," he said. The two of us were standing beside the car and that weed poked up into my throat, threatening to choke me. Sometimes I missed the way things were too, but there was no point in getting worked up about it.

"You don't have to miss it," I told him. "It's still happening."

"Right," Dad said lightly. "You're absolutely right." He reached into his wallet and handed me two crisp fifty-dollar bills. "Safe sex money."

"Okay." I was still staring at the fresh bills in my hand. "Thanks." I shoved them down into my back pocket. In my head I was already telling Sasha and she was saying: "I can't believe you let him think that."

"Give us a call," Dad said, getting into the car. "We'd love to see you again soon." *We.* I reminded myself to give them a call the next time a new ballet opened. How would I sleep at night without a full costume and cast description? Dad honked as he reversed out of the driveway and I hauled my hockey bag into the house and IMed Sasha every word.

Sasha has this teddy bear named Toby on her bed, a real raggedy thing with stitches in its stomach. I first saw him when she gave me the official tour of her house back in July. "How long have you had that thing?" I asked. "Does he get to sleep with you at night?" I knew the answer before she opened her mouth. "That's so cute," I sang, wrapping my arms around her in the doorway. "You're so cute."

That girl had her entire history stored in her bedroom—sailing trophies, picture books with inscriptions from godparents and old aunts, even her baby album. "Shouldn't your mom have this?" I asked, flipping through the album.

"We have loads of family albums in the living room." Sasha twirled her hair around her finger. "This one is mine, for when I leave home. It's funny, you know. . . ." She glanced down at a picture of her toddler self, darting across a maroon carpet. "They don't even feel like me."

"I think that when I look at mine too." There's one in particular. I'm about three and I'm wearing these dark brown cords I was crazy about at the time. It's winter and I'm staring down at the snow like I'm mesmerized. I wish I could remember exactly what I was feeling when that picture was taken, but I can't. It's like Sasha said, like it's not even me.

"Oh, you have to show me yours," Sasha begged. "All of them."

"No way," I kidded, but I actually wanted to. Especially that one.

Sasha and I never had a moment alone at her house. Either her brother, Peter, was hopping into the TV room on one foot, telling us what had happened at school that day, or we were sitting at the kitchen table, sandwiched between her parents. It was a round table, too small for five, and I never felt right sitting there—I felt like an overgrown foster child—and that feeling made me quiet.

The five of us were sitting there, all scrunched together, one night near the beginning of October. We were having chicken and rice and Sasha's parents were talking about building an extension onto the house, while Peter methodically scooped up one grain of rice at a time and swallowed, a process that seemed like it would take a hundred years. My cell started vibrating in my pocket, but picking it up in the middle of dinner would probably count as a personality flaw so I ignored it. A couple minutes later the kitchen phone rang and Mrs. Jasinski continued chatting as she grabbed the receiver from the wall.

She offered a gracious hello and then held the phone out. "That's actually for you, Nick," she said. "Someone named Nathan."

I jumped up and took the phone, conscious of four pairs of eyes on me. "Hey, Nate," I said quietly into the receiver, "I'm sort of in the middle of something here."

"I know," Nathan said. "I'm sorry, but I really need to talk to you right now. Holland told me you were there. It really . . ." Nathan's voice cut out. "It can't wait. I told my dad and . . . I need to see you, okay?"

"Yeah, sure." My blood was rushing under my skin, but I didn't want to give off any signs of anxiety. Everyone's eyes were back on their plates, but I could sense the whole family listening. "Where are you?"

"At the mall." Nathan barked out a high-pitched laugh. "I couldn't think of where else to go."

"Okay. Give me a few minutes to get there. I'll see you in the food court."

"Okay," Nathan said faintly.

"Hey, it's gonna be okay, Nate. Just wait for me, right?"

"I'm waiting," he confirmed, and then he was gone.

All eyes zeroed back in on me. "Is everything all right?" Mrs. Jasinski asked. She looked concerned and that made me like her more.

"It's my friend. I have to go."

"Do you need a ride?" Mr. Jasinski was already pushing away from the table.

"It's okay," I told him. "You're in the middle of dinner." I could just imagine the scene in the car—Sasha's dad staring expectantly over at me, waiting for me to explain what the emergency was. I wouldn't even blame him; I'd probably want to know too.

Sasha walked me to the door and squeezed my arm. "Call me when you get home," she said.

I walked down to the end of her street, fishing for change in my pocket. There was a bus stop around the corner and with any luck a city bus would swing by soon. An old woman in a long cardigan was waiting too. She looked through me, making me feel like a juvenile delinquent. "Do you know when the bus will be here?" I asked. She shook her head mutely, still avoiding eye contact. "Do they come by often?" I persisted. Ditto on that.

When the bus arrived ten minutes later, it had an NYC logo painted on its side that the Courtland bus company hadn't bothered to paint over and I glanced back over at her, determined to score a positive response. "You headed for New York City too?" I asked with a neighborly smile. The woman glared at me and stepped towards the curb. I started to wonder if she had a couple screws loose, but she began chatting, quite sanely, with the bus driver as soon as the doors had closed behind us.

Fifteen minutes later I was racing through Courtland Place.

Nathan was sitting at a table in the food court, pale and alone. I slid into the seat across from him and plunked my hands down on the table. "Sorry I took so long. Are you eating anything?" He wasn't, but I didn't know what else to say. "Do you want me to get you something?"

"I'm not hungry," Nathan said into his palm.

"So can we talk here?" I lowered my voice. "What happened?"

"I got tired of being chickenshit so I told him the truth and . . ." Nathan scanned the immediate area. He rested his head in his hands, his fingers hooked around his ears. "He said that it was just a phase, like an experimental thing that would pass. I told him it wasn't like that—that I'd always been this way, as long as I could remember."

"As long as you can remember," I repeated. "Like when you were six?"

"Always," he confirmed. "Before I even thought of what it was called. I always knew there was something different." I nodded encouragingly, thinking of the two of us at eleven, skateboarding at the park, and of him knowing, even then. "But he won't let it be that way. He said he won't accept that coming from me at sixteen and that he doesn't want to hear another word about it. He said when I get older and move out, I'll be able to do whatever I want but not now. His house. His rules."

"Maybe he just needs time," I offered. "It has to be a shock."

"It wasn't a shock to you." Nathan sighed. "You know how he is, Nick. He thinks it's weak somehow." Nathan squinted down at the table, his eyes lined with red, and I knew that we had to get moving before he lost it in the middle of the food court.

"Come on." I reached across the table and bumped his arm, reminding him that I was still there. "Let's go back to my house."

"I don't know." He looked up at me with shining eyes. "I don't want to talk to anyone else."

"They'll leave us alone," I promised. "We'll hang out in my room. Come on." I stood first. Nathan rubbed his eyes hard before hauling himself to his feet. I felt drained watching him. I wanted to tell his dad that Nathan was fine the way he was and that *he* was the one that needed to change. There was way too much macho bullshit going on at Nathan's house all the time. It made me glad to have my parents. If I told my dad I was gay, he'd probably just look scared and hand over more safe sex money.

I wondered how Nathan's mom would've reacted. She died of cancer when Nathan was eight and his dad didn't like to talk about her. I was sure his dad had never sat Nathan down and said, "We need to take a little time to adjust to this as a family."

Nathan glanced wearily over at me as he matched my stride. "Thanks," he said, hunching over like he was bracing against the cold. "I didn't know what to do."

Nathan had more friends than anybody I knew. There were so many people he could've called, but maybe he wasn't sure they'd understand. I wasn't sure I understood one hundred percent either, but I knew I'd be there no matter what.

He'd do the same for me. He always has.

nine

NATHAN ENDED UP staying with us for four days. Mom made him call his house and leave a message about where he was and it took Nate's dad three days to phone back. They had a huge fight over the phone and Nathan said he wouldn't pretend to be something he wasn't and hung up. His dad came with the car the next day. My mom put her arm around Nathan's shoulders and asked if he would at least try to talk to his father. Nathan's dad had dark shadows under his eyes and he spoke to Nate alone in the kitchen. They left together forty-five minutes later.

When I asked Nathan what'd happened, he said, "He told me he loved me. He never says that."

"What about his rules?"

"I don't know," he replied. "He just said the most important thing was that I come home."

Sasha came over once while Nathan was with us. He told her

everything that he'd told me over the summer, including the stuff about Xavier, and she said, "You know all the really good-looking guys are trouble." They both looked pointedly over at me, grins creeping across their faces.

"Shut up," I protested, breaking into a smile too.

"You need a nice guy," she continued. "The good-looking ones expect you to fall all over them. You have to do all the chasing. And then there's the sexual expectations." She poked me in the ribs.

"Sexual expectations are good," Nathan said keenly. "I have sexual expectations." He forced his features into a serious expression and added, "With the right guy, of course."

We laughed at that, but it still felt serious. Watching Sasha with Nate made me aware of how restrained I was. She was completely natural about the whole thing. She hugged Nathan and said, "I'm sorry this is so difficult when it shouldn't be anything." She rubbed his back. "Anybody who matters will be okay with it in the end. Even your dad."

That was hard for me to imagine; for Nathan it must've been near impossible. But maybe she was right. After all, he did tell Nathan he loved him. Love does strange things to you sometimes. It can twist you into saying and doing things that you know you'll regret and still, you do them.

I didn't spend my dad's safe sex money. I put it in my camera box, on the top shelf in my closet along with a pack of condoms I'd bought at the beginning of summer when I thought it might happen with Dani. I'd even practiced putting one on so I wouldn't fumble around like an idiot when the time came. Only the time didn't arrive, not then.

Of course I never forgot the condoms were there. I was conscious of them every time Sasha was in my room, but I never mentioned them. I didn't want her to think I had a timetable in my head; I wanted to be the patient boyfriend. Most of the time I was surprisingly good at that. The more I liked her, the easier it got.

She was so beautiful naked that it almost hurt to look at her. Sometimes I'd watch myself touch her, as though I was standing over my own shoulder, and hardly believe I was allowed to do those things with her. Sometimes I felt so lucky that the feeling almost made me sick. Then I'd wonder if it was because those moments alone never lasted long enough, if it was like having a drop of water when you were dying of thirst.

Maybe I wouldn't feel so crazy if I could have more, but there was no way to work that out. Normal life swallowed up most of my time and those days with Nathan took an even bigger chunk. Sasha and I talked on the phone, IMed, and saw each other whenever we could, usually in the presence of family or friends. One time Nathan's dad let him borrow the car and five of us (Sasha, Lindsay, Yasmin, Nathan, and I) went bowling. Yasmin talked too loudly and Lindsay kept ushering Sasha away to discuss some secret crush, but it was still a pretty good night. Everything was pretty okay at the time, except that I was still crazy.

When Sasha stood by my desk at the end of a Wednesday afternoon law class and asked if she could come over for a while, I beamed at her like a toothpaste commercial. We rushed back to my house after school and headed straight for my bedroom. Holland came home five minutes later and blasted Metric through her speakers. The music was so loud that she'd probably never even discover we were next door, but I got up, banged on her door, and told her to leave us alone, just in case. She was used to me doing that by then and she just nodded, moving her head in time to the music.

Sasha and I started peeling off each other's clothes. She was wearing this preppy white V-neck with a blue collar and she had blue bikini briefs on under her pants. I was already poking out of my unzipped jeans and she slid her hand into my boxers and said, "When was this last time we did this? It feels like so long ago."

"Nine days," I said, adding it up in my head as I pulled down her underwear. "Way too long."

Sasha smiled and pulled me nearer. "I missed it too."

I felt so close to her that afternoon on my bed, closer than I'd ever felt before. Everything was right between us. I wanted her so much that I couldn't stop shaking and I knew we could end that feeling without the whole thing, like we'd done before, but I didn't want to. "I have condoms in the closet," I said softly, running my fingers over her nipples. "Do you want to try?"

Sasha's eyes opened wide. It was bright in my room and her pupils were tiny. "You know when I do that, it'll be with you."

"I know. I just want you so bad. I think about you all the time." I rested my right hand along her rib cage, my chest tight. "Not just sexually. I think about you all the time, you know? I think I'm going crazy."

Sasha laughed gently. She reached up and threaded her fingers through my hair. "If that's going crazy, then I'm crazy too." She sat up and slipped her tongue into my mouth. I thought that was the end of it, but she put her hand on my chest and stopped kissing me. "Okay," she said. "Get them."

I got up and stepped towards the closet, trying not to look shocked. I guess I never thought she'd actually say yes, not for months and months, maybe longer. I tore the package open as I walked back to the bed and was about to turn away again when it occurred to me that if we were going to do it, I shouldn't be shy about putting the condom on.

Sasha watched me do it. She lay back and spread her legs and I positioned myself between them, wishing that I'd done it with Dani so I wouldn't feel so nervous.

I pushed slowly into her. It wasn't easy. She was really tight down there. She gasped under her breath and I looked into her eyes. "Do you want me to stop?"

"No." She had that concentration look on her face, almost like a frown.

I pushed in deeper, still feeling her frown up at me. Then I started moving, as gently as I could, but I couldn't enjoy it. "I'm hurting you," I said.

"Keep going," she told me, her voice like cut glass.

So I kept going, but it didn't get any better. I felt like I was torturing her and that stepped up the pressure to finish. But I couldn't. Not with her looking at me like that. Everyone knows the first time usually isn't any good for a girl, but I thought it would be okay for me. The truth is I didn't even get off. In the end I just stopped. My hard-on disappeared the moment it hit the air and I pulled off the condom and stared down at Sasha.

Music was still booming through the wall and I felt empty. I grabbed my clothes from the floor and began putting them back on. Sasha didn't move. "You know you should've told me if you didn't really want to do it," I said.

"What're you talking about?" Sasha's face went blank. It was like I didn't even know her. She could've been practically anyone.

"You were just lying there the entire time. You looked like you hated it."

"What did you expect?" she cried. "It was my first time."

"Yeah," I said, "and you were so obviously not into it. It ruined it."

Sasha sat up in bed and then I noticed it—a spot of blood on my striped sheets. My chest tightened again. I pointed down and said, "Do you want me to get you something?"

Sasha peered down at the spot. I thought she was going to tell me what an asshole I was being, but she mumbled, "I guess you better."

I grabbed one of Holland's pads from the bathroom and handed it to Sasha. She had her clothes on by then and she brushed past me and into the bathroom. I closed the door behind her and sat on the edge of the bed, hating myself.

She gazed down at me as she swept back into the room, that blank expression hiding whatever she was feeling. I should've apologized right then, but I couldn't do it; I could barely look at her. "I better go," she said dully. "Your mom will be home soon."

"Do you want me to walk you?" I asked, although it was the last thing I wanted to do.

"It's okay," she said. "It's still light out."

"Okay." I walked her to the front door. It killed me to do it. Sometimes I think something must be really wrong with me. It shouldn't be that hard to apologize when you know you're wrong. But I didn't want to think about it anymore. I thought I'd feel better if Sasha wasn't standing there next to me.

I did one thing right. I put my hands on her shoulders and kissed her forehead before she left. Then I went upstairs, pulled the bottom sheet off my bed, and washed the blood off in the bathroom sink. I threw the wet sheet into the back of my closet and grabbed a new one from the hall closet. I felt like a complete fugitive doing it; I was convinced Holland would bound into the hall and give me the third degree, but she never left her room.

I didn't know what to do with myself after that. I went downstairs and flipped through zillions of TV channels. My stomach growled, but I wasn't remotely hungry. I kept my hand on the remote. *Judge Judy, Dr. Phil,* and an ancient *Sabrina, the Teenage Witch* repeat flickered before my eyes. It was enough to make anyone sick.

Finally I grabbed the phone and called Keelor. "Hey," he said. "What's up?" His voice sounded the same as always and that was exactly what I needed.

"Bored," I told him. "I'm on my way over."

"Cool. We can watch the game." Right, the Leafs were playing the New York Rangers at seven. It'd slipped my mind somewhere between losing my virginity and walking my girlfriend to the door.

I wrote a note to Mom, stuck it on the kitchen table, and bladed over to Keelor's house. His dad answered the door and sent me straight up to Keelor's room. He hadn't been quite as friendly lately and I wondered if it had something to do with Keelor's weed. Actually, I really could've used some just then. I seriously needed to unwind.

"Does your dad think I'm your dealer or something?" I joked.

"It's not you," Keelor assured me. "He's still pissed with me. He thinks I'm two steps away from being a crack addict." If you knew Keelor like I did, you'd realize how messed up that thinking was. Keelor liked to keep his head on fairly straight. We both stuck to weed and alcohol. "Do you mind if we watch the game up here? I'm trying to keep a low profile around the house."

"Sure." We grabbed pizza slices from Gino's across the street and settled into his beanbag chairs to watch the game.

His dad knocked at the door just before the start of the game. "Are you two coming down to watch on the plasma?" he asked. The 46 inch down in the basement was reserved for hockey during the season. Keelor's entire family were big fans. His mom shouted louder than his dad during the games and his twelve-year-old brother played defense for the Pee Wee league.

I shrugged, letting Keelor know that it was up to him. "Yeah, all right," he said.

It should've been a tense first period. The Leafs' first-string goalie was out with a knee injury, but their backup kept them knotted at 0–0 despite being outshot ten to three. Keelor's mom thought she was in the stands. She screeched encouragement at the screen, giving me a massive headache. Normally her enthusiasm wouldn't bother me, but I was having trouble concentrating. Sasha kept jumping into my head, looking at me like I was a stranger. I could barely keep up with the game.

During the intermission I broke down and told Keelor I needed a few minutes to make a call. "Did you two have a fight or something?" he asked, sizing the situation up in a heartbeat.

"Something like that," I replied, and bolted up to his room.

I tried Sasha's cell first, but it was no surprise when she didn't answer. I took a deep breath and dialed her parents' number. Mrs. Jasinski picked up and went to get Sasha. A few seconds later she was back on the line saying, "Nick, she's just started her homework. Can she call you back later?"

"Sure," I said anxiously. I hadn't expected Sasha to talk to me in the first place, but it still felt like a shock. I started to explain that I wasn't at home, but Sasha could get me on my cell.

"All right, then," her mother said. "Maybe you'll hear from her later."

Maybe later. Just like that. *Maybe later or maybe not.* Would you talk to someone who didn't even walk you home afterwards? What the fuck was I thinking?

I went down to the basement and told Keelor I had to go.

He stood up, tapped my arm, and led me out of the room. "She'll wait, Nick. Relax. Stay and watch the game."

"No." I'd already made up my mind. "I have to talk to her tonight."

Keelor leaned back against the wall and sighed like I was a lost cause. "You're really letting this girl get to you, man. Don't you see it? It's too much, Nick. You're not married, you know. You can watch a game once in a while."

"You don't know what you're talking about." I was getting worked up and I didn't want to. I needed to be calm when I talked to Sasha. "I barely even see her outside school."

"Yeah, but look at you. You're acting like it's the end of the world here. Everybody fights, Nick, but you gotta stay cool."

"Why?" I folded my arms in front of me. "Why do I have to stay cool? You think it's better not to give a shit about anything?"

"Who says I don't give a shit about anything?" he said loudly. "I'm only saying this because it's you and I don't like to see you in knots. You've been different ever since you started seeing Sasha. It's like you're someone else."

"I'm not someone else," I protested. "This is me." I unfolded my arms and lowered my voice. "I know you don't like her, but I do."

Keelor pushed off the wall, frustration in his eyes. "It doesn't have anything to do with me not liking her. I just think maybe you like her a little too much."

Or maybe I was just doing a shitty job of handling it. "I have to go."

"Okay," Keelor said. "Come back if it doesn't work out—or if it does or whatever. We can talk about it." He jutted out his chin as he smiled. "Nathan doesn't have the market cornered on that, you know."

I thanked him and bladed over to Sasha's house, my stomach stuck in my throat the entire time. It would've been so much easier to apologize when I'd had the chance.

Sasha's mom answered the front door. "Nick, you're persistent," she declared, obviously surprised to see me.

"I won't stay long," I promised. "I just need to talk to Sasha for a minute."

Mrs. Jasinski glanced hesitantly over her shoulder. "Wait there." She disappeared into the house and I overheard her say: "He seems upset. Are you two fighting?"

Sasha whispered something back. Fifteen paralyzing seconds later she came to the door. Her hair was in a ponytail and she was wearing plaid pajama bottoms and a black sweatshirt. "This isn't good, Nick," she said under her breath. "My mom is asking questions."

"Sorry," I told her. "Can I come in?"

"I'm busy now," she said. She smelled like watermelon and I thought about her coming home and taking a shower. I wondered if she was still bleeding.

"Just for a few minutes? I won't be able to sleep tonight if I don't talk to you." Sasha shrugged like that wouldn't bother her. "Are you okay?" I continued. "I mean, at my house you were—"

"Actually, I feel like shit." She said that so coldly that I actually shivered.

"Me too. Are you going to let me in?"

"I don't want to talk," she said. "Do you still want to come in?"

"I still want to come in."

We walked through the hallway and into the empty kitchen. I was so grateful to be inside her house that it made me nauseous. Sasha pulled a chair away from the table and sat down, scratching at her plaid-covered legs. I sat next to her, sweat pooling at the back of my neck as I whispered, "Sasha, I'm really sorry."

"You're sorry now?" she said, her face blank. "That doesn't make any sense, Nick."

"Yeah, I know." I touched her arm. "But I am. I couldn't stop thinking about you. Can we go outside?" I motioned to the sliding door.

Sasha shrugged and slid the door open. Her parents would

really wonder now, but I couldn't worry about that; I had to talk to her in private.

We stood outside, staring wordlessly in at the warm glow of the kitchen. "That was so shitty, you have no idea," she said finally, her cheeks puffing out. "And then you let me leave like it was nothing to you." I winced and kept listening. "I ruined it. That's what you said."

"I know that's not true," I said quietly. "*I* ruined it. I don't know what my problem is." Sasha's mom stared out from the kitchen, looking displeased. Her dad would probably be next, ordering us to come back inside. "I just felt really bad before—like it was my fault that it wasn't any good. I mean, I couldn't even finish. We could still be there, waiting. It was never going to happen and you . . ." I gulped down oxygen and forced myself to continue. "You're amazing. Everything about you. The way you are with other people. The way you are about yourself. Just everything and . . ." Sasha was looking deep into my eyes; I wanted to disappear. "It was like I wasn't good enough for you, like I was the wrong person for you to be doing that with." I shrugged helplessly. "I'm really sorry."

Sasha smoothed her palm against her cheek, her forehead creasing. "Look, I wanted to be with you because it's you. Don't you get that?"

"I wish I could take it all back." I would've done anything to take the entire day back and make it happen right, but my brain was a blob of cottage cheese. I could hardly string a sentence together. "It should've been special and instead I acted like a loser. I don't know what else to say. I'm sorry."

We stood there in her backyard, watching each other in silence until Mr. Jasinski opened the sliding door and poked his head out. "It's getting late," he said. "I want you inside in five minutes, Sasha."

He motioned to her pajamas. "You're not even properly dressed to be out there."

"Five minutes," she said dutifully. Mr. Jasinski pulled the door closed and left the kitchen. Sasha pressed her hand to her head and turned towards me. "I have to go."

"Can I see you soon?" I asked. I felt better for getting everything out in the open, but that didn't necessarily fix anything.

"Call me, okay? We'll talk about it." She took a step towards the door, then reached back and touched my sleeve so delicately that it made me flinch. "I don't know what you expected. I thought it only mattered that it was us."

Me too. How did I ever forget that in the first place?

ten

THE NEXT TWO weeks were a blur of serious discussions, long pauses, and front door kisses. Hockey, school, and work happened in the background. We lost one game but won three. I did my own law homework and survived. I don't even know how to describe it. It was kind of like Sasha and I went back to the very beginning but with bad karma. One night we watched TV with Mom and Holland and froze the minute they left the room, like it was the worst thing in the world to be left alone.

It probably sounds worse than it was. We were still together. We still kissed goodbye at the end of the night. One time we actually made her family dinner. Okay, it was only pasta and garlic bread, but it was dinner and it wasn't half bad. It's not even that I minded us not being alone anymore; it was the self-consciousness that bothered me. Even kissing was weird the first few times after that day.

Nathan noticed and asked what was up with us. I told him that we'd done it and wished we hadn't and he didn't ask why. Sasha told Lindsay everything and Lindsay acted like I was a serial killer for a week. At first I felt really weird about it, but Sasha said she had to talk to someone. Lindsay advised her never to sleep with me again and Sasha said she didn't intend to. I already knew that. I didn't even want to do it again; I just wanted to go back to the way things were.

Dad had said that I could always talk to him. Imagine me phoning him up and telling him about Sasha and me. A guaranteed conversation stopper.

Some things are better left unsaid and sometimes you just get tired of talking. Take Nathan. He'd gone very quiet on the gay thing lately. His dad wanted to turn off the lights and make the issue disappear. He had this bizarre idea that Nathan could lock up his identity for the next two years. At first we'd talked about that a lot, how weird it was that someone could say he loved you and wanted the best for you while essentially rejecting who you were. After a while it got so we were having the same conversation over and over, kind of like Sasha and me with the sex fiasco.

"I'm too young to be this bored with myself," Nathan complained over lunch at the mall one Saturday. He set his chili down and rapped the table. "This is what a rut sounds like, Nick. Why do you put up with me?"

"Like I have a choice," I kidded. Then, to take the emphasis off his dad for once: "Whatever happened with that Xavier guy?"

"Nothing. Still an asshole. Probably still thinks I'm lusting after him too." He swallowed a spoonful of chili and added, "Which I am, but he's straight. You know Courtland: homosexual population of three."

"Two," I corrected. "Dakota is bi." She and Jeremy Eastman were the only out members of the school Gay-Straight Alliance, although there was constant conjecture about Ms. Navarro, the GSA advisor. "You know there's gotta be more, though—we just don't know about them yet."

"Probably all the wrong people." Nathan's voice dropped to a whisper. "Like, none of the athletes."

It was around about this stage of the conversation that I always started to get edgy, as though specifics made Nathan's homosexuality too real. Sometimes I wondered how I'd react when he actually hooked up with someone, if I could stand to hear the details.

"You can't categorize people by whether they're into sports or not," I told him. "That's what your dad does and you know it's bullshit."

Nathan scraped his front teeth across his lip. "You're right. I don't know what I'm talking about. It's just that I can't let myself get my hopes up about anyone. You're really lucky with Sasha, you know."

"I know." I believed that more every day, despite the awkward pauses and sober discussions we'd been having recently.

"I can't imagine what it's like to feel so connected to someone," he added.

"You'll know. It'll happen." My head skipped back through our conversation and snagged on the word *athletes*. "But exactly who are we talking about anyway? Who's the athlete?"

Nathan paused before stirring his chili and telling me I had an overactive imagination.

"Bullshit!" I sang, curiosity edging out nerves. "It's somebody I know, isn't it? Come on, Nate. I told you about Sasha before it went anywhere."

"Man, this is too big a deal now." Nathan dropped his spoon and stared at me like he wanted to burn a hole in the middle of my forehead. "You're a pain in the ass sometimes, Severson, you know that?" He blinked heavily and slouched in his seat. "Diego, okay? I was talking about Diego—not that I like him, just that he's good-looking and not full of himself."

"That's a popular opinion," I said, trying to act like it was no big deal. "I think Holland might have a thing for him too." I'd noticed them talking in the hallway a few times. The last time Holland had glared over at me like I'd stumbled across her diary.

"Then I'm sure she knows he's with that girl in Quebec and that he's used to girls throwing themselves at him," Nathan said definitively. "Temptation has been tried and failed."

I finished my lunch, told Nathan I'd see him later, and headed back to Sports 2 Go. A bunch of us were going to Lindsay's Halloween party later that night and Nathan had agreed to play chauffeur. His dad was all right about letting him use the car as long as he approved of who Nathan was with and where he was going and let me tell you, there wasn't a parent on earth who could object to a party thrown by Lindsay. The event was bound to be composed of board games, finger foods, and a prize for best costume.

Anybody will tell you that I don't do costumes. Even the coolest costume, in my opinion, is too lame for words. Bobbing for apples, which had a high likelihood of occurring at the party by virtue of Lindsay being Lindsay and not knowing any better, was worse. My only hope for the party was that Sasha and I could relax a little.

Sasha, of course, was really into the costume idea and that was part of what I liked about her. She'd tolerate bobbing for apples for Lindsay's sake, but she was genuinely excited about dressing up like someone else for the night. She was so cute about it; she wouldn't even tell me who or what she was going as. I had to wait until she climbed into Nathan's car, black streaks in her hair and her body cloaked in a ridiculously long trench coat that covered her ankles.

"I thought you said you were going to wear a costume," she said, eyeing my clothes.

"No, you said I should wear a costume." I was wearing a gray crewneck sweater over a white T-shirt and the same jeans I'd worn the day before.

Nathan shot a look over his shoulder and said, "Come on, Sasha. Don't you know Nick is too cool for costumes?"

"You too?" Sasha asked. It was a fair question considering the fact that Nathan was wearing a red hoodie and old jeans.

"In there." Nathan motioned to the plastic bag next to Sasha in the backseat. She reached in and pulled out a bald wig. "Instant Moby," he explained.

"Smart," I told him. "Wish I thought of it." I peered at Sasha in the backseat. "So who are you? Or do we have to wait until we get there?" She smiled, unbuttoned her jacket, and wriggled out of the trench coat, revealing this sexy as hell Gothic top, tied all down the front. Her breasts were nearly popping out of it and her belly button peeked out from the bottom. A long cross dangled from the black velvet choker around her neck. I couldn't quit fixating on her matching black skirt, slit all the way up to her thigh to reveal a gorgeous bare leg.

"Maiden of darkness," she announced. "What do you think?"

"Man." I held my breath as I grinned at her. "You look incredible." Did I say costumes are lame? I don't know what the fuck I'm talking about.

We picked up Yasmin next and she insisted on showing off her cat costume, tail and everything. The lumpy Lycra bodysuit and thick purple eye shadow gave me scary visions of what the party was going to be like, but there were no apples in Lindsay's basement after all. A girl dressed as a Hershey's Kiss and some guy in a mask were playing with a Ouija board, though, and Lindsay was walking around with a deck of tarot cards. She dragged me over to the leather couch and made me shuffle. I watched her deal and then listened to her feed me some bullshit about unexpected financial gains and an approaching betrayal. I had to pretend to be interested in what she was saying because I knew she was still trying to get over hating me.

"Sasha said you wouldn't wear a costume," she said, wrinkling her nose.

"I don't look good in them," I said apologetically. Lindsay was a nice person; it wasn't her fault she couldn't throw a decent party.

Yasmin bounced over and asked to have her cards read and I went to check out Lindsay's CDs. Four of them were stacked on top of the stereo with *Halloween Mix* printed on the labels. "SOS" was playing. According to Lindsay's bubbly handwriting, the Pussycat Dolls were next and then Pink's "Get the Party Started." In fact, it didn't look like the music would improve anytime soon.

Nathan had already slipped his bald Moby head on and was making the best of it, dancing around with his hands in the air. I grabbed a can of soda and hung out in the corner, scanning the room for Sasha.

Jeremy Eastman, in gray dress pants and wearing a humungous class ring, cocked his head and pulled a bottle out of his burgundy blazer. "Party booster?"

I nodded, gulped down more soda to make room for the gin, and then poured a shot's worth into my can. Sasha bounded over to us and grabbed me around the waist. "Dance with me," she said. I followed her across the room and danced to Lindsay's crappy *Halloween Mix* until I was dehydrated. Jeremy seemed to have the only supply of alcohol and everyone kept sidling up to him for party boosters, even Lindsay.

Sasha and I sat on the couch with our doctored sodas. I had my arm around her and she was cuddling up to me, looking content. I wished we could sit there all night—even though my eyes were starting to water and my arms were beginning to itch. I rubbed my eyes with my other hand, determined not to disturb Sasha. "Are you having a good time?" she asked.

"With you," I said honestly. "Yeah."

She lifted her head and kissed me on the mouth. It started off very sweetly. Like a first kiss when you don't plan on anything else happening. But we'd been alone so rarely lately that even kissing had been limited and soon that kiss began to remind our bodies of something else. Before I knew it, we were making out on the couch, Sasha's hand flat against my back under my T-shirt, barely aware that we were in the middle of a Halloween party.

Then someone nudged my shoulder, reminding me. I looked up and saw Lindsay's mom staring back at me from halfway down the stairs. Sasha saw her too. She stood there long enough for us to get the message and then turned and went back upstairs.

"God." Sasha groaned. "A kiss, big deal."

My eyes were worse by then and I went at them with both hands, although everyone knows the last thing you're supposed to do with an itch is scratch. "I'm allergic to Yasmin," I complained. "I'll have to go."

"Uh-oh." Sasha examined my eyes and pressed her lips together. "Lindsay's cat. He's upstairs, though."

"Doesn't matter," I said, pulling up my sleeve to inspect the growing collection of hives creeping up my arm. "Its fur is probably all over the place."

"I didn't think about that." Sasha ran her fingers over my exposed arm. "Do you have any medication for it?" I shook my head. "We should go outside for a while," she said decisively, pulling down my sleeve. She rushed over to confer with Lindsay, who went upstairs to get our coats.

Sasha and I sat on the porch swing, watching our own breath. It was so cold that it wouldn't have surprised me if it started to snow. "It's freezing," she said, her teeth chattering away. "It feels like January."

"Well, get closer." I folded her into my arms and kissed her cheek.

"You know this is the most alone we've been in weeks," she said, hugging me back.

"I know."

"So is it safe?" She pulled away and looked into my eyes. "Can we be alone together without anything happening?"

"Of course it's safe." I laced my fingers through hers. "I know things have been weird and I hate it. I just want to go back to the way things were before. Do you think we can do that?"

"I don't know." She rocked the swing. "It's different, isn't it?"

"Only if we let it be."

"Maybe, but . . ." The wind blew between us, tossing Sasha's hair forward so that I couldn't see her face. "I think . . ." The sentence hung there ominously in the breeze. I was terrified that she was going to break up with me.

"What?" I asked.

She pushed the hair out of her eyes and kissed me again. Her tongue was colder than mine. I curved my hand around her neck and kissed her back. I wasn't gentle this time. I could tell that wasn't the way she wanted it.

"What?" I repeated when we came up for air. The curiosity was warming me from the inside. I needed to know what she was going to say.

"My parents aren't home," she began. "They're in Pickering for my aunt's Halloween thing and they won't be home for ages. Peter's there too. Everyone's there. All my uncles and aunts. They do it every year." Her words were spilling out fast and that made me nervous again. "The only reason my parents didn't make me go was because I was coming here and you know how they trust Lindsay." I nodded quickly. "And I didn't tell you before because I thought maybe we'd end up over there alone and I wasn't sure I wanted that to happen." Sasha pressed her hair back behind her ears and touched my knee.

"It's okay," I told her. "I get why you didn't say anything, but I don't want you to worry about that stuff. It's like what you said before about being on opposite sides and I don't want that. I just want us to be us."

"Okay, I'm glad."

"*But*," I prompted. That unfinished sentence from before was still twisting in the wind. I could feel it the way I'd felt her disappointment that day in English class.

"But," she repeated, sitting up straighter, "I want you to come back to my house with me."

I leaned forward, sitting on my hands. "Now?"

"Yeah."

"Like as a test or something?"

"No." Her voice sounded small but clear. "Not really."

"So." She was really freaking me out. "What *exactly* do you want?" The hair on the back of my neck was standing up. I hadn't noticed that before.

"Just to see what happens." She clasped her hands together, rested them on my knees, and added, "We don't have to. It was just an idea."

"Okay," I said slowly. My mind had isolated the idea and was scrutinizing it from every possible angle. It didn't realize that I'd already agreed. "If that's what you want."

We made a production of reappearing in the basement and Sasha and Lindsay did some more intense deliberating in the corner. Lindsay kept looking over at me, pursing her lips just like her mother had on the stairs. I wanted to go over, spread the tarot cards out in front of her, and say: "A good friend will dismiss your advice and you won't be able to do anything about it."

There were enough people at the party to disguise the fact that we'd left, but Lindsay had instructions to call us if her mother happened to notice our absence. Then I'd race back, using the allergies as an excuse for being outside, and Nathan would swear he'd driven Sasha home earlier. When we left, Nathan was talking to Jeremy Eastman and I had to interrupt them to tell him the plan. I hated to do it because they were probably discussing GSA business, but I didn't have much choice. We couldn't afford to leave any loose ends.

Sasha's house was only a fifteen-minute walk away and neither of us said much. I held her hand and tried to talk myself out of the anxiety rushing through my veins. Some nerves are good. Like before a game when they get the adrenaline pumping. Other nerves refuse to work with you. They demand to be in control. They ruin everything and think it's funny. Ha Ha Ha. Look what happened to Nick. I couldn't afford those kind of nerves.

Sasha hung our coats in the front closet and said, "They won't be back for hours. Come upstairs." I followed her up to her room; of course I followed her. Who can resist a maiden of darkness? I did what I'd been wanting to do all night, I snaked my hand inside her skirt and touched her bare leg. The only thing she had on under that skirt was silky underwear and I touched that too. She stepped out of the skirt and looked at me. *Ha Ha Ha.* Instant hard-on.

Sasha noticed it right away. She unzipped my jeans and started touching me. She knew what she was doing. I tried to clear my head to make it last awhile, but I knew it wouldn't work so I put my hand down her underwear and touched her too. I hoped that's where we were going. Only there. I could do that.

Then Sasha said, "Do you want to try again?"

I stopped what I was doing and stared into her serious brown eyes. *Yeah, of course I did.* I was programmed for it, right? But my throat was vibrating and I couldn't breathe.

"Nick, do you want to?" Sasha repeated, and then I realized I hadn't answered, that I was standing in the middle of her bedroom, debating it in my head.

"I'm not sure it's a good idea," I said honestly. "I don't want it to turn out like last time."

"I know," she said. "And it's not going to be perfect, so if that's what you're thinking, then we shouldn't." What I was thinking was like an equation that I didn't understand. Also that I wanted to take off Sasha's underwear, lay her back on the bed, and kiss her somewhere new. My stomach flipped into my throat just thinking about it. "But it's like I have last time stuck in my head," she went on. "And now it seems like we're spending all our time avoiding this one thing and if we could just get it over with . . ."

"Imperfectly?" It was an effort to say that. Standing in front of her was an effort. I had no idea she'd been feeling like that.

"Imperfectly." She fiddled with her top. "But only if you want to." She sat down on the bed, pulled her knees up to her chin, and smiled nervously up at me.

"But I don't have anything on me." I grabbed my pockets as though that explained everything.

"Lindsay swiped some condoms from her brother's room for me," she said, smiling into her knee. "You know, you're making me really nervous standing there like that."

The hair on the back of my neck was standing at attention again. Either I was about to get hit by lightning or we were going to do it. I sat on the bed next to her and ran my hand up her bare leg. We kissed fast and hard. I pulled her top off over her head and touched her everywhere. I wasn't thinking anymore. I wasn't going to stop and say we shouldn't.

Sasha tugged off my clothes. She reached into her purse, pulled out a condom, and held it in the space between us like she was holding her breath. I reached out and took it.

"Hey," she cried, flipping my arm over. "You're cured."

And sure enough, no more hives. I rolled the condom on and kissed her. She grabbed my hair and wrapped her legs around me and I didn't feel sick. I didn't feel anything except what we were doing.

"It might hurt less if you're in control," I said. "Why don't you get on top?" I didn't want to hurt her. That's what had ruined things the first time.

"I don't know what to do up there," Sasha protested.

"Right," I said, smiling. *"Like I do."*

"Okay, but help me," she said, climbing on top of me.

So I did. We did it together. And it wasn't perfect, but it was good. Her bed started squeaking and it made us laugh. Afterwards we wrapped our arms around each other and Sasha said, "That was nice. Can we consider that our first time?"

We could do anything. She was perfect, that girl. "Absolutely," I whispered into her hair. Her nipples were hard against my chest. I couldn't remember the last time I felt so happy.

Toby was lying face-first on the floor. I pointed him out to Sasha and she said, "He must've fallen off was when the bed was shaking." I grinned when she said that. It killed me that we'd made the bed shake.

We dove under the covers and lay there making out and talking. Sasha made me admit that I thought Lindsay's party was boring. "I knew it," she cried. "I knew you'd think that."

"Her parents were *home*, Sasha. And Yasmin was dressed as a *cat*."

Sasha snorted and licked the bit of skin between my nostrils. It was gross and funny at the same time. "You're such a snob sometimes," she said. "You complain about everybody at school being cliquey, but you want everybody to live up to your idea of cool."

"I can't help it if people look up to me as a model of coolness," I cracked.

She took a swipe at my nose again and I groaned and fought back. Nude wrestling in Sasha Jasinski's bed. Man, life is weird. I grabbed for her right hand and pressed it between my palms. I loved how her tiny hand made mine look freakishly enormous.

"Hey, I can't believe Lindsay stole condoms for you," I said suddenly. "I love her for it, but Lindsay! I thought I was on her hit list."

"She's a good friend—even when she doesn't agree with what I'm doing." Sasha poked my stomach, threatening to start the battle over again.

Okay, so I owed her brother one. And Nathan and Lindsay for covering for us. I owed Sasha's parents big time. Maybe I could send them a thank-you card with a big bouquet on the front. *Thank you, Mr. & Mrs. Jasinski, for giving Sasha the opportunity to get on top. You have no idea how much I appreciate it. Love and kisses, Nick.*

Man, I was giddy. It was a natural high, lying in Sasha's bed. I knew I wouldn't come down all night, that I'd be lying in bed at home, thinking about her, and knowing that made it easier to put my clothes on when she said, "You should probably go soon. They might not be home for a while, but I don't want to cut it too close."

Got it. Whatever she wanted me to do. *Whenever. Wherever.* That stupid Shakira song from Lindsay's *Halloween Mix* was playing inside my head and it didn't sound half bad.

My cell phone was dead so Sasha lent me hers for the walk home. She was paranoid that some badasses would jump me along the way. Courtland was pretty quiet, but weird shit happened on Halloween. Last year someone's dog got shot in its own backyard. The year before three guys threw a fourteen-year-old girl into their car and told her to take her clothes off, but the cops showed up while she was doing it. Some people are seriously fucked up, but I knew nothing bad could happen to me that night.

"I want you to keep talking to me until you get home," Sasha insisted. "That way I'll know you're okay."

Whenever. Wherever. It took me nearly half an hour to walk home and we talked the entire time. I got so used to having her there in my ear that I didn't want to tell her I was home yet and when I said that, she laughed into the phone. "You're so sweet," she said. And you know, at that moment it was the truth. I felt like the newest person on the planet, more innocent than Lindsay, more innocent than anyone. I almost felt like bobbing for apples and singing along to Rihanna.

Well, I did say *almost.*

eleven

COACH HOWES LIKED to say, "The minute you guys feel unbeatable, we're in trouble." He said that a lot during our winning streak. "Overconfidence makes mistakes." It was his favorite warning and we tried to listen. The coach wasn't the type of guy that slapped you on the back or punched your arm. He didn't build you up or cut you down. When he said something, it was because he meant it and believed you truly needed to hear it. He was levelheaded but not very friendly. Like a machine really. All about the game.

So I was kind of surprised when he clapped me on the back after an effortless win, grinning from ear to ear, and said, "Nice defensive play lately, Nick. That's what we like to see." See, defense wasn't usually my strong point. I had speed, scoring ability, and could make crisp, accurate passes. He was right though, lately I'd been on a real hot streak all around. I wasn't crazy enough to think it had anything to do with Sasha, but I loved it when she was in the stands, even though she didn't have a clue about hockey.

Anyway, like I said, the team tried to listen. I tried. But I could never quite swallow what Coach Howes was preaching. Confidence feels good. More is better. Better is better. Sure, moderation in all things, but you could never have too many good feelings. Not that I'm the guru of good feelings or anything; it's just common sense.

No one can ever really tell you anything anyway. They can try, like my dad and his fifty-dollar bills or Keelor's parents flushing his weed, but in the end you either buy into their advice or you don't. Take Keelor. He was lying low, waiting for his parents to relax again, but he was guaranteed to score more weed and when he did, I'd probably smoke it with him.

Safe sex was a different story. The condoms weren't a problem for me. We needed them. We had them. I put them on. No problem.

I actually felt calmer once Sasha and I started sleeping together. It was like confirmation that we were right together. Sasha would never have done it if she didn't believe that—not the first time and definitely not the second. The other thing is (and I know this sounds weird) that it kept the sweetness alive. That's honestly what it felt like. You'd think sex would make you less innocent, but it didn't work that way for me. I felt new for most of November. We were closer in every way. We talked and texted each other constantly. I didn't even care about the hot girls who came into Sports 2 Go and touched my shoulder like it was something else. Seriously, they weren't a temptation.

I felt so calm that I didn't even worry about Sasha being around Holland or my mom anymore. Mom's birthday was near the end of November and Holland and I made fettuccine Alfredo and Greek salad. The old me would've avoided inviting Sasha, but the new me told her it'd be great if she could make it.

Mrs. Jasinski dropped Sasha off with a bottle of wine and Mom let Holland pour out a glass for everyone. Mom was in a mellow mood that day. She said she'd wasted too much time complaining about Mrs. Scofield and that she was making a birthday resolution to begin looking for a new job. We all cheered at that. Then Holland brought out the marble cake she'd bought at Loblaws and we sang off-key.

"This is lovely," Mom said. "Aren't you three sweet to do this."

Holland bent down and kissed her cheek. "Happy birthday."

"This is lovely," Mom repeated. "I feel so spoiled."

That's the kind of thing that would normally make me flinch. I'd stare at the wall or pretend I wasn't listening, but inside I'd be thinking that she was the opposite of spoiled. She never went back to school like she wanted; she didn't even talk about it anymore. She hadn't dated any other guys after Dad. Maybe he'd ruined relationships for her or maybe she was just too tired or thought it would upset Holland or me. That had to be lonely and to make it worse, sometimes I didn't even want to talk to her.

But I didn't think that on her birthday. I accepted a huge piece of marble cake, devoured it, and asked for seconds. Then we went into the living room and watched her open birthday cards. Holland and I had sprung for a bouquet of lilies and a bottle of Mom's favorite perfume. Sasha had picked out bath beads and a salad recipe book that was nearly as thick as my law textbook.

Mom sucked in her breath as she unwrapped the book. "That's perfect, Sasha." She flipped through the glossy pages, pointing out recipes she intended to try. " 'Tossed mushroom and walnut salad,' " she read, tilting her head to one side. "I think I have the ingredients for this one in the cupboard." I groaned jokingly and Mom tapped my knee, her lips zooming into a smile. "Thank you, Sasha. You'll have to come over and share one sometime."

The cards were mostly from people Mom had worked with at the library. She still went out with them for dinner on the last Thursday of every month. There was one from my aunt Deirdre and her family too and Mom's parents in Thunder Bay. They'd called to wish her a happy birthday just before we'd started dinner. There was only one true surprise in the pile. A card from Dad. It had a picture of a champagne bottle on the cover and said:

Celebrate your birthday in style.

Dad had signed it: *All the best, Cole.*

Mom flipped back to the cover and then opened the card for the second time. "Funny," she said, more to herself than to us. "He didn't send one last year." Holland and I exchanged worried glances, but Mom just set the card down with all the others.

Sasha helped me load the dishwasher. We kissed in front of the fridge. Mom caught an eyeful when she walked into the kitchen but pretended she hadn't and squeezed by us. "It's so nice that you could come, Sasha." She patted Sasha's shoulder, poured herself another cup of coffee, and went back to the living room.

"You know you didn't have to get her anything," I said. "How much did you spend on that book?"

"My mom put some towards it too," Sasha said.

Mrs. Jasinski was okay when it came down to it, a little uptight but a good person. She didn't dislike me nearly as much as Mr. J. did, which was another point in her favor. She asked about my hockey games, although she knew even less about the game than Sasha did, and kidded around with us in the kitchen sometimes. There was no doubt in my mind what'd happen if she or Mr. J. found out that Sasha and I were having sex, though.

So we'd make sure they never found out. We had my dad's one-hundred-dollar insurance policy waiting to be spent and we were careful. We were so careful that it didn't even occur to me to worry. Not even when we had the accident. Maybe because it didn't seem like an actual accident at the time, if you know what I mean. More like a blip. We were on round two when it happened and we fished out the condom, tore open a new one, and kept going, like it was no big deal.

Afterwards Sasha swung her legs over the side of the bed and said, "You're okay, Nick, right? I don't have to worry about that."

"I'm okay," I promised. "There hasn't been anyone else, you know that." Dani hadn't put her mouth on anyone but me. That was practically like zero sexual contact.

"Okay," Sasha said, grabbing her underwear from the floor. "I know." She buttoned her top and then tugged her jeans on while I did the same next to her.

I walked her home and we talked about my mom sending out her first batch of resumes and how more people were coming to GSA meetings since Nathan had joined at the beginning of November. They were doing an awareness campaign with posters and stuff around school and Ms. Navarro stressed that she was always available if people wanted to talk.

I was thinking about that, wondering why it was so hard to talk about certain things even when people offered, as we turned onto Sasha's street. She stared down at the end of the street, her eyes as big as tennis balls, and let go of my hand. "Shit!" she exclaimed. "My dad's already home."

"So tell him you were at Lindsay's." I reached for her hand and squeezed.

"And if he saw you?"

"Okay, then *we* were at Lindsay's."

"Great, it's nice you don't have to worry about it anyway," she said curtly.

"Hey, I worry."

She looked straight ahead, her bottom lip wobbly. "Right, like before."

I stopped walking and started worrying. Just like that. One minute everything was fine and the next we were heading for a meltdown. "In my room?" I asked. She stopped next to me and bobbed her head. "Okay, you're right," I agreed. "We should be more careful. Maybe we should use something else at the same time."

"You mean the pill?"

"Or the patch or whatever." I knew we had to have that discussion sometime. I just didn't think it'd be so soon and now that we were getting down to it, I realized I was pretty wound up about how she'd react.

Sasha's eyes settled on mine and it was like her entire face had changed. I couldn't tell what she was thinking and that made me feel worse.

"What about today, then?" I added. I hated to say it, but now that we'd started down that road, I couldn't ignore it either. "Maybe we should go to the clinic on Fairmont—get those Plan B morning-after pills. Just to be on the safe side.

"It couldn't hurt, could it?" I continued. "We could go tomorrow morning before I go to work." The more I thought about it, the more it seemed like the right thing to do. Responsible. I should've thought of it before, but other things took over.

"Okay," she said in an almost whisper. "Call me when you wake up tomorrow."

I thought that's exactly what would happen. I'd get up at seven-thirty, shower, and take the bus over to Fairmont. We'd get it taken care of and catch a cab back. She'd probably feel sick later, but it'd be for the best. Then we'd get serious about other birth control. We could handle it. People dealt with this stuff all the time.

That's not the way it went, though. Nothing like that. Sasha called my cell two minutes after my alarm went off on Saturday morning and said, "I forgot that I have to babysit Peter this morning. My parents are going to a home-decorating show." She breathed into the phone and waited for me to fully wake up.

"What time will they be back?" I mumbled.

"I don't know—you'll probably be at work by then."

My brain was starting to fire up and I could hear the tension in her voice. "I'll call in sick," I offered. "They can't be gone the whole day."

Sasha hesitated for a long moment. It felt like yesterday all over again, almost like she didn't even want to be on the phone with me, but then she said, "I wanted to talk to you about the whole thing first. I'll come over later tonight, if that's okay. I think . . . I think it would be good if we could really talk."

"I have a game tonight." I didn't like the way the conversation was going. How was I supposed to concentrate on selling sports equipment and playing hockey when I didn't know what was going on between us?

"Tomorrow, then."

"Okay." I was pissed off with her for making me feel like what'd happened was my fault, but I didn't let it show. I thought about Sasha's parents and the stupid home-decorating show, messing up the plan. There must've been something Sasha could've said to change their minds. She could've tried a little harder.

The situation was in the back of my head all day, but I worked around it and the next day Sasha came over with her parents' permission, smoothing her hair nervously back behind her ears and whispering something about going outside. I threw my coat on and followed her out the front door. She shoved her hands deep into her pockets, sniffling in the cold. "You look mad," she said. "Are you mad at me?"

"I'm not mad." Edgy, more like. "Tell me what's going on, Sasha. What happened to the plan?"

"Plans don't always work out the way you want them to." Lines crisscrossed her forehead as she curved inward. "I've been thinking a lot the past couple days and the problem is . . ." She skimmed the back of my hand with her fingers. "The problem is when I'm around you, I don't think clearly. I just get caught up in . . . everything that goes along with being with you." Her words were getting choppy and she was blinking like crazy. "Not that I didn't want to *be with you,* but it's like . . . I can't get a grip . . . so maybe I'm still not ready for . . ." She searched my face. "I thought maybe if we took some time . . ." Her voice trailed off and the dread was so thick in the air that it stopped me dead in my tracks.

"You're breaking up with me?" I winced as I said it. I couldn't believe we were back there again after everything we'd been through. "This is because of Friday. You're freaking out, I know. We should just go and—" I was freaking out too, but it was because of her. She couldn't break up with me for something I wanted to fix.

"I'm not breaking up with you," she cut in, her eyes as unhappy as I'd ever seen them. "But something like Friday happens and it turns into this big thing we have to deal with on our own so, yeah, it freaks me out. I don't want to have to worry about things like that now. I want to worry about school. Stupid things even. What I'm going to wear to Lindsay's Halloween party. Not about trying to get on the pill in case we have an accident."

"Sasha." I put my hand on her back. She squashed her lashes shut, her spine shaky under my palm. It killed me to see her worked up like that. "It's okay. We'll stop doing it if that's how you feel." I didn't want to stop sleeping together, but I'd do it for her. It wasn't the worst thing that could happen.

"I knew you'd say that." She reached out and squeezed my other hand. "But it's not that easy when we're alone and in the middle of things. I mean for both of us. If we took some time off—"

"What do you mean by time off?" My neighbor Mrs. Ghomeshi strolled past with her daughter, the two of them in identical plaid scarves, and I waved at them, but I wasn't smiling. "It sounds like breaking up."

"It's just temporary. So we can get a handle on things." Sasha dug her fingers into my skin. Her mouth dropped open as she watched me. "*I'm sorry.* You know how I feel about you, don't you? I just . . . *I need this.*"

"This is another test, isn't it? Like Halloween." My eyes were burning from the inside. I hated that she could do that to me. I was trying to be careful with her and she was breaking up with me. "So how does this one work? If we don't talk for three months, you'll be my friend?"

Sasha exhaled. Her breath was white on the air. "You're twisting my words. Would you please just listen to what I'm saying? I need to slow this down and get my head together. *But we can still talk.* And if we can handle that, maybe we'll be able to handle other things too."

"That's great," I said bitterly. "So generous of you. Thank you." I pressed my palms together and bowed.

"Nick!" She called for me as I turned away, but I kept walking. I walked all the way out to the main road and stared at the traffic. Somebody honked at me. A girl in a cheap domestic car. I didn't recognize her, but she pulled up to the curb, rolled down her window, and motioned towards me. I trudged, zombie-like, to the car.

People could've walked straight up to me and asked me to tie their shoes or drop their letters in the nearest mailbox. I probably would've done those things too.

"What?" I said. And then I saw it was Dani, looking as blond and gorgeous as ever.

"Well, hi to you too," she said, frowning. "I just wondered if you needed a ride. It's pretty cold."

It was cold, but it didn't matter. "Okay." I shrugged. "Thanks."

"No problem." She'd never been to my house, so I had to give her directions. I must've sounded strange because she said, "Are you okay?"

No, not really. I mumbled something about Sasha breaking it off and Dani's eyes rocketed over to mine. "You're kidding," she said. "I was sure you'd be the one ending it." She reached over and touched my shoulder. "Sorry you're upset and all, but I just couldn't ever see the two of you together." *Whatever, Dani.* "Trust me, you'll be okay."

"Yeah, maybe by graduation," I muttered as we pulled into my drive.

Dani gave me a weird look, like she didn't know whether I was joking or not. I smiled, but I could feel it come out wrong. Like a psycho that hunted down young girls in cheap cars or old ladies who took the bus. I thanked her for the ride and got out of the car. Dani would tell Vix and the rest of the girls and the girls would tell the guys and the guys (especially Keelor) would give me spaced-out looks and say Sasha wasn't worth worrying about. This would all happen before eleven o'clock Monday morning and I seriously thought about staying home on Monday. Not to avoid that but to avoid Sasha.

What actually happened was even more pathetic. Sasha texted me at nine-thirty Sunday night and asked me to meet her at Coffee

Time during law class on Monday. Sasha skipping class would've been a first and I didn't want to look at her face and her stupid little hands on the coffee cup, but I went. I couldn't stop myself.

I finished a hot chocolate before she got there and when she walked in, my chest started to collapse. Two older guys in short leather jackets turned to eye her up. Their crooked smiles made it obvious they were having dirty thoughts about her and that got me so mad that I wanted to kick their teeth in. Sasha went to the counter, bought two coffees, and sat down across from me. "Are you still talking to me?" she asked, sliding one of the coffees over to me.

"I'm here, aren't I?"

"Yeah, thanks. I was scared you wouldn't come." She took a sip of coffee, her focus shifting between me and the laminated table.

"So what's this about?" I demanded. "Are you gonna tell me what I'm doing here?"

Sasha knotted a strand of her hair tightly around one finger, her face sinking into her hands. "You're not going to let me do this, are you? Can't we at least try? Maybe if we take it slow for a while, we could get back to the way things were in the beginning and—"

"You keep saying that like it's not breaking up." I leaned over the table, steam from the coffee warming my chin. "So did you get things taken care of?" I thought it'd probably be okay anyway, that it was the least of our problems, but she was making such a big deal about cutting out sex.

Sasha shook her head and played with her plastic lid. "I almost did. I was going to. I chickened out, I guess." She lowered her voice and added, "You didn't finish until you put the other condom on anyway, right?"

She knew the facts as well as I did. She was there.

I was still angry, but I was so far from being over her that I shoved my hard feelings aside and said, "I'm sure you're okay, but look, we'll stop all that. I get that you're not ready for sex. It's not a problem—and that's not just something I'm saying."

"It's a break, Nick. I need one." Her voice cracked in frustration. "We'll see each other at school. We'll talk."

"Go out with other people," I added sullenly. "Because that's the way it'll turn out, you know."

"No, it won't. Not for me." Sasha's tone was definite, but her eyes were glossy. She smeared her tears across the bridge of her nose and stared me down. "What you do is up to you."

And suddenly it was. I didn't have to worry about being careful anymore. I could do whatever I wanted. There was no one to stop me. I wanted to feel happy about it. *Fuck you, Sasha. You think you're so much better than everyone else, but you're nothing special. I don't know why I wasted my time.* But inside I just felt cold. Like nothing mattered anymore.

I stood up and zipped my jacket. "So I'll see you at school, then."

"Nick!" She followed me outside and cut in front of me. I laughed hollowly, but she was crying. My chest filled with salt. It stuck to my ribs and rushed up to my throat, burning my insides raw. Sasha wrapped her arms around me and hugged me like it was the end of the world. "Trust me; we can do this," she said.

But we couldn't.

By the end of the week I was avoiding her in the halls and by the end of the next week she was avoiding me too. I wanted to talk to her. Every time I saw her in law class, her head facing front like she couldn't feel me staring at her, I wanted to stand next to her desk and ask if we could start over. At first I was too angry to do it and by the third week I was sure she hated my guts.

Everything started to suffer. I didn't bother with law homework and got a D on a math test. I was rude to Sports 2 Go customers and told Grayson he was the biggest asshole I'd ever met. I cut Mom off when she tried to talk to me. Everything I did only made me feel worse. My game turned to shit and there was nothing I could do about it. I smoked so much weed with Keelor that my brain oozed out of my ears, into the street and down the sewer and then Keelor, the last person who should've complained, told me I was doing too much shit and ruining my game. "This isn't the way to get over her, man," he said. "Hook up with someone else. Then she'll beg you to take her back." He snapped his fingers. "It's a classic."

Classic head games. What a fucking sad concept.

I missed her. I hated her for hating me. And then Christmas Eve happened and made those things look like the easy part.

twelve

I CLIMB INTO Dad's car and stare past the windshield wipers. The snow's coming down heavy and it looks like magic in the air. The way Christmas is supposed to look. For a second I think everything will be all right now that Dad knows, but by the time he opens the back door, the feeling's already fading. He hands me my backpack and gets into the front seat. "We're taking Nicholas back to Courtland," he announces, not looking at Bridgette.

"What's happening here?" Bridgette asks.

"We're taking Nicholas back to Courtland," Dad repeats sternly.

"Yes," Bridgette says in her stupid clipped voice. "But why?"

I don't answer. I'm not there in the car with them, not really. I close my fingers around the backpack straps and think about Sasha waiting for me. It's us in the situation. Her and me. Everybody else is on the outside. That's the way things are.

"I'm dropping Nicholas off at a friend's house and we're not going to discuss it any further at the moment." That's Dad's *don't argue* voice and Bridgette doesn't argue, but she gapes at me in the backseat, frowning so hard that the line between her eyebrows deepens into a crevice that begs for a plastic surgeon.

"You have something to say to me, Bridgette?" I ask, my voice full of attitude.

"Nick, don't," Dad says. "That's the last thing we need."

So what's the first thing we need? A truck to ram into the side of Dad's car and kill me instantly? Things like that only happen when you don't want them to.

I let go of the straps and stare numbly out the window. The car is quiet all the way to Courtland. Dad remembers the way to Sasha's and when we get there, he steps out of the car with me and plants his hand on my shoulder. "What happened, Nick?" he asks. "We had that talk."

Yeah, I remember. I still have the fifty-dollar bills to prove it. "That's not the cure for everything, Dad." I laugh under my breath. "Sorry to disappoint you."

"I didn't say you disappointed me, Nick." Dad's green eyes flicker. He looks so much like me that it's like staring thirty years into my future. "Is there anything I can do?"

"I don't know." My nose is running from the cold and I sniffle like a kid who's played too long outside. I feel like I should be wearing wet mittens or something. It's crazy. I can't keep my head in one place long enough to form a sentence. "I want to talk to her first."

"You two should do that." Dad nods and I nod along with him. "And I assume you'll be going back to your mother's tonight?"

"I guess so." My shoulders drop. "I guess I'll miss Christmas."

Dad sighs and tries to smile. "Well, don't worry about that, Nicholas. We can catch up on that later."

"Yeah." I laugh again. It's impossible to imagine the next three minutes. Tomorrow seems like science fiction.

Dad clutches my shoulder harder. "Are you going to be all right? Maybe we should stay."

"No. It's okay. I'll call you tomorrow." I have no idea how long I'll be and the thought of Dad's car idling in the Jasinskis' driveway, Bridgette silently fuming in the passenger seat, doesn't calm me down any.

"Okay." Dad stares at the car, then back at me. "We'll work this out somehow, Nick. It's not a good situation, but we can work it out."

"Thanks." He's being good about this, I know. It's just that I can't feel anything.

I watch him get in the car and drive away. Then it's just me standing there alone in Sasha's driveway. I don't want to move, but I lurch towards the front door and ring the bell.

Mr. Jasinski answers. His eyes fill with suspicion and he says, "Sasha mentioned you'd be dropping by. This is Christmas Eve, you realize. We have people over and Sasha doesn't have much time."

Mrs. Jasinski steps up behind him, her hair swept into a bun and a Christmas tree pin clipped to her velvet top. She steers her husband out of the doorway and says, "Come in, Nick. Sasha's waiting for you in the den, but we'll all be off to church shortly."

I don't know what to say to any of that so I don't say anything. I take my shoes off at the front door and walk along the hall to the den. Sasha is sitting on the couch in a long burgundy skirt and white sweater, watching *How the Grinch Stole Christmas!* She looks at me and hikes up the volume. I stand there in my socks, the sound of cheery Jasinski voices floating in through the hall.

"You're going?" I say.

"To church," she tells me. "I have to. I tried to get out of it, but my grandparents are here too." She motions to the hallway.

"Shit. I thought we had some time to talk." I sit down beside her, my heart racing.

"I know." Sasha's voice is dull. "I had to tell them we were thinking of getting back together—otherwise they'd never even have let you in." She stares over at the TV, but I can tell she isn't really seeing it. "My dad was freaking before you got here. He said, 'Nick always brings drama with him.' "

On any other day that would've offended me. Today it barely registers. "Do you have any idea what you want to do?" I ask patiently. I don't want to push her, but I need to know.

"Am I going to have it?" She lets the question hang there until I can't take it and look away. "I don't know yet. I'll have to tell my parents either way. I just wanted you to know first."

"Okay." I don't know what she wants to hear. "Can you do me a favor? Can you take another test? It was just that one time and I wasn't even finished when it—"

"These tests are pretty accurate, Nick."

"Yeah, I know, but it won't hurt, right? Can you do that? Just to be sure before you tell them?"

"Okay," she agrees. She reaches down, her chin trembling, and smoothes invisible wrinkles out of her skirt. "I'm so stupid." She folds her left arm in front of her stomach and kneads her forehead with the other. "I'm sorry."

"No." I touch her sleeve. "You were just scared."

"And stupid."

I'm not up for this. I can't sit here and tell her she's not stupid until her parents drag her off to church. I don't want to feel any sorrier for her than I already do. It won't help. "So you'll do it?" I say. "You won't tell them until you take another test?"

"Yeah." She smiles bitterly. "Don't get your hopes up too high."

I nod. "I just don't want to make another mistake if we don't have to."

"What about your dad?" she asks. "What did he say?"

"He asked if he could help." I shrug. "I told him I wanted to talk to you first."

"He wasn't mad?"

"He couldn't understand how it happened." I hang my head and laugh at that; I can't help it. "I think he's in shock." I think I am too. One minute I can't stop laughing and the next I feel frozen from the knees up. "I didn't want to tell him, but it was the only way I could get here."

Sasha makes a clicking noise with her mouth. Her hand brushes against mine. "Thanks. I know things have been really rough between us."

"There hasn't been an us for the past month," I remind her. "You didn't want me around until today." Harsh but true. "It didn't have to turn out like this, Sasha. I would've gone with you, you know. Everything would've been okay." Suddenly I'm angry, just when I least expect it.

"I know." The words are so low that I can't hear them over the sound of the TV; I read them on her lips and think how unfair this is. We could've been okay, the two of us, but I never had a choice.

"You didn't need to break us up," I say. The words feel jagged in my mouth.

"I know," she repeats. "I never thought it would turn out this way." It's my turn to go quiet. Sasha makes everything she says sound right, even when I know it's wrong. "You think it was easy for me? I wanted to talk to you so many times, but you had to have it all or nothing."

"I never said that!" I shout. I glance at the hallway, half expecting Mr. J. to skid into the room and do something crazy.

"Keep your voice down," Sasha hisses.

"You know I didn't say that," I continue, forcing my voice into a carefully modulated Jasinski-approved tone. "I told you we could stop sleeping together."

"You said that, but it wouldn't work." She charges off on a tangent, explaining that was the whole purpose of the break, to see if we could handle a platonic relationship. Another test, like I said in the first place.

Mrs. Jasinski walks in at the end of Sasha's speech, her Christmas tree pin glittering like a dozen diamonds, and something clicks in my head and reminds me why I'm here. "Sasha, we'll be leaving in about ten minutes," she says. She turns towards me and adds, "Sorry to rush you out, Nick, but it's a busy family time. I'm sure you understand."

"Sure." I'm already getting to my feet.

"Oh, no." Mrs. Jasinski motions for me to sit down. "You still have a few minutes."

So I sit down again and that stupid knotted weed twists back and forth in my stomach. I want to throw up, but I know I won't. This is what it must be like to swallow poison ivy. "Sasha." I dip my head towards hers. "We have a lot to think about. Can you meet me after you take the test?"

"You're not going back to your dad's?" Her face is flushed from arguing.

"I told him to go. I'm working the twenty-sixth—do you think you could meet me at the store around one?"

Sasha slides a finger across her lip and says: "One o'clock. Okay."

I get back up. This time I'm really going and it feels wrong, everything undecided between us and that weed flapping its leaves inside me like it wants to fly. Sasha stands up next to me. Her cheeks practically match her skirt and I hope her parents won't ask too many questions about us; I don't think she'll be able to handle that right now. "Are you gonna be okay?"

She opens her mouth but closes it again before saying: "I guess I can act like I am for a while."

"You can IM me later if you want," I offer. "Not like I'll be getting any sleep tonight."

"Okay, I might. I'm glad you came over anyway."

"You are?" I say it lightly. I'm not sure this meeting helped either of us any.

"Yeah, I am. Thanks, Nick." She takes a step towards me and puts her arms around me. The hug catches me off guard. You'd think it would take longer than a month to forget how to hug someone, but my arms feel heavy and stupid at first. Then my hand reaches for her hair. It's soft like it always was and I hug her back the way I used to.

It feels so good to do that. So good that it's scary.

How many times can one person break your heart?

I look like a snowman by the time I get home. My socks are wet, my toes are frozen, and my teeth hurt, but I don't care. I could take off my clothes and lie down naked in the backyard all night and I wouldn't feel much different than I do right now.

The icicle lights are still on, but inside, the house is dark. I can't remember what Mom and Holland are doing tonight, but I hope they'll be gone a long time because I don't think I can pretend I'm okay. At the very least I need an explanation for my presence, but I can't think. My brain is stuck on Sasha in that burgundy skirt, staring at *How the Grinch Stole Christmas!*

I pull off my shoes and socks and tell myself what to do. *Change your clothes, you're cold. Get some food, you haven't eaten.* It's like I'm on autopilot, like I'm sleepwalking. I change into sweatpants and throw two Jamaican beef patties in the microwave. I eat half of the first one in the kitchen, but it sounds like a cemetery in there so I stretch out on the living room couch and turn on the TV. There's a lot of Christmas stuff on—*The Nightmare Before Christmas, Elf, A Christmas Story, The Santa Clause*—but I'm not exactly in a festive mood so I keep flipping until I land on *Minority Report.* I've already seen it twice, but it's good so I stay with it.

The year is 2054 and Tom Cruise is being framed for murder. He keeps saying, "Everybody runs." It's the best line in the movie. *Everybody runs.* It's inevitable. Sometimes there's only one thing to do. I wish that's how it was with Sasha and me because I don't know what I'll say to her in two days. See, I don't think I want her to go through with it. I'm like that asshole I told you about, the guy that convinced his girlfriend to have an abortion. I just want it to be over with and I want Sasha to want the same thing so I don't have to feel bad about it. But this is Sasha we're talking about. I don't want her to hate me again. Maybe that's the most important thing. I'm not sure.

Anyway, Tom Cruise is on the run with that precog girl he kidnapped. She's the most fragile person you've ever seen—pale skin and huge eyes. I'm seeing her and I'm not seeing her because the whole mess with Sasha is squirming around in my head. Then next thing I know, I'm blinking up at Holland. Her mostly pink bangs are back in barrettes and she stares down at me and says, "What're you doing here?"

I catch a glimpse of the TV and notice *Family Guy* is on. I'm not fully awake yet and part of me knows that I don't want to be. "I came back," I mumble.

"Obviously. Did you have a fight with them or something?"

"No, I . . ." I struggle into a seated position and notice that Holland's wearing her coat. She must've heard the TV and headed straight for it.

Mom steps into the living room behind her and says, "Nicholas, honey, what are you doing home?" She sounds soft and worried, but I'm not ready to lay the truth on her. She won't sound that way when she hears it; she'll sound more disappointed than ever.

"I don't want to talk about it now, okay?" I flip weary glances at Holland and Mom. "I'm gonna be home for Christmas. I hope that's all right."

"Of course it's all right." Mom's still in her coat too. She hardly ever wears high heels anymore, but she's wearing them now. Blush and eye shadow even. "Is this about *her*?"

I shake my head. I think I'm pouting and maybe that's a good thing. Maybe they'll lay off me for a while if I keep it up. "Mom, I really don't want to talk about it right now. Everything's okay. I'm just gonna be here for the holidays. I might see Dad in a few days."

I can tell I've totally confused them. It would've been smarter to let them believe this was about Bridgette or Dad, but I don't have the energy to lie like that. I squint at the empty plate on the coffee table. I must've eaten the second Jamaican patty too, but I can't remember doing it. I remember Sasha in that burgundy skirt. She's pregnant. My kid. I already know the second test will be positive.

I should check my IM, but I can't get away. Holland and

Mom have me cornered. "So where have you guys been?" I ask, rubbing my eyes and milking the little boy lost look for whatever it can get me.

"Church." Holland sits on the arm of the couch. "Then Christine's."

Christine is one of Mom's old library pals. She got divorced a year before Mom did and then married a guy who grooms pets. He offered us a lifetime of free pet grooming, should we ever decide to "take the plunge and buy a furry friend."

"Barry and Christine asked about you." Mom unbuttons her coat, slides it off, and folds it over her arm. "He's a big hockey fan, you remember?"

I don't remember, but I nod anyway.

"They bought a macaw for Christmas," Holland adds. "It speaks German."

"German?" I repeat.

"*Wer sind Sie?*" Holland offers, gazing at the ceiling like she's trying to remember more. "*Bitte bringen Sie Erbsen.*" That's just like Holland. She probably even knows what it means. "Who are you?" she translates. "Please bring peas." See what I mean.

I glance over at Mom. "So now she speaks German."

"*Nein,*" Holland says. "Just 'who are you' and 'please bring peas.' "

"The two most important phrases in the German language," I joke.

Holland smiles and I can't believe I made a joke. It must be that voice in the back of my head again—the one that told me to change my clothes and eat something. Maybe it means things will be okay. Maybe you can make it through your whole life feeling like shit, as long as you have that voice taking care of you. I glance from Holland to my mom and back to Holland. It's like they're scared to move, afraid to leave me alone in the living room with my secret. They're my little support group, only I don't want to talk to them.

"I can barely keep my eyes open," I tell them. "I think I'll go to bed."

"We were about to make hot chocolate," Mom says, her eyes lighting up. "You love hot chocolate."

And she's right, normally I do. Hot chocolate with shortbread cookies is a Christmas Eve tradition. Six years ago Holland and I snuck downstairs in the middle of the night and finished off half the shortbread cookies while diving under the tree and searching out our presents. We weren't going to open them. We just wanted to examine their shapes and test their weights. Then Holland lost her balance and landed full force on one of her own presents, instantly flattening it. Something snapped inside and Holland's eyes popped out of her face like she was being squeezed. Man, she looked funny, but I didn't laugh.

"We'll hide the evidence," I suggested. "Maybe they won't notice it's missing."

And you know, it actually worked. We unwrapped it and it was one of those paint by number sets, the little brush snapped in two but the miniature paints miraculously intact. A few days later we managed to smuggle the numbered landscape into the garbage. It was from some great-uncle and not something a kid would normally be interested in painting, but I think Holland used the paints during her angels and castles phase.

"Okay," I say. "I guess I'll have some hot chocolate first."

The three of us sit in the kitchen sipping hot chocolate. It feels like we'll never be done and the moment we are, I trudge up to my room and check my e-mail and IM. There are four new messages, but none of them are from Sasha. I told her to IM me because I thought it might be good for her. Now I realize it's what I need too. We're connected, her and me and what's happening inside her. I'm more connected than I've ever been to anything in my whole life, but I've never felt more alone.

thirteen

HOLLAND WAKES ME up at 9:48 the next morning. Nothing registers at first. I'm plain old Nick scowling at Holland for waking me up so early. Holland's bangs are hanging in her eyes and she's wearing one of her many black T-shirts. This one says *Angry Young Girl* on the front and has a pink cartoon face with squiggly long hair on the back. The face is baring its teeth in an angry young frown.

"We're about to do presents," Holland says, watching me struggle towards consciousness.

I'd like to stay in that moment where I don't remember anything, but sure enough it all rushes back to me as I look at Holland. *What happened, Nick? We had that talk.* I sit up in bed. It's one of many things I have to do while I'm waiting for tomorrow. I have a whole Christmas Day to get through.

"So what really happened yesterday?" Holland asks. "I won't

say anything to Mom, I swear." She folds her arms in front of her angry declaration. "It was them, wasn't it?"

"Holland, it's Christmas," I rasp. My voice box has accumulated a hundred years of dust overnight. "I don't want to think about this shit. Go downstairs and wait for me. I'll be down in a second."

Holland cocks her head and stares at me. I know this look. She's trying to decide if she should keep pushing. Well, push away, Holland. It won't get you anywhere.

"Fine," she says, and turns on her heel.

I jump in the shower, change into my clothes, and set a course for the Christmas tree. Mom and Holland are sitting on the couch, waiting for me. "Merry Christmas," Mom says. I go over and kiss her on the cheek. She smells like the perfume Holland and I gave her for her birthday.

"Merry Christmas," I tell both of them. It sounds okay, I think. It only feels wrong.

"Merry Christmas," Holland says. "Are you playing Santa Claus?"

"You can do that." I motion towards her.

"I did it last year. It's your turn."

So why ask? Shit. But Mom looks genuinely happy and I don't want to mess with that if I can help it. I root around under the tree and pull out present after present, reading the tags and passing them on.

Afterwards Mom makes blueberry pancakes, another Severson family Christmas tradition. It's funny, Dad doesn't do any of the stuff we used to, but Mom's kept it all up. Maybe that's why she normally looks so unhappy over the holidays. She hasn't moved on. Maybe I'm wrong about that, though, because her smile looks real today, unlike mine.

"I'm glad you're here for Christmas this year," she says as I load the dishwasher. "But are you going to tell me what happened with your father yesterday?"

"Who says anything happened with him?"

"Nicholas." Mom stands with one hand on the counter and watches me, but I don't stop loading. "There's obviously a problem here and I'd like to know what it is."

The phone rings just then and we both step towards it, but Mom gets there first. She frowns at the voice on the other end of the line and says, "Yes, he is, Cole, but he won't tell me a thing. Maybe you can fill me in on what happened last night." She holds the phone tight to her ear and my stomach sinks. This isn't the way I want things to go. Not on Christmas. Not before I've seen Sasha again.

"Let me talk to him," I say. I can hear Dad's voice, but I can't make out what he's saying. "Mom, give me the phone."

"Well, at least he'll confide in you," she says, glowering at me as she continues speaking to Dad. "I still haven't heard a word about it. I came home last night and found him asleep on the sofa."

Mom hands over the phone, which I promptly put on hold. I rush upstairs, pick up the phone in my room, and yell for Mom to hang up.

"You haven't told your mother yet," Dad says, sounding tenser than he did last night.

"Not yet. Sasha and I want to get some things settled first."

"And how'd it go last night?"

"We didn't have long," I explain. "Her family was going to church. I'm going to meet her again tomorrow."

"And her family? What do they say?" Dad exhales heavily.

"They don't know yet either."

"Nick, I know you just found out, but don't wait too long on this. Her parents could be some help." A single note of laughter shoots out of my mouth and slides under Dad's words. "They seem like good people," he continues.

"Yeah, I know." I've had as much of this as I can take. He can't help me. He doesn't know how. "So how was Christmas Eve? You guys got back okay?"

"Fine. Nicholas, look, I want to hear from you again soon. I know it's early, but there are different options that could be set in motion."

"I know." I don't mean to say more; it just slips out. "Maybe she won't have it."

"That could be the best thing, but this is her decision, you realize," Dad says cautiously.

I do realize, but I don't want her to ruin both our lives. Sasha's got more plans than I do; you'd think she'd want to keep them.

Dad and I don't talk for long. He tells me he's glad I trusted him enough to tell him. I don't point out that it was an act of desperation. I thank him for calling and promise to get in touch with him in a few days.

There're a few hours before Aunt Deirdre and Co. show up and I spend most of them in my room. My Christmas gifts are piled at the foot of my bed—new shoulder pads, a waterproof clock radio for the shower, gift certificates for clothes, a collection of CDs and DVDs, and a Magic 8 Ball. The Magic 8 Ball is from Holland and I swoop down and pick it up. I don't even know if you're supposed to ask the questions out loud or what. It's a stupid ball, after all.

Is Sasha pregnant? Magic 8 Ball: *Better not tell you now.*

Will she have the baby? Magic 8 Ball: *Concentrate and ask again.*

I drop the Magic 8 Ball on my bed, disgusted with myself. Next thing you know, I'll be phoning a psychic line that charges by the second. Still, I retrieve the ball and try to focus. The Magic 8 Ball says: *Signs point to yes.* I give it another shake and read the next reply: *As I see it yes.* I keep flipping it over, waiting for a message I can live with.

Yes definitely.

It is decidedly so.

Outlook not so good.

Really? I have no idea what that's supposed to mean. I balance the Magic 8 Ball on top of the DVDs and stand in the middle of the room. I need to get out of the house and do something. I'm not up to the turkey dinner with my cousins. Mom always forces me and Holland to hang out with Simon because he's fifteen, right in between our ages. She thinks that automatically means we have something in common, but I don't understand half the stuff he says. He speaks fluent computer-geek. It's not my language on a good day.

Taking off on Christmas Day isn't an option, though. Where would I go anyway? Everyone I know is locked into family plans. So I plant myself in front of my computer and check my e-mail and IM again. Not one word from Sasha.

We used to e-mail and IM all the time. A bunch of our conversations and e-mails are sitting on my computer, evidence that we actually used to be together. The funny thing is that I wouldn't let myself reread any of them. It was proof that I was in control, I guess.

But I'm not in control of anything. I see that now, and I click on her e-mail from Halloween and read it through three times before pushing my chair away from the desk. I remember everything about that night as though it just happened—kidding around with her in bed, singing "I'm with You" in my best Avril imitation, Sasha wrestling with me, grinning at me, telling me how special I was and how it felt like we'd just started over.

That night comes back to me in the shower, ringing up a sale, or warming up on the ice. Lots of things about us come back to me. That hug from last night. Does she still believe anything she said to me on Halloween or is it all past tense? It's the last thing I should wonder about, but I can't help it.

Somehow I survive the turkey dinner with Aunt Deirdre, Uncle Martin, and my cousins. I'm quiet, but the giddy noises coming from my two youngest cousins disguise that. After dinner Simon follows me up to my room, sits at my desk, and tries to pretend we have something in common. I try to pretend too, but I know I sound moody and bored. I'm relieved when they leave at ten o'clock, but by ten-thirty I'm bouncing off the walls again.

I don't sleep until after three and Mom has to tell me to pick up the speed a little in the car the next morning. We've been making this mall run since I got my learner's permit. In fact, I drive whenever we're in the car together. My road test is in three weeks and I need to pass; I'm tired of walking everywhere. "I don't think I've ever had to ask you to drive *faster* before," she jokes from the passenger seat.

It's not just the car. I'm slow at Sports 2 Go too. Brian, the manager, makes cracks about it all morning. By noon I'm completely sick of it and it must show in my face because he claps me on the back and says, "Why don't you take your break early? Re-energize yourself."

"I have to take lunch at one," I tell him. "Somebody's meeting me."

"Oooh," Brian croons. "Maybe she's the problem."

"Yeah, and maybe it's you," I retort. Okay, so maybe I did sound a little panicked, but is that any reason for him to act like he knows it all?

Brian's eyebrows leap up in surprise. "Steady there, Nick. This is just friendly banter. You're normally right on the ball—not like some of the other guys in here. Nobody knows that better than I do, buddy."

I nod at the ground and try to figure out what normal Nick would say to that. "Man." I rub my forehead. "Sorry. I'm seriously burnt out. I think I need a vacation."

"Yo, this *is* your vacation," Grayson says on his way by to grab a pair of shoes from the stockroom. Grayson, as you probably have already guessed, is still an asshole. He mostly stays out of my way and I mostly stay out of his. It's an arrangement that's been working for the past three weeks, but for some reason today's the day he decides to start talking to me again.

As soon as Brian fades into the background, Grayson's by my side, straightening the men's sportswear on the sale rack. "Boss-man's really on your back today," he comments. I shrug and step aside to avoid being stampeded by a sudden rush of customers. "So what's with you today? You all right, man?"

I shake my head. Spending the day after Christmas at the mall is not my idea of a good time. Between rabid customers knocking merchandise off the shelves and bitching about the lousy sale prices, Brian's "friendly banter," and my approaching lunch hour, I'm about as fucked up as I can be without completely losing it.

"Why don't you take off?" Grayson suggests. "Store won't fall apart without you, you know. You tell the man you gotta take care of some shit. An emergency."

"Someone's meeting me here at one." I guess Grayson missed that part of the conversation.

"Oh, yeah?" I wait for him to make his own "friendly banter" about that, but he just adds, "Then you go when they get here. Do I have to figure this all out for you?" He cracks a smile when I look at him.

"You're doing an okay job so far." I fire a smile back. The conversation actually calms me down for fifteen whole minutes.

I circulate through the store, looking for people to help, and a woman flags me down in sports accessories. The boy with her must be about ten years old and the woman speaks to me like I'm her shrink. She's all worried because she wants to get her kid interested in sports, but he hates everything he tries and shouldn't there be something out there for him? I could easily mess with her—say something like, "Well, have you tried chess or backgammon?" but then the kid would feel bad. Clearly he's got bigger problems than sports, you know, like his mother spilling his personal info in the middle of a sports store.

Shouldn't these things be obvious?

I give the woman and her kid a spiel about the individuality of sports and how some people are really into the team thing while others prefer solo stuff. I explain that some people like aggressive games while others are into strategy. There are some people who will play anything and some people who need to find their exact fit. It's like anything else really. Some people have a calling, one thing they were born to be (like Sasha with forensics), while others can explore a spectrum of options. A contemplative expression slips over the woman's face as she listens to me. She's buying it, I can tell, and I explain why hockey is the best sport for me. Skating. Speed. The team. The kid is staring at me too, but it's her I'm getting to. For some reason she needs to hear this and when I finish, she thanks me and walks out of the store without buying anything.

It's busier than ever in the mall and I stare out into the crowd, trying to catch sight of Sasha, although it's not one o'clock yet. I get edgier with each passing second. I haven't decided what to say yet, but I know how I feel. I'm not ready to have a kid. There's no possible way I can be someone's dad.

The minutes crawl by. One o'clock hits and still no Sasha. I hold it together for eighteen more minutes and then I break. How can she be late today? I'm hanging on by a thread, nerves shooting through my veins and making me half crazy, and she's late. I stalk towards the cash register, calling Brian's name. He cocks his head as he eyes me.

"I'm taking lunch now," I tell him. My company T-shirt is stuck to my back and my forehead is wet.

"Go on," he says, and I walk out of the store and stop by the fountain. Sasha's cell phone number is burned into my brain and I fish my phone out of my pocket and punch in her number.

She picks up on the first ring. "Nick?"

"Where are you? I've been waiting since one."

"It's positive," she announces hollowly. "I took another test this morning and it's positive."

"Shit." It's what I expected, but that doesn't make it any easier. I grip the phone tighter. "I'm sorry."

"Yeah," she says quietly. "Yeah."

"You need to get over here. We need to talk."

"Nick, I can't . . . all those people. I can't deal with going anywhere today and you don't know anyway, do you? You don't know what to say to me or what I should do. It all comes down to me and I need to stay here and think right now."

"That's not fair," I protest. "I can't keep doing this, Sasha, pretending everything's okay when it's all I can think about. We need to make some decisions, the two of us, and we can't do it over the phone." I pull at the back of my T-shirt and wipe my forehead. "If you're not coming here, I'm coming there."

"Don't," she commands. "Not now."

"You're kind of limiting my options," I say bitterly.

"Fine, come over!" she cries. "Help me tell the folks. They'll be glad to see you, I'm sure."

"Sasha." I say her name gently. I need her to calm down. "Don't you think we should get some things straight before you tell them? Do you even know what you want to do?"

"No, but it sounds like you do."

"I know we're not ready. We're sixteen. You can't tell me you're ready for your whole life to change." My throat shrinks as the words slip out. "Maybe we can take care of this ourselves. Maybe they don't even have to know."

Sasha's silent on the other end of the phone. I have no idea what's going through her mind and that scares me. "Nick, I don't know if I can do that." Her voice is brittle. "You think you can just make this disappear. Maybe that would work for you, but it's not that easy for me. *I need to talk to my mom.*" She sniffles into the quiet between us and it's such an awful sound that I'm almost relieved when she finally whispers, "I told you first because you have the right to know, but I can't get through this on my own."

"You're not on your own, Sasha."

"No? I woke up this morning, walked to the drugstore, and bought a pregnancy test. Me. On my own. You say you can't think about anything else, but I'm living it. It's with me every moment."

I draw in a long breath, like I'm testing out a new pair of lungs. "So what happens now?"

"I tell my mother," she repeats.

"When can I see you?"

"I'll call you in a couple days, okay? When I'm ready."

"And that's it? I'm out of it. Don't call me, I'll call you."

146

"It's not like that," she says. "I just need some time to figure out what's best for me."

I can't believe she's doing this again, shutting me out like this isn't even about me. "Okay, so do it, but don't act like I'm on the outside of this, Sasha. I know it's your decision, but it affects me too. This is about us whether you like it or not."

"I know." She says that like she hasn't heard a word. "I'll call you in a few days. I promise."

A couple days, a few days, next thing you know it'll be a week. What am I supposed to do until I hear from her? *Press end. Get lunch in the food court. Go back to Sports 2 Go and pretend you give a shit about the post-Christmas blowout sale.* That's what the voice tells me, but I can't do it. The sound of Sasha hanging up echoes in my ear and I keep holding on, cell phone pressed against my ear and my shirt melting into my back. I keep holding on. The sound dies and then there's just silence. I keep holding on.

fourteen

KEELOR AND I lean against the boards and watch the Zamboni flood the ice. Keelor is permanently wired when it comes to hockey. He can't wait to get out there and he bursts onto the ice the moment the Zamboni doors are closed. Gavin is right behind him. Me, I'm not in a hurry for this practice; my impatience comes from somewhere else. I don't even know what I'm doing here; that's the truth. I'm no good at anything since Sasha told me on Christmas Eve. I'm just waiting. It's only been one day since she said she'd call and I can't stand it anymore.

I drag my ass out onto the ice and Coach Howes orchestrates the warm-up. We run lines. Skate hard from the goal line to the blue line and back. Red line. Goal line. Far blue line. Goal line. And finally all the way down the ice. Coach Howes blows his whistle. "Drop!" he orders. "Push-ups." Everyone knifes to a stop and falls to the ice. My body isn't anywhere near tired and I do the push-ups without thinking. Coach blows the whistle again. Circles this time.

Two laps forward and two laps backwards for every circle on the ice. My feet know what to do and they do it. I've been playing hockey for so long that the basics come naturally.

The shooting drills are a different story. Every pass is in my teammates' skates and my shots couldn't hit the side of a barn. No one except the coach gives a shit if you're crap in practice, but I keep my eyes down in the dressing room afterwards. I don't want to talk to anyone and I don't want to listen. Keelor's busy ribbing Gavin about something, but just when I think I might pull off my invisible man trick, he pulls me aside and asks if I'm going to Marc Guerreau's New Year's Eve party.

I've received at least fifteen messages about this party in the past twenty-four hours, but it's the last thing on my mind. "I don't know," I tell him. "Maybe."

"You have other plans?" he says mockingly. "Come on, Nick. It'll be good for you. All of us are going—Gavin, Hunter, Scotty, Vix, Dani."

"Nathan?"

Keelor shrugs. "Ask him." I can tell you right now there's zero possibility Nathan will be at Marc's party. It's not his crowd anymore; bringing up his name to Keelor is a reflex action from years gone by.

I shrug like it doesn't matter anyway. I have no intention of showing up and Keelor knows it.

"We'll pick you up," he says. "No excuses."

"Whatever."

"Hey, fuck *whatever*, Nick. I'm serious. You're going to this party if I have to throw your ass into the back of Gavin's car." Keelor's eyes are blazing. "You're a walking disaster, man. You gotta shake this. Something's gotta change."

He's serious, all right, but he doesn't have a clue. A New Year's

Eve party won't solve my problem. "I said I'd be there, didn't I?" It's not worth an argument at this point. I can get out of it later.

I head for the shower and stand under the stream of hot water, wondering if Sasha's told her mother. Will her parents let me see her again? I need to see her.

It was different during my parents' divorce. My life felt unchanged when I was on the ice. Now I can't forget anything for more than a minute and it turns my judgment to shit. We lost our last game because I screwed up a perfect opportunity in the last minute of the third period. We were down 2–1 when the puck sprung loose in front of the Northam Blue's net. I was closest to the puck and I sped towards it, swung my stick back, and tried to slap it into the net while it was still in motion. That was the idea anyway, but I fanned on the shot and the puck dribbled into the corner. So much for our tie.

Sometimes the puck finds the net and sometimes it doesn't, but I've never had it quite this bad before. Somehow I have to get it together before the tournament in Buffalo tomorrow. I can't let this shake me up forever. It's not fair to the team and it's not doing me any good either.

I do the only thing that will help. I catch a ride home with Keelor's dad and start typing out an e-mail to Sasha. I know I'm supposed to leave her alone for a few days, but this is the best I can do. No voices. Just words.

There's a knock on the door before I get far. "Nicholas?" Mom peeks her head around the door. "Can we talk?"

"I'm kinda in the middle of something." I already have everything written out in my head and I don't want to forget.

"Put that aside for a few minutes," she says, stepping into the room and closing the door behind her.

I stop typing and glare at her. "So you're not really asking."

"Don't be difficult." Her voice tenses. She used to sound like this a lot just before the divorce.

I drain any hint of expression from my face as I swing around in my chair. Mom sits down on the edge of my bed with her hands resting on her knees. "I'd like to know what's going on with you, Nicholas. You still haven't explained what happened on Christmas Eve. I'm glad you can talk to your father, but we should be able to talk, you and I. You're unhappy, that's obvious."

My chair creaks as I lean back and fold my arms in front of me. "Maybe it would help you if I talked about it," I say flatly. "But it wouldn't help me."

"What's that supposed to mean?"

"You don't really want to know what's going on. You just think you do."

"That's not true, Nicholas." Mom's eyes soften as her neck cranes forward. "I do want to know."

And you know, I almost believe her. Almost but not quite. She probably still thinks this is about Dad and Bridgette—some big blowup we had on Christmas Eve and are in the middle of working through. Then she could be sympathetic and tell me that just because my father is self-centered at times doesn't mean that he doesn't love me.

"Mom, I'm trying to work things out for myself for now." I give her the responsible tone so she won't worry too much. "You can't fix everything for me anymore. There are things I need to take care of for myself."

Mom sighs and shakes her head. "I don't know what to say to you."

"Don't worry so much." I roll my eyes. "You take every little thing so seriously." Okay, I know that's not fair, and that this is no little thing but she keeps pushing me.

"Every little thing," she repeats. The words make a pinging sound, like a leaky kitchen faucet.

"*Here we go again.*" I mean it and I don't.

Mom marches indignantly out of the room, closing the door snugly behind her, and I stare at the barely begun e-mail, trying to recapture my thoughts. I had it perfect in my head a few minutes ago, but now I'll have to start over.

> Sasha, I know you need time but I also need to hear from you. Maybe you think this is easy for me but it's not. I was never even over you and there you were at my house telling me you were pregnant. I was mad at you. I shouldn't have made you go. A lot of things should've happened differently than they did. I'm sorry for the things that are my fault and I want you to know that I do want what's best for you—not just what's best for me. I know you'll tell me when you figure that out and I know this is harder for you than it is for me but it isn't easy for me either. Nothing else matters right now. Please e me and let me know you're ok.
>
> Nick

I press send before I can change my mind and then IM Nathan and ask him what he's doing on New Year's. There's too much time to kill while I'm waiting for Sasha's reply. I feel like a monkey on speed, staring at the monitor with beady eyes and banging wildly on the keyboard. Next thing you know I'll start shrieking and jumping around the room and Holland will burst in, hand me a banana, and start speaking to me in sign language.

I go downstairs before that can happen. I don't want to run into Mom, but I'm going stir-crazy. Holland is talking on the phone and watching music videos in the living room. She tosses me the remote as I sit down and then walks away. I ride up and down the channels and land right where I started with Eminem's "Lose Yourself." It's his best song and the music pounds in my chest and grabs me by the throat.

I love music that can do that. Just not now. I flick through channels for the next thirty minutes. Two minutes of *Entourage*, ninety seconds of *Battlestar Galactica*, three minutes of *Miami Ink*. After a while I don't even know what I'm watching. The flipping itself is the activity. I don't watch much TV normally. I don't have time and 90 percent of the shows suck anyway. Today is no exception and the therapeutic effects of flipping wear off fast. Maybe it's *Maury* that does it or maybe it's cumulative. Whatever it is, I have to stop and check my messages.

I sprint upstairs to find Sasha's reply waiting in my in-box. The subject line's blank and I hold my breath as I open her e-mail:

Thanks, Nick. I know this isn't easy for you. It's not that I want to keep you in the dark or that I don't want to talk to you. I'm just very confused right now. I talked to my mom after we got off the phone yesterday. She was more upset than mad—and not just because we were having sex but because we should've been protecting ourselves properly and she wishes that I'd gone to her about that. She said if she'd known about the accident she could've taken me to the drugstore for Plan B pills.

When she asked what I wanted to do I didn't know what to say. She said some of the things you said about us being young and that having it would be very hard and she doesn't want things to be hard for me. She also asked if you'd be involved if I had it and I said I didn't really know. I know we need to talk about that and I promise I will try to consider

153

your thoughts but first she's going to take me to a clinic to speak with a counselor.

I'm really scared but it helps that she knows—and that she said she'd be there for me no matter what I want to do. Maybe I shouldn't say this to you because I think it's what you want too and I haven't made up my mind yet but now I won't feel like such a bad person if I can't go through with it. Please give me a few more days and I promise I'll come by and talk to you about it.

My dad doesn't know anything yet. I'm not ready for that. Have you told your mom?

Sasha

I don't reply right away. I sit down on my bed, the exact spot where Mom was sitting an hour ago. There's nothing else I can do; I have to let Sasha figure out what she wants. Things feel different now that her mother knows. I'm glad, I guess—relieved—but the bad feelings don't go. Maybe I should've told Sasha I'd be there for her no matter what. I mean, I can't picture it. Our kid. But I know that if it comes down to it, I won't be able to ignore it either. He or she will probably be at the school day care, three doors away from my math class. Sasha will be running in and out of there all day, checking on the kid while she tries to keep up with everything. She'll have one of those giant diaper bag things people carry around and her parents will probably buy her a car to get them both to school. Her parents have money; they can do that. Money isn't the issue here. The issue is me running into Sasha and the baby in the parking lot and in the hall, acting like they don't have anything to do with me. It's not right.

So it looks like I'm in. Parental visits to the Jasinski house. Babysitting maybe. It's the only thing to do. And Sasha might not have the baby anyway. I crouch in front of the monitor and read her e-mail a second time. Her mom thinks it'd be better if she didn't have it. I'd feel the same way if I were her mother. She wants Sasha to have the perfect future and this isn't it. I'm the wrong guy and this is the wrong time. This isn't anything like her life is supposed to turn out. She's supposed to go to university, do Europe, and then start this incredible career. Abortion is so obviously the right thing to do that I feel like crying. This kid never had a chance from the start. They suction it out or something, right? I know it's not a real baby, but it's something and it's not its fault. But that's not the worst part about this. I don't want that to happen to Sasha. Nobody should ever have to do that, but I can't stand to think about it happening to her.

I sit down at the computer and type out this e-mail:

> Sasha, I just want you to know that I'm ok with whatever you decide and that I will be involved if you decide to have it. I don't know if that changes anything but I wanted you to know.
> Nick

I mean it and that surprises me. Suddenly I also know that I can't go to Buffalo with the team. Not only that, but I can't say when I'll be able to play hockey again. I lunge for the phone and dial Coach Howes. The coach's usually solid voice bends with concern at my tight-lipped mention of personal problems. He's really bighearted about the whole thing and doesn't slam the door on the possibility of me rejoining the team later in the season. It helps me to hear that. They're not just a collection of hockey players; they're in the game together and that's rarer than you'd think. But the hardest part is breaking the news to Keelor. I know he won't let me

155

do it without an explanation and my chest starts pounding again as I punch in his number, just like when I was listening to Eminem.

"I'm not going to Buffalo," I blurt out. "I already called the coach and told him. I'm quitting the team—at least for a while. They're calling up some guy to take my place. I don't know how—"

"Don't be an asshole," Keelor cuts in. "Everybody has bad games, Nick. Okay, I know you've been having them a lot lately, but it won't last. You're too good to—"

"Shut up for a second, man. Just listen, all right?" I pause to make sure I have his attention. "This doesn't have anything to do with hockey. It's personal. Really personal. I don't want anyone else to know this, you get me?"

"Yeah, sure, Nick. Of course."

"Okay, then." I swallow hard. "It's Sasha—she's pregnant."

"You're sure?" he asks gravely. "She might just be late. Stress can do that, you know. It can, like, throw their whole cycle off."

"It's been confirmed," I tell him. "Twice."

"Oh, shit." His voice is heavy with dread. "Shit." Yeah, that was my first reaction too. "Sorry, that's not what I was expecting," he continues. "So what is she gonna do? Do her folks know?"

"Her mom knows. She's taking her for counseling—to help her figure out what to do." I tell Keelor most of what's happened since Christmas Eve. Saying it out loud cuts some of the tension in my stomach and I keep going, explaining about my dad wanting me to call him with an update and my mother on my case for being secretive. "I'm not ready to tell her yet," I admit. "I need to disappear for the next few days."

"You can still come with us," he suggests. "The hotel's already booked."

"But everyone would wonder why I wasn't playing."

"You sure you can't play? Maybe it'd be good for you. Kill some

156

tension. You can't hole up in your room forever. You said that was already making you crazy."

"Everything's making me crazy, but I can't play. Trust me."

"Got it," Keelor says. "So then it's Nathan's place, isn't it? Crash with him until we get back."

"Yeah." The thought of spending forty-eight hours with Nathan's dad doesn't give me a warm fuzzy feeling. Nobody's family is perfect, but the tension between Nathan and his dad is too close to the surface. I don't know how Nathan lives with it day in and day out; I guess there are a lot of things you can do when you don't have a choice.

I talk to Keelor for a few more minutes. Our conversation gives the situation a weird kind of normality that it didn't have before. "I'll call you when I get back," he says. "And don't think this gets you out of New Year's."

"I'm not in a party frame of mind," I protest.

"We'll just chill," he promises. "We can leave early if you want."

"Shut up. You know you never leave a party early."

"Well, this time I will. Look, take it easy the next few days, okay? Maybe you should give the old man a call, make him feel useful."

Maybe he's right and maybe I will, but it's Nathan I call next. Telling him is harder than telling Keelor because he understands right away. It's not just about being scared shitless and I know he knows that. His voice is clear but quiet. "When're you going to see her again?" he asks.

fifteen

I TELL HOLLAND that I'll be at Nathan's for the next few days and swear her to secrecy. She gets mad all over again because I won't tell her what's going on. Believe me, I don't even want to tell her about missing the tournament, but someone needs to know where I am. "If Sasha or Dad calls, tell them they can get me on my cell," I instruct.

"Sasha?" Holland repeats. "Are you back together? Mom said she was here on Christmas Eve."

"We're not back together. We're just friends."

"Friends?" Holland says skeptically.

"Trying to be, okay, Holland?" I frown and dig my hands into my pockets. "You're as bad as Mom sometimes, you know that? Can you mind your own business for five minutes?"

"You want me to lie for you, but you don't want to tell me anything. You think that's fair?"

"Okay, so do whatever you want." I throw up my hands in defeat.

"God," Holland growls. "Fine. Okay. Whatever you say, Nick. Just remember that you owe me."

"Fine," I growl back. I'm in a bad mood with almost everyone, but it's worst with Mom and Holland. They've been talking about me, you see, trying to figure out what in the world is the matter with Nick. I expect that of my mother, but Holland should know better. I don't talk about her behind her back.

I toss some clothes in my backpack and walk over to Nathan's. It's not snowing, but the wind is fierce and Nathan does a double take when he sees me. "Look at your face," he says, motioning to the mirror behind him in the front hall.

I peer at my reflection and study my icy red cheeks. They don't actually feel cold; they feel warm. "Christmas Eve was worse," I tell him. "I'm fine."

I take off my coat, drop my backpack in Nathan's room, and join him in the kitchen. He's in the middle of making hash browns and he throws a couple in the frying pan for me and makes me a cup of coffee. "So you never told me what you were doing for New Year's," I say.

"Yeah, we never got around to that." Nathan grabs the spatula and flips over a hash brown. "This girl at work, Bethany, invited me to a party in Toronto. Her sister is this wild librarian there and her and her roommate are having a party in their loft. I'm not sure I'm gonna go, though."

"Why? Sounds cool."

"Well." Nathan looks up at me. "What're you doing? I thought we could hang out or something."

"Thanks," I tell him. "But you should go to the party."

"There are always parties." Nathan shrugs.

"Not at lofts in Toronto." There aren't any remotely cool librarians among Mom's acquaintances, but I've heard rumors of their existence. "Besides, Keelor wants me to go to Marc Guerreau's party."

"Who cares what he wants?" Nathan says. "You're the one dealing with shit."

"He's just trying to help."

Nathan shrugs again. "It's up to you what you want to do."

We eat the hash browns and then watch TV and play video games until his dad gets home. After dinner Nathan drives us over to the theater and we catch a spy movie based on a bestseller neither of us has read. I can't keep track of the plot, but the action sequences are semi-distracting.

When we get back, Nathan's dad stands in the hallway jingling his pockets. "You're staying the night?" he asks, scrutinizing me.

"Jesus, Dad," Nathan snaps.

Nathan's dad nods as his gaze leaps over to his son. "I know he has a girlfriend, but you young people are all so flexible now that I have to wonder if that even matters."

"Look, I'm straight," I assure him. "You don't have to worry."

"I didn't think so, but I have to check." His dad's staring at me like I understand, but I just feel embarrassed for him. "Nathan and I made a deal. He can be in that club at school, but I don't want anything else going on. Somebody has to look out for him and I'm all he's got." I focus on a spot on the wall behind his forehead as he continues. "I don't want him to make mistakes. He's young now. He doesn't know what he wants." Of course he does, I think, he wants Xavier or Diego. "I have to limit the damage."

"I don't think you can limit damage like that," I say, peeling my eyes off the wall to meet his. "People can try and tell you not to do things, but sometimes you do them anyway. Everybody does things."

His dad's eyes get really small. He tells me I can sleep on the pullout couch in the living room.

When Nathan and I are alone in the living room later, I apologize. "I don't know why I said that. I should've kept my mouth shut—I don't want to make things any worse."

"They're not worse." Nathan grins. "Just more interesting. Maybe you shouldn't have mentioned you were straight."

"Hey, I need somewhere to sleep tonight," I remind him, cracking a smile.

Nathan points out that I'm probably not sleeping much anyway, which is true. I describe my recent consultations with the Magic 8 Ball. It sounds pretty weird, I admit, and Nathan starts laughing under his breath. The rasp of air seeping out between his lips and through his nostrils sounds hilarious, like a snoring asthmatic, and he tries to stop, but the noise only gets louder until we're both laughing so hard that tears run down my face.

"Sorry," Nathan splutters. "It's not that funny."

"It's you." I shake my finger at him. "You laugh like a freak."

"I *am* a freak," he says, gasping for breath. "Didn't you hear my dad?"

I howl at that, although it's not that funny either. The last time I laughed this hard I got the hiccups. Holland was pinching me around the neck during a road trip up north to see Mom's parents. You wouldn't think that'd be so ticklish, but it totally disabled me. All I could do was shake with laughter. Mom made Holland stop, but the hiccups started up as soon as the laughing stopped. Those hiccups were painful, extra-strength, but I wouldn't mind having them now.

"So do you think you'll be able to sleep tonight?" Nathan asks once we've calmed down.

"Maybe I won't even try," I tell him. "Maybe I'll just watch TV."

"Yeah, that might be better," he says sympathetically.

"Otherwise I'll probably just lie here thinking too hard." I slouch down on the couch and push my legs under the coffee table. "Do you remember when you were talking about having a connection to someone?" Nathan tilts his head and nods. "I still feel it, you know. I don't know how she feels, but it's still there for me."

"Yeah, I know."

"If we were still together, things might be different. Maybe we could do this."

"She might have it," Nathan says. "Maybe you will do it. You told her you'd be involved, right?"

"Yeah, but we won't be together. Not in the same way. I keep thinking . . ." I clear my throat, which is dry from laughing. "I keep thinking it's my fault."

"You can't let yourself think like that, Nick. Accidents happen." Nathan sits forward and turns towards me, as though there's an invisible booth between us. "You said you wanted to go to the clinic with her. What else were you supposed to do?"

What Nathan's saying is a version of the truth and I appreciate it, but I know what I know—I convinced her to sleep with me the first time. I got us started. "I'm a natural predator," I quote. "You said it yourself."

Nathan shakes his head. "You weren't like that with Sasha." I stare down at my jeans and nod unconvincingly. "Believe it's all your fault if you want to, Nick, but she messed this up too."

"It doesn't make any difference." I run my left hand roughly through my hair and glance at Nathan. "It's done."

But it's not nearly done. Everything is undecided and I'm more confused than ever. I fall asleep with the TV on and sleep all morning. My cell phone wakes me up just after noon. At first I'm too dazed to understand what's happening, but then it hits me. I roll onto my chest, grab hold of my backpack, and dump its contents onto the floor. The still-ringing phone slides under the pullout couch. My hand shoots in after it and yanks it to my ear. "Hello?"

"It's me," Sasha says. "I was wondering if I could come see you, but Holland says you're at Nathan's."

"Yeah." I rub my eyes with my other hand. "Do you want me to come over?"

"Peter and my mom are still home. I can get her to drive me over there."

"No, meet me at home. My mom won't be home for hours." Somehow I don't feel right about talking things over at Nathan's. My mom's house is the most comfortable option—even if Holland's home.

We arrange to meet at one-thirty, but I make sure I'm early. I expect to find Holland watching TV in the living room or holed up in her bedroom working on her mysterious blog. I'm part right. She's in the living room—a guy's body stretched out on top of hers on the couch. They're making out like they mean it and my neck jerks in surprise. I swing out of the room, pad noisily into the kitchen, drop my backpack on the tile floor, and wait. Holland rushes in twenty seconds later, her hair full of static electricity and her lips puffy.

"What're you doing here?" she demands. "I thought you were staying at Nathan's."

"Sasha's coming over." I stare at the empty space behind her. "So who is it?"

"What difference does it make?" She looks anxiously over her shoulder before adding, "It's Diego, if you must know." She juts her chin out. "You weren't supposed to be here."

"Diego," I echo. The guy is seventeen years old and all but engaged to some girl in Quebec. Or is that just something he uses?

Holland holds her head steady, her chin up like she's daring me to say something and I mean to, but the doorbell rings. "That'll be Sasha," she says, shoulders relaxing.

I stride out of the kitchen without another word. Sasha's standing on my doorstep. Her mother's car is idling in the driveway and Sasha turns to wave goodbye before stepping into the hallway. I squeeze her shoulder and she hugs me quick. I catch a whiff of watermelon before she pulls away and I want to pull her back towards me, but I don't. Sasha struggles with her coat. The buttons are stiff. I know this from working them myself in the past. She drapes her coat over the banister and stands with her arms by her sides.

"We should go upstairs," I say in a low voice. "Holland and Diego are in the living room."

"Diego?" Sasha repeats. "What's he doing here?"

"Crushing Holland into the sofa."

"For real?" Sasha's eyes widen. "Since when? What about Elodie?"

"I don't know. It's news to me."

We walk up to my room and Sasha sits down at my desk. The Magic 8 Ball is resting on top of my computer monitor and Sasha picks it up, silently reads the message, and flips it back over again. She's wearing a brown turtleneck and her hair looks freshly washed, like a shampoo commercial. I feel myself staring at her, taking in every single thing about her, and I try to stop, but it's hard. "How're you feeling?" I ask. The words sound as awkward as I feel, but it's better than silence.

"My body feels weird," she confesses, looking over at me on the bed. "Extra-sensitive, like things smell stronger than usual—I can smell the Christmas tree no matter where I am in the house—and my breasts are heavy."

"I thought that kind of stuff didn't happen until later."

Sasha chews her lip. "I read about it. The counselor gave me some pamphlets and some women can feel it even earlier—nauseous and peeing a lot too."

I'm about to ask if the counseling helped, but there's something I need to get out first. "I've been thinking about it and I really think we can do this if you want to," I say, my voice as level as I can manage under the circumstances. "I know it won't be easy. I have no idea what it's like to have a kid and I don't know if I could be a good father, but I can try." I smile, but my eyes don't meet hers. "I'll do whatever I can to help—babysit, do your homework for you, whatever you need."

Sasha studies my face. One of her tiny hands disappears into her sleeve. "That wasn't what you wanted, Nick."

I hunch over and scratch my head. The weed wedged inside my stomach is actually a man-eating plant. It's chewing its way out into the world bit by bit. What happens once it's loose is anybody's guess. "I know," I tell her. "It was a shock, but I've been thinking about it the past couple days and maybe it's the right thing."

"Nick." Sasha blinks quickly. "I don't think so." Her fingers peek out of her sleeve and then disappear again. "It's great that you want to help, but I don't think I can do it. At first I really thought I should have it, almost like I didn't have a choice. It was like *it happened* and this is what *I have to do,* but . . ." Sasha rests her weight on her knees and looks into my face like it pains her to do it. "It was destroying me. It was like I couldn't want anything for myself anymore. There was just this thing I had to do and that's all that was left of me."

"This isn't because of your mom?" My throat's sore as hell. It's a miracle it even works.

"It's not because of her and it's not because of you either." Sasha's words are thin. They slow to a trickle as she continues. "The appointment's next Wednesday. My mom's bringing me. I'll probably take the whole week off school."

"Wednesday?" I repeat. "That's so soon. We've barely even talked about it."

"The sooner the better." Sasha steps towards the bed. She sits down next to me. Our legs are touching and my face sinks into my hands. "You said you wanted what was best and this is best for both of us."

"You're fucking with my head," I say. "It doesn't even matter what I want, does it? It never mattered in the first place."

Sasha reaches out and strokes my hair. "Don't make it harder, Nick."

My face is hot and I never want to look at her again.

"Nick?" she says softly. "Nick, are you going to talk to me or what?"

I close my eyes and listen to the sound of her voice. It's still sweet and it shouldn't be, considering what we're talking about. "I don't want to care what happens to you anymore," I croak. "All this shit with you and you don't even care. I'd get back together with you right now, you know that?" I raise my head and look at her. "Whether you want to have the kid or not because it's you and it's us. All that stuff you said about being on the same side—what happened to that? Because I was on your side, Sasha, and you weren't on mine."

"I was," Sasha says sadly.

"No, you were on your side, looking out for you."

"Then I didn't do a very good job, did I?" Her eyes are red and

166

I think I want to make her cry. She could cry over me at least twice. Anybody is worth that.

"This isn't all my fault," I rasp. "You were in this too, Sasha. I never made you do anything."

"I never said you did," she whispers.

We sit silently on the bed, avoiding each other's eyes. My head is throbbing. Everything I do is wrong. There's no right thing between us anymore. "This isn't going anywhere," I say, and for a second it's like I've been unplugged, like I can't feel a thing.

"It's not what I came to talk to you about."

"I know," I bark. "I'm still crazy and you're fine. Don't worry about it—I'll get over it."

"I'm not fine!" Her hands fly into the air. "I have bigger things to think about. This isn't just about us. How do you think we'd get back together after this? Nothing would be the same. Look at us. We can't even talk like normal people."

I'm not sure that should be a goal—talking like normal people. I never thought we were normal people in the first place. Anyway, what I think doesn't matter. It's all over. I nod numbly and stare at my knees, feeling like a dead person.

"You think I'm not crazy anymore?" she cries hoarsely. "You think I don't give a shit about you? You have no idea how much I wish this never happened." She gets to her feet and grabs for the doorknob.

"Sit down," I plead, reaching for it too. "I'm sorry." My fingers automatically skim her hair. "I'm so fucked up, I don't know what I'm saying."

Sasha sits down on my bed and presses her palms between her knees. "I feel sick," she says, bending at the stomach. "Can you get me some water?"

I touch her shoulder. She looks pale as snow, almost translucent, just a turtleneck and wet eyes hovering above my bed. I bring her water and sit down at my desk. "I'm not over you," I say honestly. "That's the problem."

Sasha lowers her glass and stares at me. "I'm not over you either."

My stomach drops. I can't take my eyes off her. "It makes it harder," I confess. "I don't know what to do." I never knew what to do about Sasha anyway, but this is different. I have no chance of forgetting about her now.

"There's too much to deal with between us," she says. "I can't do it, Nick. I miss you, but just being near you hurts."

"But that's the way relationships are—if you're with someone long enough, there'll always be stuff to deal with." I'm so happy that I think I'll burst, but it hurts too. This isn't what breaking up should feel like.

"Maybe you're right, but I can't," Sasha says, her voice hushed and slow. "I'm sorry." I nod wearily. I don't know if we'd work out either, but I don't know how to let go. "Are you okay?" she asks.

"Are you okay?" I motion to her water.

She swallows the last mouthful and hands me the empty glass. "I'm going to Lindsay's for a few days. I need some breathing room—away from my parents. My dad hasn't spoken to me since I told him and he and Mom are fighting all the time. They're making me crazy."

"Your dad knows?"

"Yeah." Sasha grimaces. "He thinks I'm a slut now, but whatever."

"He doesn't," I tell her. "You just caught him off guard."

"I spoiled his perfect vision of me. He said that he feels betrayed."

"*Asshole*," I say vehemently.

Sasha flashes a hint of smile. "My mom's taking me over to

Lindsay's after we're finished here." She stretches her arms into the air and arches her back. "I want to eat junk food, watch movies, and pretend this isn't happening for at least two hours."

"I tried that." I describe the conversation with Nathan's dad.

"What is it with you and parents?" Sasha teases.

"Just the fathers," I correct.

"Right," she scoffs, "because the women are crazy for you."

"It's a problem." I pull a serious face.

Sasha groans, reaches for the Magic 8 Ball, and pretends to hit me over the head with it. It's the second-best thing that's happened all day.

"Call me when you get back from Lindsay's, okay?"

"I will," Sasha says. "I should call my mom to come get me."

I hug her again before she goes. This one lasts longer and while it's happening, I'm sure everything will be okay in the end. It doesn't feel awkward this time; it feels natural. I kiss the top of Sasha's head and stroke her white cheek. Her dark eyes stare up at me and we stand there, caught in the moment. A second can change everything. I bend towards her, our faces so close that she blurs in front of me. "Nick," she whispers. Does that mean stop? I don't know, but I wait, frozen in time, and she inches forward and presses her lips against mine. It feels so real. I don't know any other way to describe it. It's her and it's me and the last five weeks never happened.

"Nick." She takes a step back and pokes her chin into her turtleneck. "I have to go."

She puts her coat on. Buttons one stiff button at a time. Her hands smooth her hair back behind her ears and then burrow into her pockets.

"Call me when you get back," I remind her.

And then she's gone.

sixteen

HOLLAND IS ALONE when I officially return home the next day. Whatever I was going to say about Diego has dissolved and been absorbed into the rest of my brain, but she has no idea about that; she looks dubiously over at me and rushes up to her room before the non-questioning can begin. Actually, I do have a question (although it has nothing to do with that) and I follow her upstairs and knock on her door.

"Blogging," she shouts. "Do not disturb."

"Two minutes," I shout back.

Holland opens the door and tosses me an impatient look. "Two minutes."

I slouch in the doorway. "I just want to make sure everything's okay with Mom, that she doesn't suspect anything."

"And what would she suspect?" Holland raises one eyebrow. My eyes get that glazed-over look that says I'm never going to answer and probably didn't even hear the question in the first place.

"You're safe," she grumbles. "She doesn't know anything. Nobody knows anything. Whatever is going on with you is safely shielded from familial eyes—except Dad's, of course."

Familial eyes? I told you Holland was a freak, didn't I? "Okay, good." I knock on the door frame. "Thanks."

"Nick." Holland calls my name as I turn to go. "Are you okay?" I swing back towards her, but the answer doesn't come. "You're not, are you? What's going on?"

"I . . ." I lean back in the door frame, instantly heavier. "I can't talk about it right now, Holland. I'm working on it."

Holland nods. "But you'll be okay?"

"Yeah, hopefully." I force a smile. "After years of intensive therapy."

"If you do want to talk about it, you know I won't say anything, right? I'm not gonna bug you about it, I'm just putting it out there."

"Okay, thanks. It's just, you know, not a good time for it right now."

"Mmm." Holland looks thoughtful. "You're not gonna say anything about yesterday with Diego?"

"Right." It's not my job to say anything. This is a whole other family department, but nobody else knows. "So what's that about anyway? I thought Diego had a girlfriend in Quebec."

"Yeah. He did." Holland scrunches her lips together. "She said they should start seeing other people."

"So you're one of these other people?" The old Nick, even yesterday afternoon's Nick, would've been more concerned about this, but I'm so tired, you have no idea.

"We're just friends." Holland shrugs. "He's having a hard time getting over her."

"So you thought you'd help out." It makes perfect sense and

171

I'm not even saying it in a sarcastic way, I swear, but Holland's head twitches and her cheeks flash pink.

"It's none of your business, Nick." She throws her head back and rolls her eyes. "God, for a second I thought you were actually going to be cool about this and let it go."

"You brought it up," I remind her. "Just be careful, okay?"

Holland scoffs at that. "I don't need to be careful. Nothing's happening."

Where have I heard that before? "All I'm saying is you roll around on the couch with someone and things can happen that you don't anticipate." I wince at my choice of words. Suddenly I'm Dad spouting off about complicated situations. Next thing you know I'll be handing over my fifties as some kind of dysfunctional family heirloom.

"Well, we're not all you," Holland says frostily. "Sometimes making out on the couch with a friend is just making out on the couch with a friend."

And sometimes a blow job is just a blow job and sex is just sex and getting your ex-girlfriend pregnant is just getting your ex-girlfriend pregnant. It doesn't necessarily have to mean anything, but then again, sometimes it does.

"I'm not ragging on you, Holland," I say. "I'm just saying be careful. It's good advice no matter who it's coming from."

I retreat to my room and call Dad. I don't particularly want to talk to him, but the call is overdue. Bridgette answers the phone in her country club voice, but her syllables tighten the moment she hears my voice. Dad, on the other hand, is weirdly ecstatic. "I've been thinking about you," he tells me. "You know your presents are still under the tree here. I'd like to drive up and give them to you— it'd give us the chance to talk."

"Yeah, I guess," I say. "When?"

"What about tonight?"

Canada is playing Finland in the World Junior Hockey Championship tonight, but I tell him okay. Nathan and I watched Canada kick Sweden's ass last night and it felt pretty good, but I can't blow Dad off for hockey when he's trying to help. Besides, I doubt that good feeling will happen twice, even if we win.

"I'll pick you up around seven," he says. "We'll go somewhere quiet."

That's hours away and I check my e-mail. Dani is wondering if I'm going to Marc Guerreau's party and Ronnie, one of our goalies, wants to know if I'm okay. There's nothing from Sasha and I don't expect there to be. I know she's at Lindsay's trying to keep things straight in her head and that I shouldn't mess with that. She's okay there, I'm sure, but I keep thinking about yesterday. She kissed me and then she left and I don't know what the right thing is anymore.

I look up abortion on the Internet, not the pro-life stuff—I don't want to hear people tossing around the word *murder* or talking about God like they know him personally—but clinical information on the procedure. There's a pill the girl can stick up inside herself during the first eight weeks. The pill makes the uterus contract and get rid of the tissue. In the first trimester there's also the vacuum method. They give you a shot to numb the cervix and put these metal things called dilators in to gradually open it. Then they put a tube through the cervix into the uterus to suction out its contents. The whole thing only takes about five minutes, but it sounds painful. You can be asleep through it if you want to, but I don't know if she will be. After the first trimester you have to get a D&E (Dilate and Evacuate), which sounds even worse.

I stop reading for a while and concentrate on breathing. She'll be okay in the end. It's a surgery. People recover from surgeries. I look at a list of possible complications and it says that first-trimester abortions are nine to ten times safer than normal childbirth. The complications they describe have really small percentages attached to them and I know her mom will look after her. It'll be okay, I tell myself. I say it over and over, although my stomach hurts and my throat is swelling shut.

I never thought this would happen, not even when I suggested that we get those pills from the clinic. Stupid people get pregnant. Girls that sleep with guys at parties or girls that don't make their boyfriends use condoms because they love them and want it to feel special. That wasn't us.

But why should anyone care how bad I feel about it? It's not happening to me.

And then, because Dad's arrival is a long way off and Mom isn't due home yet either, I look at pregnancy sites. Sasha's five weeks pregnant, but they count back to your last period, which makes it officially seven. I didn't even know that about the counting. Either way it's not very old, but the embryo, just over half an inch long, already has the beginnings of eyes and the lungs have formed.

It's not an actual baby yet, but it could be. Somebody else would be happy about this. Instead it's a mistake. It's doing all this growing and forming for nothing. It's a waste and I feel sorry for it and that makes me feel even sorrier for myself.

I need to talk to my dad, whether he can help me or not. But Mom comes home first. She asks me about the tournament and puts her hand to my forehead. "You look clammy," she says. "Are you feeling all right?"

I try to conjure fictional tournament details, but I'm not feeling creative. Sick is easier to do and I touch my own forehead and say, "Bad headache. I think I'll lie down for a while before Dad comes."

"You're going out with your father?" Mom's eyebrows pull together.

"Yeah, we still have to do the present exchange." I haven't explained Christmas Eve to her yet and I'm not going to do it now.

I go upstairs, lie on my bed, and wait for Dad to show up. The waiting gives me more time to think and I congratulate myself on not calling Sasha while I'm desperate. It wouldn't be fair to her, and besides, Dad will be here soon.

Some people's divorced parents are friends. Some of them still sleep together. My parents only speak when it can't be avoided. Dad has never been inside the house we moved into after he left, and Mom has never met Bridgette. I can't imagine either of these scenarios actually happening. See, Dad honks. That's what he does. He doesn't even venture as far as the front door. He sits in his car and honks twice. I thought it was funny when it first started happening. What would happen if some divorced family with the exact same signal moved in next door? Imagine the confusion.

But today there's no honk. Mom knocks on my door at five to seven and says that Dad's waiting for me in the living room. It's a surprise, but my brain is overloaded and I just stand up and go downstairs, like it happens every day.

"I thought I'd have a look at the house," Dad says when I step into the living room. "Very nice."

"Yeah." I run my hand over my head. "Did you see Holland?"

Dad nods. "We talked a little."

About what? What do you say after nearly a year? "That's good," I tell him. "And Mom?"

"Oh, yes." Dad's nostrils flair. Aha, familiar family tension. "You still haven't told her?"

I shake my head and point to the door. Dad follows me into the hallway, where I slip on my coat and shoes. He looks lost out there, but I have no time for that. "Come on." I open the door and guide him outside.

We climb into the car, the promised presents in the backseat, and drive. I don't know where we're going and I don't care; I need to talk and I need him to start. "There's a nice place on Ridgeway," he says. "Great steak."

"Whatever." I'm not hungry.

"Okay." We keep moving in the same direction and I think I'll be sick, that I'll have to tell him to pull over and let me out, but just then he looks over at me and says, "I've been thinking about you a lot, Nicholas. I would've called, but I wanted to give you some time to talk things over with Sasha."

I nod, my eyes staring straight ahead. "She's not gonna have it," I say in a low voice. "She told her parents and her mom thinks she's too young."

"I think her mother's right," he says carefully. "It would be quite a burden on a young girl and you two aren't even involved anymore."

"That wasn't my choice." I bend my neck, fold one hand in front of my stomach, and hold my head up with the other. I can't say any more. My eyes sting and my throat is closing up.

Dad touches my shoulder and pulls off the highway and into a parking lot. My fingers sink into my hair and I'm shaking. Dad rests his hand on my back. "It's all right," he says. "You'll be okay." Then I break. Tears squeeze out of my eyes and soak my face and I sit there, letting it happen. "Listen," Dad says. His voice is surprisingly soothing. "This is a tough thing for anyone, but you'll get through it, Nick. I swear. You take it day by day and it happens. Day by day."

Dad keeps his hand on my back long after he's stopped talking. My eyes feel like they've been rinsed with bleach. They probably look that way too. My throat's too raw to speak. "We'll sit here awhile," Dad says. "How about I put on the radio?"

I nod and he switches the radio on. It's an easy-listening station and now I know why people listen to that stuff—it doesn't touch you. It's there, but it's not. It just fills the silence.

After what seems like an eternity but is probably less than ten minutes, we start driving again. "So you tell me where you want to go," Dad says.

"I'm not hungry," I tell him. "Anywhere quiet is good."

So we're back to the original plan, cruising towards steak to the sound of easy-listening favorites.

I don't say much in the restaurant and Dad doesn't make me. I order bruschetta and keep asking for refills of Coke. Dad has a beer with his steak and the two of us eat, drink, and stare at each other across the table. The restaurant looks like the inside of an Ikea catalog and the food speeding by me on its way to hungry diners smells terrific, but I can barely manage what I have.

"So what's Bridgette doing tonight?" I ask.

"I don't think she has any particular plans."

"Did you tell her?"

Our eyes lock and Dad shakes his head. "Are you going to tell your mother?"

"I don't know." I fill him in on the last few days—about me quitting hockey and then faking participation in the tournament while sleeping over at Nathan's.

Dad leans back in his chair and taps his temple. "I know it's hard to talk about, but what about Sasha's parents? You don't think they'll want to discuss it with us?"

177

"Maybe." I think they'll never let me see Sasha again once this is over. Does that leave anything to discuss?

"I'm going to leave this up to you," Dad says. "But for what it's worth, I think you can tell your mother."

"And maybe you can start talking to Holland some more," I suggest.

"I never stopped talking to Holland; she stopped talking to me." Dad tilts his head. "Of course I'd like to talk to her."

"Then you could try harder." I'm not mad at him; I just know how it feels to think he won't make the effort. I was there when he left and he did a bang-up job of edging himself out of the picture.

"She holds me responsible for your mother and me breaking up—there's nothing I can do about that." So why even try, right? Good plan, Dad.

"It didn't help that you hooked up with Bridgette so soon afterwards," I tell him.

"It was a *year* later," Dad says sharply. "And that has nothing to do with anything."

"Maybe, but it's not like you have a lot of time. You're always together."

"You and Holland live two hours away. You know I wanted you to come down more often during the summer, and I came up specifically to see your game in the fall. There's only so much I can do, Nicholas. If you want to see me, all you have to do is ask."

"If I want to see *you*," I repeat. "But it's never just you."

Dad takes a sip of beer and sets his glass back down on the table. "I'm here now, Nick. You have my undivided attention."

I pick up my fork and hold it at both ends. The sick feeling never completely goes away anymore. It's better and it's worse, but it's always there. Right now it's a little better and I wish Dad didn't have to go back to Toronto later.

"Hey," he says. "We still have to do presents. I should've brought them in with us."

After we finish eating, he orders a coffee and heads out to the car to get the gifts. He sets the presents on top of the trendy pseudo-Ikea table and smiles. "I opened mine on Christmas," he explains. "Hope you don't mind—you left it in the car."

"That's okay." I pick up the smallest box. It's wrapped in green metallic paper and the gift tag reads: *TO: Nick* and *FROM: Bridgette.* I rip the paper off, pry open the box, and stare down at an ultra-expensive-looking Seiko.

"Kinetic," Dad says. "You never have to change the battery."

"Nice." I look up at him. "Thank her for me."

"You can thank her yourself next time you talk to her."

I slide the other two presents towards me, but it's the card I pick up next. It's signed by Dad and Bridgette and inside there's a check made out for three hundred dollars. "Thanks," I say. The other gifts turn out to be a new MP3/video player and a video game and I thank him for those too. Everything is great, really. It's all stuff I would've been excited about six weeks ago, but six weeks ago I wouldn't have had a breakdown in Dad's car.

Dad sips his coffee and then charges the dinner to his Amex gold card. "We should do this again soon," he tells me. He drapes his arm around me as we walk to the car. "You'll be all right," he says. "You'll see. Just give it some time."

I nod and keep walking. It's what I want to hear, but I don't trust it.

Dad stops walking and faces me. "You know you can call me anytime, Nicholas. I want to know how you're doing, especially now."

"I'll call," I promise.

"Good." Dad sighs softly. "Let me know if there's anything else I can do."

Just be around, I think, but I've spilled my guts enough for one night. I climb into the car and switch on the radio. Phil Collins fills the air and I sink down in the seat and let my head empty out, one agitated brain cell at a time until there's only one thought left: Sasha, I can't do this anymore.

seventeen

Keelor calls as soon as I get home from work. The
team won bronze in the tournament and Patrick, my replacement
on the first line, got two assists. I should be happy for them, but I
don't care one way or the other—hockey and me feel like ancient
history. I tell Keelor that's great anyway, then ask what time he and
Gavin are picking me up. Until last night I fully intended to opt
out on Marc's party, but what good would that do me? Sure, I
could sit in my room and reread Sasha's e-mails like a loser, wondering why she hasn't called from Lindsay's and bending myself
out of shape worrying about the operation. But I won't. I can't.
Not anymore.

"You're going?" Keelor asks, sounding surprised.

"Absolutely."

"We'll be there sometime after ten," he tells me. "Does this
mean you're feeling better?"

"I don't know. Maybe it just means that I can't sit here any-more."

"For sure, for sure," Keelor says encouragingly. "That's why I thought you should play, but it's good you're taking some time to deal with things. So have you heard from Sasha?"

I tell him what I know and he's so relieved for me that I cringe inside. "Look, I don't want to talk about it tonight, okay?"

"Hey, nobody knows, man," Keelor says. "Unless you told them."

"No, I mean you and me. I don't want us to talk about it. I was with the old man last night and that's all it was—us having this serious conversation about it and I don't even know what to say anymore."

Keelor is happy to drop the subject and soon we're talking about Marc Guerreau's party, which I picked up some weed for earlier today. Keelor can always be counted on for that, but I do my part. Somebody always knows somebody and in this case the transaction was done in the privacy of the Sports 2 Go stockroom.

Anyway, almost everyone we know is going to be at Marc's tonight to take advantage of his family's trip to New Jersey. Party rules are minimal. Park a street over. Don't hang out in the yard forcing the neighbors to call the cops. Don't leave evidence (dirty sheets, beer bottles, cigarette butts, muddy footprints). Marc has already assembled a voluntary cleanup crew to implement the third rule; it's the second rule that's the real problem. People get a little wasted and they want to drift out onto the deck and grill hamburgers or hop over the fence and throw things into the lake, even in the middle of winter.

In case you haven't already figured it out, Marc's family has this big house on the lake. His dad is a financial controller, his mom's an accountant, and between them they make enough money to cover the house in Courtland and a one-bedroom condo in Toronto where his dad stays during the week. To tell you the truth, I don't even know Marc that well, just well enough to get invited to this party with a hundred other people.

Gavin and Keelor show up just after ten. I say goodbye to Mom and Holland, who have dedicated themselves to watching the ball drop on television, and pop out the front door with my weed in my coat pocket. It feels so familiar, me patting the weed in my pocket to make sure it's there and stepping onto the freshly salted driveway, that I think I must be back on track. It's a good feeling, only I wish Nathan were with us.

"Hey," Keelor says as I slide into the backseat, "this is my cousin Jillian." The girl next to me is long and thin with curly blond hair and a face like Kate Hudson. She smiles and turns towards me as Keelor points in my direction. "This is Nick."

"Hi," she says.

"Hi," I say.

Then Gavin jumps into the conversation, steering it somewhere I don't want to go. "Coach said you left the team. *That's fucking huge.* What's the story?"

"Man." Keelor glares at Gavin. "I told you he didn't want to talk about it. What word didn't you understand?"

My heart jumps and for a millisecond I wonder what else Keelor told him. But that's paranoia, plain and simple. Keelor would never tell anybody anything I wanted kept secret; he never has.

"It's family stuff I . . . can't get into," I stammer. This is what happens when you make up lies on the spot. I should've planned this better, but it's too late, everyone will be wondering what my big secret is: What made Nick Severson give up hockey? "The coach was cool about it," I add. "Said I might even be able to rejoin later." That's huge too. The team doesn't have to put themselves out for me like that. It would mean bumping my replacement down to his old league.

Gavin's still semi-gaping at me from the front seat when Jillian springs forward and taps Keelor's shoulder. "Hey, who's throwing this party anyway?"

"What does it matter?" I say in my antisocial voice. "It's not like you'll know anyone." Okay, so maybe the party isn't such a good idea. Or maybe I'm just not in the mood for conversation.

Jillian's face folds into a frown. She doesn't look like Kate Hudson when she frowns; she just looks like a teenage girl. "Nice friends you have, Owen," she says, both hands gripping the seat in front of her.

"Hey, I didn't say anything," Gavin reminds her.

"It's just a guy we know from school," Keelor explains, ignoring Jillian's criticism. "His folks are in New Jersey with his sister."

Gavin cranks up the music so we don't have to talk and soon we're sauntering through Marc's front hall and checking out the action. Keelor introduces Jillian to people as we move through the living room. The music is pounding and the girls all look hot—plenty of bare bellies, tight pants, and criminally short skirts. Vix, hair straightened for the night, dances over to us and pushes her tongue into Keelor's mouth. He squeezes her ass, which is barely covered by a brown suede skirt, and I keep moving, into the equally crowded kitchen where Marc, Scotty, Hunter, and a bunch of other guys are knocking back beers.

"Nick!" Marc shouts over the sound of the music. He pulls a beer out of the fridge and hands it to me and I'm instantly one of them. We talk shit loud and fast until a girl named Denise teeters into the kitchen and drags Hunter into the other room. I down the rest of my beer and move on too, past the kitchen and into the den. Six people are sitting in a circle on the floor, sharing a bowl of weed. This is exactly what I'm looking for and I sit down next to a girl from last semester's math class and wait my turn. The bowl is cashed before it gets to me and I hand over my weed to this guy named Jonah who repacks it, takes a hit, and then hands me the bong and the lighter. The girl next to me reaches for the lighter and when I'm ready, I nod and she gives me a light. I breathe in slowly, careful not to suck in so much that I'll cough. I do this once, twice, and then pass the bong to the guy on my other side.

He smiles and I smile back. I can already feel the difference. My body's letting go and waking up all at once. The girl from math class has long eyelashes and huge pores. I've never been close enough to her to notice. The music is sharper, better, and I listen and look and wait for my turn, no hurry, wait for my turn and then begin the process over again. This could be my whole night, this room and these people, but there's that beer I finished earlier and eventually I have to take a piss.

I kick off my shoes before heading upstairs to explore. Nobody is using any of the bedrooms, all the doors are wide open, and I walk through each of them, the carpet soft under my feet, before using the bathroom off the master bedroom. The bathroom has two sinks and a whirlpool and I think about locking the door, filling it up, and climbing in, but by now my mouth is dry so it's back to the kitchen for more beer.

"Hi," someone says as they edge by me. It's Jillian with a beer bottle in her hand. She's wearing one of those beaded peasant top things and hip-hugger jeans. The outfit is new to me and I realize I must not have seen her since she took her coat off.

"Hey," I say back. "How ya doing?"

"All right. Probably not as good as you." She points to my eyes and I nod to acknowledge that yes, I'm aware they're dilated and weird.

"Where's Keelor?" I ask, for no reason really, except he's our only connection.

"Owen's in there." She motions to the smoke-filled living room, which has become the main dance floor, and I guess she doesn't seem thrilled at the prospect of talking to me due to my antisocial episode in the car.

"You actually call him Owen, huh?" It's one of the worst names I've ever heard. Like Frederick or Alastair. Besides, he looks exactly like a Keelor, which is why everyone calls him by his last name.

"It's what I'm used to," she tells me. "You seem marginally more communicative now."

"You caught me at a bad time earlier." I make sure I sound friendly to make up for before. "But I shouldn't have taken my frustration out on you. Don't hold it against me, okay?"

Jillian takes a swig from her beer and hoists herself onto the counter. "Here's to second chances."

I grab a beer from the fridge and take a step towards her. "So what are you doing here anyway? In Courtland, I mean."

"Staying with Owen's family for a while," she says. "Have you guys been friends a long time?"

"A long time." My mouth is drier by the second and I gulp down beer and stare at her tits. They're small, but that doesn't bother me.

"Hello," she says loudly, waving into my face. "You're supposed to look at the girl's eyes."

I smile, swallow more beer, and apologize. She really does look like Kate Hudson and I try to remember what Kate Hudson's tits look like, but I'm not sure I've ever seen them. "I should get higher," I say, excusing myself. "Don't let any other guys talk to your tits, okay?"

Jillian makes a face, jumps off the counter, and slips into the living room. And me, I follow my feet back to my favorite room and continue to get ripped. By the time I finally leave the room again, I have the munchies bad. People are hanging out on the deck, just like I predicted, but sadly, there's no barbecue. Marc lures most of us indoors with a jumbo box of Oreos and multiple bags of potato chips. This is my cycle. Smoke. Drink. Food. Drink. Food. Well, you get the picture. I'll be out of balance for the rest of the night, but it doesn't matter. It's only an external problem. Inside everything's cool. Calm and easy.

The music rushes by my ears. Nelly, Nickelback, Jay-Z. I dance better when I'm stoned and so I dance and then I drink, vodka this time, and then there's more pissing and my eyes can't focus, but I don't care. I amble into the kitchen, which is now full of girls making toast and sitting around the table talking. Eljeunia and Dani are there too and I stand in the doorway and listen to them console the crying girl at the table. Her father's been arrested for fraud apparently and everyone's saying that it's gonna be all right because it's not a real crime, like armed robbery, and then all of a sudden Eljeunia notices me hanging in the doorway.

"You want some peanut butter toast, Nick?" she asks.

Dani looks over at me too and I say, "I would *love* some peanut butter toast."

Eljeunia grabs two slices of bread and lays them out beside the toaster, ready for the next batch. "I'll bring them to you," she offers.

This is clearly a private conversation, and I slink over to the TV room on the other side of the kitchen and sit down on the floor to catch the video game in progress. "Hey, Nick," somebody says.

"Hey," I say back. I'm not really following the action; I'm staring at the screen and thinking about peanut butter toast. In fact, most of my body is parallel to the floor, silently praying for the swift appearance of peanut butter toast, when Dani steps into the room.

I sit up, like a fully functioning member of society, and she hands me a plate of peanut butter toast and a glass of orange something. "What's this?" I ask, holding up the glass.

"Just OJ," she says, sitting down next to me.

"Thanks." I take a sip of the orange juice and place the glass carefully down on the carpet.

Dani's blond hair floats down over her shoulders as she bends her head close to mine. "So how was your Christmas?"

"Okay," I say, nodding. "How was yours?"

"Great, the three of us went skiing for two days." The three of them is her, her mom, and her older sister, Lenore, who goes to university in Montreal. I think that's what they did last year too and because I remember that, I say it out loud and Dani smiles and bobs her head. "Yeah, every year since my dad moved to Seattle."

She goes on about the ski trip for a while as I devour my toast, which is so amazing that I have to stop myself from holding it up and announcing how amazing it is, and then she says, "I didn't think you were coming. You never e-mailed me back."

It never occurred to me to answer any of the messages about the party. For one thing, I didn't know I was coming until last night and for another, it didn't seem personal. This is exactly what I tell her and she picks at the carpet and says, "Are you still messed up about Sasha?"

"No," I lie.

Dani keeps picking at that carpet, like it contains the solution for world peace. "You are," she says knowingly.

Guess what? I don't want to do this. "Whatever you say, Dani."

My words sound like they're coming out of a stereo speaker. Hers do too. Everything is happening in slow motion.

"That hurts a little, you know," she slurs. "You being so messed up over her."

"Hey, don't take it personally." I put down my toast and touch her leg. "It has nothing to do with you. I always thought you were great."

"Or maybe just fuckable." Dani's head droops, her hair falling forward like a curtain.

Yeah, that too, only we both know we never fucked. "Are you drunk?" I ask, parting her hair so I can see her eyes. "I thought you were okay about us. That time in your car you didn't even—"

"Yeah," she says suddenly. "A little drunk." She gets to her feet, stares down at me, and says, "I never think about you." Then she turns and leaves the room.

I finish my toast and go back to watching video games. Gavin, who at some point slipped into the room without me noticing, announces, "Nick, Dani's looking for you."

"Not anymore," I tell him.

I scoop up my plate and glass and put them on the coffee table. I want to be closer to the music. My feet take me back to the living room and as soon as I get there, I wish I hadn't. I hear Avril Lavigne's voice before I hear the music. It's like she's whispering straight into my ear: *I'm with you.*

That sick feeling rises up in my throat. The man-eating plant pokes a hole in my stomach and sticks one of its leaves into the outside world. I hate myself. I can't get drunk or stoned enough to forget and I edge by people slow-dancing, with no idea of where I'm going.

In the corner of the room, a ninth-grade girl named Meaghan

is sitting on Marc Guerreau's lap, facing away from him. His hands are fondling her tits while this other guy, sitting in the chair across from her, holds her knees and sucks her face. She's giggling and kissing him at the same time and I'm not the only one watching. Everybody in the room sees it.

"Waiting for the live sex show?" a girl whispers into my ear, and I turn my head and find myself looking at Jillian. "It looks like you have ten minutes before they really get down to it."

She whirls off before I can say anything and I search out someone to talk to, anyone who won't ask me stupid questions or accuse me of fucking them up somehow, and I end up sitting down on the couch next to Hunter, who has lost the girl from earlier or is already finished with her or whatever. I crane my neck and scan the room for Keelor, but I can't see him anywhere.

Jillian is dancing nearby. I see her body through the cracks in the crowd. She dances like a hippy, but it looks right on her and I keep looking away and looking back while Hunter laughs at some joke I didn't catch. I bet Jillian's the tallest girl in the room, taller than me, and I'm wondering just how tall that is—checking her out from the ground up—when she catches my eyes on her. She smirks and looks away. I look away too and when I look up again, she's standing right in front of me, grabbing my hand. I stand up, but I don't want to dance and I tell her that.

"I don't want to dance either," she says. "Come upstairs."

She has ahold of my hand and I follow her, the carpet tickling the soles of my feet through my socks. We get to the top of the stairs and I stand there like a statue. Some of the doors are closed now and I guess I should warn her, but by the time that occurs to me, she's already opening the door to the master bedroom. Keelor and Vix are going at it full throttle on the bed inside and I start to laugh. Jillian slams the door shut before they can turn to look at us. She frowns at me like I'm being an idiot and I laugh again.

I can't see straight and I can't stop laughing. I'm really pissing Jillian off and I don't care. I don't even know what I'm doing. She tries the next door, which doesn't budge, and peers back at me with an expression that says: Why aren't you doing something? But I am doing something. I'm laughing hard. Until the third door opens.

We step inside and she closes the door behind us. The walls are peach-colored and covered with posters of horses. Medals and trophies top the bookcase and there's a photo on the bedside table— a girl in riding clothes with an old couple, too old to be her parents. "This must be Marc's sister's room," I say, walking around and picking up the trophies. They all have the name Celine Guerreau engraved on them.

Jillian sits down on the bed and glances uneasily over at me. "Maybe we shouldn't be in here."

"I think it's okay," I say, sitting down next to her. "All the doors were open before—like they were left open on purpose."

Jillian nods at me. "Are you going to start laughing again?"

"I'll try not to." I straighten out my face.

"What about the door? There's no lock."

"Oh, yeah." I get to my feet, wedge the only chair in the room under the doorknob, and sit down on the bed again.

Jillian slips off her shoes and lies down. I can make her nipples out under her top and I stretch out next to her and rub one with the tip of my finger. We kiss. I roll on top of her, slip my hands under her shirt, and unhook her bra. Man, she feels good. I push her top up and stare at what I'm touching. They're small, like I thought, but cute and my hard-on presses up against my zipper.

Jillian can feel it too and she pulls my face back towards her and kisses me some more.

I want to do it so bad. I want her to touch me and let me do everything to her. Something tells me she'd be really good. Maybe it's the way she's smiling.

"Jillian," I say. My voice still sounds funny, disconnected. "I don't have anything."

"We don't need anything," she whispers. "I don't want to do everything. I just want to fool around a little."

That could be okay too, that could cover just about anything, and I sigh when she strokes my jeans. Nice. I miss this. Maybe I shouldn't, but I do and I didn't even know it until this moment.

But I can't. Not even this.

I grab for her hand. "I don't think I can do this." Jillian looks up at me in surprise. "It's not you," I add swiftly. "I can't do this with anyone right now."

She sits up, gathering her knees towards her.

"Sorry," I tell her.

"It's okay. I just thought by the way you were watching me . . ."

"Yeah, I was watching—you're a good dancer." I glimpse down at her feet. I can't remember seeing her take her socks off, but her feet are bare and her toenails are painted cotton candy pink. "You have really nice feet," I add. It's a stupid thing to say given the circumstances, but I'm too out of my head to come up with anything smart.

"Thanks." She looks at me hard.

I'm starting to wish I'd kept it clean and passed on the beers. That twisted plant is poking around inside me again and I don't know how to stop it. "It's complicated with me," I explain. "It doesn't have anything to do with you as person."

"I said it was okay," she insists. "I just wanted to let off a little steam, you know? Keep things simple. And I thought I could trust you—with you being Owen's best friend."

"Shit." I smack my hand against my forehead. "What am I doing?" I completely forgot about Jillian being Keelor's cousin. How could I forget that?

"Relax." Jillian crosses her ankles and flexes her candy toes. "Nothing happened."

But I wanted it to and the thought of that, of what was running through my head only minutes ago, makes my stomach drop.

"Well, anyway . . ." She reaches down and picks up her socks. "I guess I should go downstairs."

"And find someone else?" I ask.

Jillian shrugs and scans the room for her shoes.

"You won't have any problem."

"Gee, thanks." She makes a sour face and gets to her feet.

"Don't go yet." I reach for her arm. Desperation is pathetic—you think I don't know that? But I don't want to be alone and I don't want to go back to the party. "Why don't you stay awhile and talk?"

"Talk about what?"

"I don't know, anything." I scramble for something sane to say. "How's it going over at Keelor's? How long are you staying?"

A trace of a smile passes across Jillian's face, but she's still standing. "It's okay. I really like his family." She crosses her arms in front of her. "Are you changing your mind?"

"No, no. I just want to talk for a while."

"Funny, you didn't seem interested in that earlier," she says flippantly. She sits down next to me again and I'm so grateful that I smile like an idiot. "So what's your story? Having a good time tonight?"

"I was," I reply truthfully. "But I think that's changing."

Jillian stares at me and I stare back, her face fuzzy. "Why?" she asks finally.

"Because I shouldn't have come in the first place." I've known this girl for a total of three hours, but it doesn't matter. My resistance is breaking down and I can't hide.

"Are you okay?" Her eyes are concerned.

"I'm fine," I say in a surprisingly steady voice. "But my ex-girlfriend is pregnant." Jillian doesn't blink. She should be a lawyer or a therapist. "I guess you're shockproof."

"Well, I don't know you." Her hands land on her denim legs. "Besides, it happens. So what are you two going to do?"

"I don't know." Heaviness settles back into my throat. I explain about Christmas Eve, my dad, Sasha's parents, and her recent trip to Lindsay's and Jillian sits there nodding and listening through the whole thing.

"One of my friends has a two-year-old," she says after I've finished. "His name is Sandy. Her ex comes to visit him every Sunday."

"How old is your friend?"

"Seventeen. It's tough for her, but her mom helps out a lot. Her and her ex still hook up sometimes." She rolls her eyes in frustration. "I've told her she should stop so many times that she doesn't even mention him anymore, but I know it's still happening."

"Yeah, that happens a lot. But not with us." I fold my arms over my knees and look at the carpet. It's peach like the walls, with fresh vacuum tracks, and I don't want to be sick on it. "I shouldn't be telling you all this. I'm spinning out. You can go if you want to." I hold my head and shut my mouth tight.

"Are you going to be sick?" She looks at me closely. "Can I get you something?"

194

"No." I prop one of the pillows up against the wall and lie back against it. "I just need to sleep it off. Thanks."

"Okay." She gets to her feet, then spins abruptly towards me. "It sounds like you need to get some stuff straight with your ex-girlfriend before you start following people up to bedrooms, but I guess you already know that."

"I know." My eyelids are ready to slam shut.

"You probably won't even remember this tomorrow." Jillian takes a step towards the bed and hovers over me. "How many times have you done this before—with some girl you barely knew at a party?"

I shake my head at her and she sits down on the bed and stares into my eyes. If we hadn't already been through this, I'd think she was going to kiss me. "I brought you up here to distract me," she says, smiling faintly to herself. "It didn't work the way I was thinking, but it's okay." *Distract you from what?* I must say it out loud because she slides one hand under her chin and says, "My mom's in the hospital. I'm staying at Owen's because I had to get away for a while."

"Why?"

"I'm sick of all her problems. After a while I feel like they're actually making *me* sick, like I can't remember what normal is." She glances at the bedspread and then quickly lifts her head. "She tried to kill herself. She talked about it before, but she never actually tried it until a couple days ago. My dad's with her in Windsor, but I couldn't take it anymore." Jillian's shoulders sag. "Anyway, so maybe that makes me shockproof, like you said."

"I'm sorry." I sit up and rub her shoulder. "Is she going to be okay?"

"Oh, she'll be okay and then one day she won't. That's how it works with her. It never really changes."

"I'm sorry," I repeat. "I don't know what to say."

"Don't say anything—I don't want to talk about it."

So I reach out and hold her hand instead. Part of me feels like I shouldn't even be doing that, that every single thing I've done tonight would make Sasha hate me again, but I do it anyway. Jillian stares down at our hands and moves towards me. "Don't get the wrong idea," she says.

Our heads settle back on the pillow and she drapes her arm across my chest. Jillian's breathing is real shallow, but she doesn't cry. It's so hard to do that with her. Almost as personal as what we were doing before. It reminds me of all the simple stuff between Sasha and me. It hurts so much that it's impossible to let go.

And neither of us do.

eighteen

MY LEFT arm is deadweight when I wake up. It's seventeen minutes after three and Jillian's breathing softly next to me. She looks really innocent in her sleep, much younger than when she's awake, and I gaze down at her pink toenails and take in a huge breath of relief. Things went farther than they should've between us, but it could've been a lot worse. I slip out of bed, swinging my left arm in the air to get the circulation working.

I don't feel completely normal yet, but I'm on my way back. I can see again, for one thing. What I need now is water or better yet, Coca-Cola, and I brush my hair into place with my fingers and head downstairs.

The kitchen is quiet and the supply of soft drinks exhausted so I rinse off one of the dirty glasses on the counter and fill it with plain old tap water. It's the best water I've ever had and I gulp down two glasses before slowing down. It's funny just how bad you can feel and continue to walk around as though nothing's the matter.

I swing into the living room. Two girls are dancing and smoking while all around them people lie passed out on the floor and the couch. Meaghan, that ninth-grade girl who was on Marc's lap, is there too and I'm sure someone will fill me in on the rest of that story later. I head for the TV room and almost trip over Keelor. He's sitting on the floor, Vix's head in his lap, watching a skin flick with a room full of semi-conscious guys and girls.

"Keelor." It's been hours since I've said anything and it comes out louder than I want it to.

He puts his finger to his lips and points down at Vix, who is nestled happily in dreamland. He shifts her weight as gently as he can and she stretches out on the floor without opening her eyes.

"Have you seen Jillian?" he asks, following me into the kitchen. "I thought maybe you guys left. Where've you been for the past two hours?"

"She's asleep upstairs. She's fine."

Keelor flinches. "You were upstairs with her all this time?"

"Nothing happened," I tell him. "We were just talking."

Keelor's mouth hardens. "You mean that, right? You wouldn't mess with my cousin. She's going through a lot of stuff. I can't talk about it, but the last thing she needs is anybody messing with her."

"Yeah, she told me about her mom."

Keelor blinks in surprise.

"I was losing it and I told her about Sasha," I continue. "Seriously, we just talked and fell asleep."

Keelor drops back against the counter with his mouth open. "I thought you didn't want anybody to know about Sasha."

"I was out of my head—it was bad. I still don't feel right." I grab the glass I was using earlier, refill it, and guzzle more water. "I'm gonna catch a ride with the next person who leaves."

"Okay," Keelor says uncertainly. I don't know if he's worried about me or if he's suspicious of my story.

"Look, you can ask her later. She'll tell you."

"No, I believe you," Keelor says. "I think Jonah's taking off soon—you can go with him."

I catch a ride with Jonah and tiptoe into my house. I'm not breaking curfew or anything, but I don't want Mom to see me like this. Once I'm safely in my bedroom, I hobble over to my bed and pass out on top of the covers. My dreams are endless. They blend into each other so it seems I'm having one epic dream all night long, only it doesn't make any sense. When I finally wake up, I feel like I've been asleep for days, but my clock radio says 7:39. The doorbell's ringing and I roll over onto my chest and ignore it. The moment it stops, I immediately drop back into unconsciousness.

"Nick." That's Mom's voice and I roll over and open my eyes. "Nathan is downstairs," she continues. She's wearing her purple terry-cloth robe and has sleep stuck in her throat.

"Nathan?" I rub my crusty eyes and sit up in bed. My tongue tastes like a Dumpster.

"I'm going back to bed," she says. "I'll let you handle this."

I stare after her for a few seconds before forcing myself out of bed. Last thing I knew I was eating oranges and arguing with Bridgette in some pointless dream. So far this isn't much of an improvement. Nathan over at my house before eight a.m. on New Year's Day can't be good news.

I go downstairs, still in yesterday's clothes, and find Nathan sitting in the kitchen, staring at the gurgling coffee machine. "Sorry, I know it's early," he says, his eyes darting over to me. "I tried to call you—your cell must be off."

I rub my eyes again and sit down next to him at the table. "It's *really* early. What's going on?"

"The New Year's Eve party last night." He taps the table. "I had a blowup with my dad about it. I got home a couple of hours ago and mentioned some things he didn't want to hear. I just need somewhere else to be for twenty-four hours while he calms down."

"Yeah, sure." The gurgling coffee looks and smells disgusting. The only thing I want in the world is orange juice so I get up and pour myself a tall glass while Nathan's waiting for his coffee. "So what'd you tell him exactly?"

"Nick." Nathan frowns and lowers his head. "I don't think you really want to know."

He's right, but I don't want to admit it. I look at the coffeepot filling up with dirt brown liquid and gulp down orange juice. How much are you supposed to know about your friends? Should I be asking him whether he's a top or a bottom or what?

"Okay," I tell him. "I don't need to know."

"You don't *want* to know," he repeats. "But it's okay."

"Look." I put my glass down and face him. "I don't tell you everything either, right? Maybe you don't need to know absolutely everything about me and I don't need to know absolutely everything about you."

"Yeah, but Nick . . ." Nathan's eyes are somber. "Someday I'm going to be with someone—I hope so anyway."

"I know," I snap. "I get it, Nate, but I don't need to know the details."

"Because you think it's sick." His voice is calm, but his eyes are angry.

"I never said that. Why'd you come here if that's what you think?"

"Because you're my best friend. I don't want to have to go somewhere else."

My fingers are wrapped tightly around the glass. I don't want to talk about this. I don't want to think about it either. "You don't have to go anywhere," I tell him. "Where are you getting this bullshit from? Are you forgetting what I said to your dad?"

"No, but I can tell when we talk sometimes, Nick. You don't really want to know. You say the right things, but you don't want anything to happen. You want me to be normal."

I don't want him to be normal; I don't want to be normal myself. The word doesn't even mean anything. "I'll be okay," I say. "I'll get used to it eventually." I lower my voice. "I just don't want a clear picture in my head."

Nathan shakes his head and tries to suppress a smile. "You picture all your friends in the act?"

"You know what I mean." Only when they're giving me play-by-plays. "So are you staying or what?"

Nathan puts both hands flat on the table. "There was a guy last night, a journalism major. We hooked up for a while—nothing heavy. I'll probably never see him again."

I nod like it's all good. Fuck Nathan for being right. "Is that what you told your dad?"

"Yeah, basically. He was the first person I kissed since I was fourteen. Pretty sad, huh?" Nathan's eyes are tight on mine. "I didn't even really like him that much. I think I just wanted to be close to somebody for a while."

"Everybody needs that."

"Try telling that to my dad."

The coffee is finished brewing and I grab a mug for Nathan and fill it. "I have to get some more sleep. I didn't get home until almost four."

Nathan yawns. "I haven't even been to sleep yet."

"Okay." I hand him his coffee. "Let's go."

201

We head up to my room and I pull my sleeping bag out of the closet and toss it onto the floor along with an extra pillow. I climb into bed and shut my eyes, but Nathan hasn't finished talking yet. He asks me about Marc's party and I tell him most of what I remember. I hesitate when it comes to Jillian, sleepy as I am, and Nathan says he knows I'm leaving something out. He thinks it's about Dani, but I break down and admit what happened with Jillian.

"I feel like shit," I confess. "I don't know what I'm doing anymore."

"You and Sasha aren't together," he reminds me. "Technically you didn't do anything wrong." He's only saying that because he's my friend. He knows it's wrong as well as I do.

I open my eyes and look at Nathan; his eyes are closed too. "I don't want to be with anyone else," I say. "I just want to be with Sasha." It's a lie and it's true. I don't know how it can be both, but that's the way it feels.

"You shouldn't be with anyone now, Nick. You're too fucked up to even know what you want."

"I know," I whisper. It's the last thing I remember before falling asleep.

It helps having Nathan around, but after he goes home to face his dad the next day, I can't avoid the fact that Sasha hasn't called. I shut my bedroom door tight, grab the phone, and sit on the floor. It takes me a minute to dial and when I do, her mom picks up. "Nick, I don't think you should make a habit of calling here anymore," Mrs. Jasinski says.

A habit, is that what this is? Before I can reply, Sasha's voice sings into my ear: "Nick?"

"Yeah." Everything I wanted to say suddenly seems stupid. I can't tell her how she's always in the back of my head or how happy she made me when she told me she missed me. "You never called."

"I just got back from Lindsay's this morning."

"Did that help?" I ask, evening out my voice.

"Dad hasn't spoken to me since I got back, but I don't know if I want him to so . . ." Sasha sighs. "I don't know. Maybe."

The pause between us lasts seconds too long and I breathe in and out, gripping the receiver. "Sasha." My voice dips. "Do you want me there with you on Wednesday?"

"I think it'd be harder." Sasha clears her throat.

"Okay." I'm holding my breath. "I just need to know you're gonna be okay."

"I'll try," she says. "How about you?"

"I miss you."

"Nick—"

"Don't worry," I tell her. "I know it's over. Will you just let me know you're okay afterwards?"

"Yeah," she promises. "I can do that. Take care, okay?"

"You take care. Call me anytime." I'm not ready for the conversation to be over. I haven't asked if she's going to be awake or even if she's scared, but I hang up. It's the story of us, I guess. I was never ready for anything.

nineteen

THE ONLY CLASS I can deal with is Visual Arts. Ms. Navarro lets us sketch anything we want all period to get us warmed up and Nathan sits across from me, drawing an old woman in a clingy, long dress. Her face is full of lines, but her body is young. He's always drawing freaky stuff like that. Mostly I do scenic stuff or real people. I can do them from memory pretty good, but Nathan has real imagination.

Nathan's dad grounded him for the next month—even from the GSA—but otherwise he's doing okay, better than me. I slept for about four hours last night, dreaming about stuff I don't want to remember. The funny thing is I really wanted to go to school this morning. Then I got here and my chest started pounding again.

I don't remember a single thing from Information Technology class. No, wait, I remember Jonah clapping my back and saying how great Marc's party was. English and physics were equally stimulating. One of the teachers made a comment about us all being "works in progress."

I could've stood up and announced, "Not me. I'm done." But I don't want people thinking I'm funny today. In fact, I don't want anyone to talk to me and I'm relieved when Dani breezes by me in the hall. She shouldn't be embarrassed about the other night, but I don't have the energy to tell her that. Anyway, it's not like we were ever really friends. I never called her just to see how she was. I didn't want to hurt her either—that's the best thing I can say and it's not great.

Keelor I can't avoid, but when he stops by my locker at the end of the day to check up on me, I can't help feeling the way Nathan felt about me: *He doesn't really want to know.* Maybe my bad luck feels contagious. Most of us could get somebody pregnant. All it takes is a little slipup.

"She'll be all right, man," Keelor says. "Those people know what they're doing. When is she coming back to school?"

"Next week," I tell him. "But we're not in any of the same classes."

"That's a good thing. You don't need that now."

I do. But he wouldn't get that.

Nathan walks by at that exact moment, says hi to both of us, and keeps walking. Once he's gone, Keelor says, "I told you he wouldn't come to Marc's party."

"He was at a party in Toronto."

"With gay people, right? I get that he's gay, but do you notice how everything's about that now?"

"Like everything isn't about you getting laid," I say with a smirk.

"Of course not." Keelor's face explodes into a grin. "There's always hockey."

"Right." It's hard to believe there was a time when the three of us were practically the same person. The only thing I can think is that it was never really true in the first place.

I sleepwalk through the next two days—classes and work—it's all the same, I'm just not there. I jump when anyone speaks to me and Brian reminds me to smile and look customers in the eye. That's something he tells you on your first day at Sports 2 Go, along with where to hang your jacket. Usually I can do this job in my sleep—people live to buy things—but that part of my brain has been switched off.

So I force myself to play Nick Severson. *Ha ha. These are good. Excellent. Whatta ya play? They're the best at their price range. On your credit card? Have a good one.*

There's no way to distinguish between real Nick and phony Nick. It's disturbing. I could play Nick Severson forever and most people wouldn't notice the difference as long as I stayed off the ice.

Mom picks me up at the end of the night. She gets into the passenger seat and shuts her eyes, like she completely trusts me to drive home unsupervised. It's like she's making a point of it. Saying she trusts me without actually saying it. I'm supposed to trust her too, you see, and I never explained about Christmas Eve. She's still pissed off about that and the feeling doesn't seem to be fading. What she doesn't understand is that I see through everything she's doing and it only makes me feel farther away.

"How was work?" she says finally, slowly opening her eyes.

"All right."

"You still enjoy it?"

"It's okay." I watch the road and feel her frowning beside me.

"I'll be gone before you leave for school tomorrow," she announces. "I have a job interview first thing."

"Great." I smile over at her. She's gotten a couple phone

interviews out of her resumes but nothing live until now. "Good luck. I'm sure you'll ace it."

"I don't know about that," Mom says with a laugh. "All those probing questions. What particular strengths do you bring to this job? Describe an instance in your current position where your efforts averted a potential disaster."

"Maybe you should bring a lawyer," I joke.

"Or maybe you could do the interview for me," Mom suggests. "You're much better at thinking on your feet—like your father."

She wouldn't say that if she knew half the things that have happened lately. I'd laugh if I had the energy. As it is, I keep driving without even a smirk to give myself away.

"Oh, Nicholas." Mom folds her arms in front of her and stares out the window.

"Oh, *what?*"

"What happened to our communication?" she says sadly.

"Mom." I'm so numb that I don't care. "Cut the melodrama. We're just talking about your interview. You always do this."

"Yes," she says coldly, "I don't know why I don't just switch off my emotions until you move away."

"Shit." *What a heartwarming thing to say. Thanks, Mom.* "I'm not playing any head games with you. Just because I don't tell you everything doesn't mean you can act like this."

"And you can't behave however you want and expect to get away with it, Nicholas."

"I'm not DOING ANYTHING," I shout.

"And you're not SAYING ANYTHING either," she yells back.

Those are our last words for the night. Mom gets out as soon as we pull into the driveway and I open the garage and park the car inside. My anger defuses the moment I step into my bedroom. I curl up on my bed and listen to Holland's music through the wall.

I'm so lonely, but nothing will fix that tonight, not even Sasha. To-morrow night everything will be different and most people won't even notice. We made such a big deal about being us all along and I'd rather think about us tonight too, but what's this thing inside her if it isn't us?

We haven't been fair to it. If there's a way to be fair to all of us, I don't know what it is. This thing inside her has a heartbeat and everything. A doctor wouldn't be able to hear it yet, but it's there and soon it won't be. Soon it won't be anything anymore and I'll walk away from this, but I won't be the same.

I'm sorry. I know that doesn't change anything. It's useless, but I can't help feeling it.

I'm sorry.

I turn the light off and slip under the covers. Sleep comes and goes in bursts. I don't dream; I just think the same things over and over and I'm wide awake way before my alarm goes off. Yesterday's clothes are plastered onto my body and I peel them off, stand in the shower, and then trudge down to the kitchen. Mom's finishing her coffee. She's wearing a light gray blazer and skirt and she looks up at me and says, "You're up early."

"Yeah. Are you on your way out?"

"Yes, that interview I told you about," she says curtly.

"I remember. Good luck."

"Thank you," she says, suddenly gracious. She sets her coffee mug in the sink and smiles slightly. "I better dash—don't want to be late."

"Good luck," I say again. You can never have too much good luck. Besides, I have nothing else to say to her.

I sit down at the kitchen table with a glass of orange juice and a bowl of cornflakes. Then I walk to school. It's the earliest I've ever been there and hardly anyone is around. I bum a cigarette from a ninth-grade kid with shaggy red hair and smoke it by the park bench just off school property. This kid, with the name I can't remember, looks at me like I'm royalty and says my name every chance he gets. A couple of his friends come over and bum cigarettes. One of them asks me if I was at Marc Guerreau's party and if the rumor about Meaghan is true. I tell him he shouldn't listen to rumors and that everybody makes up bullshit about parties, although I saw part of it for myself.

"Relax, man," the puny ninth-grade kid says. "I'm just asking."

"It's a stupid question," I say, and I must look mad because the kid's eyes get scared.

I drop my cigarette and walk back towards the school. Holland and Diego are talking in the hallway. She's stuffing her coat into her locker and he's leaning against the locker next to hers and smiling like she just said something hilarious. They don't see me and I don't stop.

I have double physics first and I prop my monster textbook up on the counter in front of me, take out my pencil, and doodle on a sheet of loose-leaf paper. Sitting still is impossible. I shift my weight in my chair and tap the countertop with my fingers. The girl on my left shoots me a highly annoyed look and grits her teeth.

The morning doesn't improve. My English teacher, Mr. Diebel, has to say my name multiple times before I hear him. I have no idea what he's been talking about; I'm just twitching away in my seat, thinking about this afternoon. I don't know exactly what time it's happening at, but I feel more panicked with every second. My voice stalls when I try to speak and Mr. Diebel flexes his right eyebrow like I'm just another brain-dead student, not worthy of his time and effort.

"Thank you for your insight, Nick," he says wryly, playing to the crowd.

Next it's on to lunch, but I'm not hungry. Socializing is out too. I don't want to sit around with Keelor and Gavin, pretending I'm all right. My body makes the decision for me. It swings away from the cafeteria and out into the winter sunshine. The air is cold but still and my feet keep walking. They take me all the way down to the lake, where I stop and stare at the water. It's hard to believe that it was ever warm enough to swim in and I think about that first day with Sasha, how nervous and excited she made me. It seems like something I made up in my head now. How could anything ever feel so perfect?

I crouch down and stick my hand in the water. It's ice cold and my instincts want to yank it straight back up again, but I hold it there for a minute, letting it ache.

My feet start up again and I follow them to the park on the hill. An old couple is pushing two little boys with fat mittens on the swings. Another woman is standing at the base of the wooden jungle gym and protectively eyeing a little girl, frizzy red hair sticking out of her hat, standing on top.

"Penny," the woman shouts, "are you getting hungry?"

"No, Mummy," the little girl calls back. She has a strong English accent and it makes her sound so proper that I smile. "Do you want me to come down?"

"Not if you don't want to," her mother says.

The little girl sits down at the top of the slide, poised to push off. "I'll come down soon," she promises, "but not yet."

She's so precise that it kills me and I look up at this Penny girl, who is bundled up for arctic temperatures, and smile straight at her. She waves to me from the jungle gym and says, "Mummy, that boy is watching us." It's funny, Penny can't be any older than four or five, but she knows I'm not a man.

210

"It's all right, Penny," her mother says, her voice registering a hint of embarrassment. "He won't bother you."

"I know that, Mummy," she says, exasperated. With that she hurtles herself down the slide.

I turn my back and start walking again, but I can still hear the girl's voice. "Mummy," she's saying, "I'll have you for a long, long time, won't I?" I'd never guess little kids would think about that, but obviously some of them do.

"Of course," her mother says. "Years and years."

"Years and years," Penny repeats, and I can tell what's she thinking: Exactly how long is that?

You can never be sure of anything, even when you're five years old. I'm tired of walking and I don't know where to go anymore. My head is pounding behind my eyes and my stomach wants to puke its guts out, only there's nothing in there but orange juice and cornflakes.

I cross the street and pass the row of stores on Main Street. A few people are taking advantage of the sun and walking their dogs. A black Labrador retriever tied to a sign outside Starbucks is devouring the remains of a bag of potato chips.

Beyond downtown it's houses again and I head north for a while before hanging a left. This is Keelor's neighborhood. I've spent so much time here over the years that it feels like a second home. Most of his neighbors still have their Christmas lights up and the family across the street has six reindeer lined up on their lawn. Santa Claus has lost his balance and is lying on his back. I go over, stand him up, and hover around the bottom of Keelor's driveway.

I should go home and lock myself in my room; I shouldn't step up to Keelor's front door and ring the bell. His cousin might not be home and what if she is?

But I can't control myself. I walk up the driveway and hit the bell. Jillian opens the door, frowns at me, and says, "God, you're pathetic."

No, she doesn't. She stands in front of me in a purple-striped sweater and jeans, looking surprised and waiting for me to say something.

"Hi," I say.

"Hi," she says. "What're you doing here?"

"I was—walking around." My mouth stumbles over the words. "And then I was in the neighborhood." I point at Santa Claus across the street.

"Don't you have school?" Her eyes rake over me, evaluating my state.

"Yeah," I admit, and she reaches for my arm and pulls me inside.

Jillian stands with her back against the wall and watches me take off my shoes. "Are you okay?" she asks. Would I be here if I was? I shake my head and stand stiffly in the hallway. "You want to talk about it?" she asks.

"No." I turn and reach down for my shoes. "I should go."

"No," Jillian says forcefully. "Come in—I'll make you something warm." She reaches out and touches my hand. "You feel cold. How long have you been out there?"

My mind skips back to Penny's mom at the bottom of the slide. *Are you getting hungry?* What makes me think I can do this to some girl I've known for six days?

"I'm okay," I tell her. "It's not that cold today."

We go into the kitchen and Jillian makes two hot chocolates, hands one to me, and leads me into the living room. Jazz is playing on the stereo and a Clive Barker novel is splayed out on the coffee table.

"I should've said goodbye to you on New Year's," I say, sitting down next to her on the couch. "I just felt kind of weird about the whole thing—not even with you, really, but about my girlfriend."

"Your ex-girlfriend," she reminds me, her curly blond head tilting.

"Yeah, well, that's the thing, she doesn't feel like an ex." I take a sip of hot chocolate, then hold the mug in front of me. "Have you heard anything about your mom?"

"Actually, yeah. My dad says she's doing better." She throws me a sideways glance. "He wants me to come home this weekend."

"I thought you were going to stay here awhile."

"I was. He deals with things better without me. When I'm there, he just gets worked up about me not being supportive." Jillian's cheeks tighten. "But I'm missing school and this is my last year before university."

"Your mom must've been pretty unhappy before." I shouldn't push it, I know, but I can't stop.

"Yeah." Jillian's face goes blank. "It's chemical. There doesn't have to be a reason for her to be unhappy. Anything can make her unhappy at any time if she's off her medication." Jillian sets her mug down next to the Clive Barker paperback and turns towards me. "Why'd you come here?"

I take another sip of hot chocolate. "I couldn't handle school." My hands are as cold as ever, even holding the warm mug, and I feel like I did that day in my dad's car, but I don't want to let go. "My ex-girlfriend is having an abortion today." I angle away from Jillian and talk to the wall. "Nobody at school . . . I mean, I can't talk to them . . . and she won't let me be close to her anymore and—" I rush to my feet, knocking the coffee table along the way. "This is stupid. I'm sorry. You have your own stuff to worry about—you don't want to hear this. I don't even know you."

Jillian stands up next to me. "Sit down," she says. "It's okay. I just don't want to dredge up all this stuff about my mom. I talked to my dad for an hour yesterday night and . . ." She takes a heavy breath. "It's hard, you know." She touches my hand again and threads her fingers in between mine. "Sit down, okay?"

I sit down and she sits down next to me. I know she heard Gavin ask me about giving up hockey on New Year's, but this time I explain it for real, along with the truth about hiding out at Nathan's during the tournament. She tells me I should start playing again as soon as I can. She says she's in this teen theater group at home and that it helps a lot, pretending she's someone else. Maybe that's my problem with hockey; I'm always me. I ask her more about the theater group and she says they did a production of *Grease* in the fall and that she got the lead.

"So you can sing?" I ask.

"Yeah, I love to sing," she tells me. "When I was younger, I used to sing for everyone that came over to our house. I'd organize pretend contests and stuff with kids in my class and get their parents to be the judges. I was a real show-off, totally obnoxious."

I smile and ask what her favorite song is.

"You mean to sing?" she asks.

"Yeah, sing a little." I fold my arms and sink further into the couch, expecting her to protest. Instead she takes a sip of water, warns me that it's corny, and launches into "Landslide." She holds her head straight and sings sweet and sad, looking straight at me. I'd let her sing the entire song without stopping her, but she stops anyway, just after the chorus.

"You're really good," I say sincerely. "You probably already know that."

Our bodies are so close they blend effortlessly together. We spent two hours spooned up together on New Year's Eve so the nearness feels completely natural between us and somehow we drift down on the couch until we're lying with our bodies wrapped tightly around each other. I can feel her heart beating against mine, racing, and I feel like crying, but I won't let myself. I nuzzle my face in her neck and kiss it softly. We lie still. I don't want to move and end the moment. I'm addicted to this and I shouldn't even be here. My fingers brush across her cheek as I pull back to look at her.

But Jillian must be able to read my mind because she turns her face away and says, "You know it's not going there with us. The timing's all wrong."

"I know," I say. "Sorry." I'm sorry for everything and I free all my limbs and feel the color drain out of my face.

"I wonder if we'd even like each other if we met under normal circumstances," Jillian muses, sitting up and grabbing for her mug. "What would've happened at that party?"

"I'd still like you," I tell her. "But I don't know what would've happened."

"I guess I probably wouldn't have been at the party in the first place."

"That's true." I guess I might have been—if Sasha and I weren't together. There's a whole alternate chain of events that could've happened to the three of us.

Jillian and I spend the next twenty minutes or so trying to talk about normal things, but I can feel both our problems trying to claw their way back to the surface, and then she says, "What're you going to do after you leave?"

"Go home."

"And then?"

"Wait for her call." My watch reads twenty-one minutes after two. It may have already happened. I hope so. My head drops into my hands and I remind myself that it's for the best. Was I going to take this kid to the park, hang around at the bottom of the slide, and promise to be around forever?

"I should go," I announce.

"No hurry," Jillian says. "No one will be home for at least an hour."

She means Keelor and his brother. They'll be the first ones back and I shouldn't be around then. Make that another reason I shouldn't be here.

"I should go anyway." I stand up and move slowly towards the door, waiting for her to follow me. "I'm sorry about before." I turn and look into her eyes.

"It's better this way," Jillian says. "I think you know that."

I do. My arms hang by my sides, feeling empty. "Can I hug you goodbye? This is probably the last time I'll see you."

"Sure." Jillian's eyes are sparkling, like I didn't need to ask in the first place. She takes a couple steps towards me and wraps her arms around my back. I hold her too.

"You never know, we might run into each other again sometime," she says.

I let go and nod. It's one of those things that'll never happen, but she's right, it's better this way. Whatever's between us is untouched. This is what pure feels like before you ruin it.

twenty

NATHAN CALLS AT four o'clock. He didn't know I was cutting art and wants to make sure I'm okay. I could tell him about Penny, the girl in the park, and how I found myself wandering over to Keelor's house to see Jillian, but it'll wait. Explaining myself is exhausting these days and besides, that's all background. He knows Sasha is having the abortion today; he knows how I'm feeling. He always knows.

"I don't know if I'm coming in tomorrow," I tell him. "I want to see her."

"I thought her folks wouldn't let you."

"Yeah," I admit. "That's the deal."

"She said she'd be back at school on Monday," he reminds me, and I try to wait for her call, I do. I sit up late Wednesday night, repeatedly checking my IM and e-mail. Someone would let me know if anything went wrong, but I have to hear her voice—to be sure—and early the next morning I cave in and text her, asking her to call me.

I lay low until Mom leaves and then tell Holland I'm cutting classes. She's not in the least surprised and she doesn't ask why—she already knows I won't tell her.

I take the cordless and my cell into the bathroom with me and jump in the shower for five minutes. My body already feels different from not playing hockey for the past week and a half—lazy from lack of use. Outside of summers this is the longest I've been off the ice since I sprained my ankle two years ago. The sprains can be worse than the breaks sometimes and my right ankle is still weaker than my left.

The smallest thing can change you.

I towel off and park myself in front of the TV. Maybe Sasha won't check her cell today; then she'll think I'm at school and the whole day will pass before she calls. But I give it a while longer. I don't want to wake her if she's sleeping.

An hour and a half goes by like that—me watching music videos on the couch and the phones not making a sound. I go upstairs and check messages again. There's spam preapproving me for a fixed-rate mortgage, advertising 75 percent off printer ink, and trying to interest me in penis enlargement patches. I delete them and wait until exactly 10:46. Then I break and dial Sasha's cell phone. Mrs. Jasinski answers on the second ring and I'm so stunned to hear her voice on Sasha's phone that I freeze.

"Hello?" Mrs. Jasinski repeats. "Is anyone there?"

"Yeah," I say. "It's me, Nick."

"Hello, Nick." Her voice is formal and stiff, like I'm trying to sell her windows that she doesn't need.

"Can I speak to Sasha?" I ask. "I haven't heard from her yet and I want to make sure she's okay."

"She's sleeping."

"But she's okay?"

"She's doing well." Mrs. Jasinski's tone sharpens. "I don't want you to call here anymore, Nick. I know you two will see each other at school, but it'd be better if you kept your distance. For her sake, you understand?"

"I just want to make sure she's all right," I repeat. "I still care about her." It's more than I want to say, but I don't stop there. "I didn't mean for any of this to happen. I know she's special."

"Yes, she is," Mrs. Jasinski agrees. "I'll take good care of her. Don't worry about that."

The phone goes dead in my hand. At first I think Sasha will call me anyway; she knows I need to hear from her. But hours go by and then it's afternoon. Monday is over three days away. It's the future, a day that may never in reality arrive.

I'm crazier now than I've ever been. It doesn't matter what her mother says. I understand it, but I won't listen. I shove my cell into my back pocket, slip my shoes and coat on, and walk over to Sasha's house. The house looks lonely without its Christmas decorations. Christmas Eve seems almost as long ago as last summer.

I walk slowly up to the Jasinski doorstep and ring the bell. Mrs. Jasinski's face falls as she opens the door. "Nick, you shouldn't be here," she says, the lines between her eyes jumping to attention. "I thought we had an understanding. This isn't what Sasha needs."

"I'm sorry." I bow my head, but I'm not going anywhere. "I need to see her."

"So I'm going to have a problem with you." Mrs. Jasinski pulls the belt on her cardigan tight around her waist and focuses an uncompromising stare in my direction.

"No, but . . ." I pinch the outside seams of my jeans. "Will you at least ask her if she wants to see me? Please." My voice is getting thick. I can't have this conversation with her mother much longer, but my feet are frozen to the spot.

"I don't want this to be harder than it is." Mrs. Jasinski tips her head. "Do you understand, Nick?" It's a plea and I do understand, but I can't move.

"Please," I say hoarsely. "Just ask her."

We can both hear the gravel in my voice and I squint into the open doorway, pleading silently back. The moment seems endless. I can't talk and she won't speak. I let go of my jeans and watch Mrs. Jasinski purse her lips. "I'll ask her," she says at last. "Wait here."

She closes the door in my face and for a minute I think that's it, I've blown my chance. Then she reappears and ushers me inside with an aggravated whisper: "Sasha's in her room."

Mrs. Jasinski lets me brush past her in the hallway. I can feel her staring at the back of my head as I walk on. Sasha's door is closed and I open it and slip inside her room. Under my coat my sweater is sticking to my back and I wipe my hands swiftly on my jeans in case they're damp too.

Sasha's sitting on the bed in dark green sweatpants and a long-sleeve top, her back resting against the pillow that's propped up against the wall. Her hair's flat and she has dark circles under her eyes, but other than that she looks all right. She's facing the TV, which is a new addition to the room, and her eyes leap over to me as I take a step towards her.

"Hi," I say quietly. "I called earlier, but you were asleep."

"Yeah, Mom told me. I was going to call you later."

"I won't stay long." I stand in front of her dresser, my throat filling up with sand. "I just wanted to see how you were."

"I'm okay." She fiddles with her sleeve. "Crampy."

Then I notice a bottle of Tylenol on the bedside table next to a tall glass of what looks like cranberry juice and her ragged old teddy bear. I lean back against the dresser, my fingers curving around its edge, and lower my head.

"Nick, don't," Sasha commands.

"I'm not." I choke on the words. "I'm glad you're all right." I swallow sharply, determined to make this okay, but when I look up, tears are sliding down Sasha's cheeks. My eyes open up. Tears run hot down my face. I suck at being steel.

"Was it bad?" I croak.

Sasha wipes her face, but the tears keep coming. "I was just scared." She looks into my eyes; I wish she wouldn't. "I never thought I'd be somebody who did this. Sometimes it didn't even seem real but not yesterday." Sasha's fingers dig into her hair. Her chest quivers as her voice breaks. "The worst part is I'm glad it's over."

I sit down on the bed next to her. I'm sniffling and wet all over and I struggle out of my coat and throw it on the floor. "You were right," I whisper. "We're not ready to have a kid."

"I know." She squeezes her eyes shut and I stroke her hair. She blinks at me and folds her hand inside mine. I wrap my arms carefully around her and she buries her face in my shoulder.

Neither of us says anything for a long time. My insides howl, my eyes burn, and Sasha keeps shaking silently against me. I kick off my shoes and pull my legs up onto the bed. Sasha moves over to make room. We lie with our heads on her pillow until I'm numb. I think the tangled weed inside me is dead or maybe I just don't know how to feel anything anymore.

"I could come back to school tomorrow," Sasha says, her face inches from mine. "But I think I'll wait until Monday." She sweeps a strand of hair out of her eyes. "I wouldn't be able to concentrate."

"When do you have to go back to the doctor?" My voice is calmer now.

"In about two weeks. Just to check things out."

I nod with my eyes. "Is your dad still mad?"

"Not really." Sasha sighs and sucks in her cheeks. "I don't think he knows what to say to me anymore." She points at the TV. "He bought that for me a few days ago. He said he was going to get one for my birthday but that I might as well have it now."

We lie there blinking and trying to catch our breath. "My mom's been great," Sasha adds quietly. "She took the day off to be with me. I know she told you that she didn't want me to see you today."

"Yeah. She hung up on me too, but I couldn't wait." I hold the air inside my lungs for a while and then let it go. "I couldn't stop thinking about you and what was happening. I cut class yesterday. I couldn't do anything."

Sasha's gaze clings to mine. The corners of her lips drop and she reaches out to touch my face. I'm still numb, but somehow I can feel that and it occurs to me that we'll never be this close again. My skin goes warm where her fingers were, but I'm too drained to be any sadder.

"Can you stay awhile?" she asks.

It's like she can read every single thing I'm thinking just by looking at me. How long does it take a connection like that to dissolve? Part of me hopes it takes a long, long time. The other part wants to stay numb. I'm a work in progress and the Nick of the moment opens his mouth and says, "As long as you want—or until your mom kicks me out."

Sasha almost smiles. "She wouldn't do that—she knows I want you here."

We snuggle up on the bed and watch a soap opera neither of us follows. To tell the truth, I'm not even watching. I'm just breathing next to Sasha, recovering. After the show's over, she sits up, picks up her cranberry juice, and drains the glass.

"You want some more?" I ask.

"Thanks." She hands me the empty glass. "There's loads of stuff in the refrigerator. Grab something for yourself too."

I pad into the Jasinski kitchen and swing open the refrigerator. It's well stocked with juices, soft drinks, and three different varieties of milk. I refill Sasha's cranberry juice and take a can of 7-Up for myself. That round table is by the wall, just like the last time I had dinner here. A package of Peter's crayons is lying on top of it. Lime green is halfway out of the box. It's his favorite color. His coloring books are full of people with lime green faces. Some things haven't changed.

Mrs. Jasinski appears in the kitchen before I can make a clean getaway. She stands in front of the closed refrigerator and says, "Is she all right?"

It's funny, I spent the past few weeks thinking I was the last person who'd be able to answer that question correctly. Now, for once, I'm the person who knows best. "She's fine," I say politely. "I'm getting her more cranberry juice."

Mrs. Jasinski nods and walks out of the kitchen. I go back to Sasha's room, hand over the juice, and sit down at the end of her bed. "Your mom was asking about you just now. She wants me to stay away from you." I don't even blame her mom; that's just the way it is.

"I know," Sasha says. "They told me to stay away from you too."

"So what happens at school?"

That concentration look slips over Sasha's face. She frowns as her eyebrows draw together. "Well, you better not ignore me," she says firmly. "I don't want it to be like before."

223

"I don't want that either." Like that's even possible. "I don't think I could do that after all this."

"Yeah." She drops her voice. "But it'll be different, you know? We can talk at school, but no more phone calls or anything. My parents wouldn't like it and I think I need some distance too." She rubs her eyes. "Right now you just remind me of everything."

"I know what you mean." I glance at her black socks, bunched up around her ankles. The last time I was on this bed so many things happened between us. Now it's all about this. "You know you can call me anytime if you want to—if you need to talk."

"Thanks," she says, but we both know she won't. I know her so well that I can do most of the translations in my head without missing a beat.

Sasha stares at me with weary eyes, her lank hair lying against her shoulders and her washed-out skin nearly the same color as the wall behind her. I love her so much, only the love is all pain now. I don't want to remember us like this; I don't want to feel this way every time I look at her, but maybe I will. It's not something I can run away from.

"You look tired," I say gently. "Maybe you should go back to sleep." Don't get me wrong, I don't want to go, but it has to happen sometime.

"Now you sound like my mom," Sasha says with a yawn.

"It could be worse, right?" I joke. "I could sound like your dad."

"Yeah." Sasha crosses her ankles next to me. "I don't think that's possible."

"I hope not." I'd like to think I wouldn't make my teenage daughter feel like crap for getting pregnant. "I think I'm gonna call my dad tonight—let him know about everything."

"What about your mom? You never told her?"

"I'm going to. As soon as I get home."

Sasha tilts her head as if to ask: Why now? And I don't know except that it's happened and it's finished. I've been doing a shitty job of acting like Nick lately and today I can't do it at all. If you tapped my chest, you'd hear the sound of emptiness.

"I should've told her before," I continue. "Even my dad said that. I should've told her on Christmas Eve."

"Your mom's okay," Sasha says. "She'll be upset, but it'll be all right."

"Yeah." I nod at Sasha. She always knows what to say—even on a day like today. "Did you talk to Lindsay?"

"She called last night, but I didn't want to talk. I'll probably call her back later."

"Nathan called yesterday when I cut art." I reach behind me, grab my 7-Up from the dresser, and down a couple mouthfuls. "Sometimes I feel like he's the only person aside from you that gets how I'm feeling." Him and Jillian, but she's going and I'm still not ready to hear any details about that journalism student. That last part is something I really need to work on. There are a few things I have to work on and with hockey on the back burner I have a lot of time.

"He's a really good person," Sasha says.

"He is," I agree. Him and Sasha are the best people I know.

"Listen." Sasha turns and adjusts her pillow. "Maybe you better go soon after all. I want to take a shower." She puts a hand to her head. "My hair's disgusting."

"You look fine."

"You must be legally blind," she says.

I stand up and hover around her dresser as she gets off the bed. "You're okay to take a shower?"

"No baths," she says. "Showers are okay." I move out of the way as she grabs a pair of underwear from the dresser. "And I have to take my temperature again later."

I read about that on the Internet. A fever can mean you have an infection. Bleeding is normal, but too much isn't. They say abortion's one of the safest surgical procedures, but there are still things to watch out for. Thinking about that makes me glad we didn't do this on our own, that Sasha's mom is right here looking out for her.

"Okay." I bend down and kiss Sasha's forehead, as softly as I can. "I'll see you Monday."

"Yeah, see you Monday." Sasha folds her arms in front of her chest, just like she did that day at school when I chased after her. "Thanks for coming by," she adds quietly. "It means a lot."

I bury my hands in my pockets and nod. We're at the very end. There's nothing left to say. All I have to do is walk out the door.

twenty-one

THere are VOICES coming from my living room, mingled with the sound of some English band's gloomy guitar chords. Holland is musically challenged and loves this shoe-gazing crap. I bypass the living room and leave her to it, but a guy's laugh stops me partway to the stairs. I poke my head into the living room and take in the scene. Holland and Diego are sitting on opposite sides of the coffee table, the Scrabble board spread out between them.

It's like I've been hurtled back in time. Our Scrabble board hasn't seen the light of day in three years. Diego bounces me a smile over his shoulder. "Hey, Nick. How's it going?"

"All right," I tell him. "You?"

"All right," he says.

Holland adds her own smile for good measure and I turn and double back to the stairs. I go up to my room and sit on the floor next to the bed. The sheets are twisted into a solid mass, leaving the mattress partially exposed. My sleep over the past few days has consisted mostly of shifting positions and I'm exhausted, but I won't lie down.

When I'm sure Mom's home, I slog down to the kitchen and catch her pulling a bag of Brussels sprouts out of the refrigerator. "Can I talk to you?" I ask. You'd think it'd be hard to say after waiting so long, but it's not. I'm on auto and everything feels the same.

"Mmm?" she says, her head darting back into the fridge. My flat tone obviously hasn't set off any alarm bells. "What is it?"

"No, I mean . . ." I point to the fridge, although she hasn't looked up at me yet. "Can you stop what you're doing so we can talk?"

Mom's back straightens and her eyes meet mine. She closes the refrigerator and motions towards the table. I pull out a chair and wait for her to sit down next to me. As soon as she does, I announce: "Sasha had an abortion."

Mom's head wilts slightly. Her bottom lip juts forward. She stares at me in silence. I look at the table, then back up at her, waiting for my words to sink in. "Is she all right?" Mom asks.

"She'll be okay."

Mom's eyes are unreadable. Her head springs up as she opens her mouth. "I didn't know you two had that kind of relationship."

"Before we broke up," I say factually. "Yeah, we did."

"And when did this happen?" Mom asks.

"Yesterday." My throat's drying out. I don't have an ounce of water left in my body after what happened at Sasha's earlier. "I just saw her today."

"Do her parents know? Is she being taken care of?"

I nod leadenly. "Her mom took her. She's at home with her now." Mom's head slopes towards mine and I keep going. "I couldn't tell you before. You take things really hard." I slump down in my chair. "I didn't know what to say."

Mom's head snaps up again. It's the wrong thing to say, I guess, but it's the truth. "You can always talk to me, Nicholas. How many times do I have to tell you that?"

"I can't always," I argue. "You can't expect that."

"But you told your father?"

"Yeah," I admit. "That's different. He's not around all the time." I'm too tired to do this with her. Why should I have to explain the way things are? Why can't she just open her eyes and see it? "Anyway, that's not the point. I'm telling you now. If you turn this into something about him . . ." My face is throbbing red. I can feel it.

"I'm not doing that," Mom says evenly. "But you can't expect me to hear something like this and not give it a second thought—because this is what's been upsetting you lately, isn't it?"

"Since Christmas Eve," I confirm. "I couldn't get away from it."

"And now?"

"I don't know." I shrug. "Nothing's the same."

"No," Mom says. "Of course it isn't." I stay quiet and stare at my knees. "This is a very serious situation. This is something you could be dealing with for a while."

"I know that."

"Okay." Mom folds her hands into her laps and squints at me like she's about to say something intense. "What do you want me to say to you?"

My head jerks up. "I don't know." I stare past her. "I don't know."

"But I'm sure you know nothing like this should ever happen again." Mom leans in so I can't ignore her.

"Yeah, of course."

"Because right now you may think you'll never find yourself in that situation again, but you will."

I've already decided to listen to whatever lecture she has in store for me. My face is fixed in a passive expression and I nod as she continues.

"I hope talking to your father helped."

"A bit." My jaw twitches in surprise. "He was pretty good about it, but I haven't talked to him for a while."

"Maybe you should give him a call," she says. "I'm sure he'd want to hear from you."

"Yeah, I might." An idea begins building in my head and snowballs with momentum. "I was thinking maybe I'd go down and stay with him for a few days. Just to get away, you know?"

Mom blinks and looks into my eyes. "It's not a bad idea if it's all right with him."

"I'll check," I tell her, and before I know it, I'm standing. "Thanks."

Mom stands too and then we're both standing there trying to pretend this isn't as awkward as it seems. "Go ahead and give him a call now," she suggests. "Let me know what he says." I take a step towards the door and she adds, "Dinner's in about forty minutes if you're interested. Holland's friend is staying."

I shake my head and Mom nods sympathetically and says, "I'll put some aside and you can have it later."

"Thanks," I say gratefully.

Upstairs, I pick up the phone and dial Dad's condo. He has a lot of late meetings and I expect to get his machine, but he answers.

"Nicholas, how are you?" he asks. "What's happening?"

He could've called me himself to find out, but I let that go and fill him in on the last few days. When I come to the point about staying at his place, he interrupts with: "Nick, this isn't enough notice. Bridgette's sister and her family are coming in from Calgary on Saturday, and you have work and school, I'm sure."

"I can call in sick," I tell him. "And I won't miss much school."

"The thing is I have plans, Nick." Dad puts on his hearty voice. "What do you say to two weeks from now? I'll come pick you up and we can get tickets to a Leafs game—the whole thing."

Two weeks seems like a life sentence and I say, "No, that's fine. Do your family thing with Bridgette. I'm cool." In fact, my words are like ice. I never ask him for anything and all I'm asking for now is time. Not even a full consecutive twenty-four hours, just time.

"*Nicholas,*" Dad says. His tone's all "don't be that way."

So okay, I won't. I hang up and flick on my stereo. After a minute the phone rings, but I don't pick up. Thirty seconds later there's a bang on my door and Holland swings it open and says, "There's a man on the phone claiming to be your father."

"Did you ask him for proof?"

"I didn't think of that," Holland says. "Are you picking up or what?"

"No." I'm not going to beg him so what's the point?

"What?" Holland scrunches up her face. "Are you guys fighting?"

"Yeah, so go downstairs and hang up the phone like a good little girl, okay?"

"I don't think so." Holland picks up the receiver and places it facedown on my bed. "Do your own dirty work, Nick." She shuts the door gingerly behind her and I stare down at the abandoned receiver.

"Hello?" Dad's voice is sputtering. "Hello? Nick? Hello?"

"Okay, fine," I say irritably, my fingers closing around the receiver. "I'm here."

"There was no need to hang up, Nick." Dad's really worked up; he sounds like my parents' divorce all over again. "If you'd listen for a moment—all I'm saying is that next week is out. We have theater tickets tomorrow and Saturday we're leaving for Montreal for two days. So, I'd really like to do this in two weeks' time." He pauses and then adds, "I'd like to see you."

"Just us?" I need to make my temporary escape now, but I can see that's not going to happen this week. "Because it'd be cool if it could just be me and you for a change."

"All right, Nick," Dad says. "We can do that, but you have to realize Bridgette is important to me and that's probably not going to change anytime soon."

"That's your business," I tell him.

"Sure, but it'd be nice if the two of you could get along."

"I'll be nice. But I'm not going to promise anything else. You can't expect me to like her just because you do."

"Okay," Dad concedes, frustration rumbling around in the back of his throat. "I'll give you a call next week and let you know the arrangements."

"Thanks," I say sincerely.

"Are you going to be all right?" Concern gives his words a razor edge.

"I'm okay. I just need to get away from everything for a while."

"Sure," Dad says genially. He's already forgiving me, silently ascribing my attitude to everything I've been through lately, or at least that's the way it sounds. "I think it's good you told your mother. Most secrets don't do people much good." He didn't say *all*, I notice, and I still believe in good secrets, but they're fragile.

After Diego's gone, I throw my dinner in the microwave and tell Mom I won't be going to Dad's for a couple weeks yet. She doesn't ask me to explain; she says it'll be good for me to spend some time in Toronto and that the time frame will give me the chance to book shifts off work. I realize I never told her about leaving the Courtland Cougars and fill her in on that too.

The next morning she wakes me up, stares down at me, and says, "I wasn't sure you'd want to go school today but I thought I'd check."

I must've forgotten to set the alarm, but I want to go to school and I mumble that in barely coherent morning English. Mom smiles and tells me that with everything that happened yesterday, she forgot to mention that the company she interviewed at wants her to come in for a second interview.

"See?" I say. "I knew you'd do good."

"They're interviewing three other people too, but I'm still in the running," Mom says, her lips stuck in a grin. "The second interview is on Monday." She tosses her head back in mock aggravation. "There goes another sick day."

Monday's also Sasha's first day back at school and the thought of that makes me shudder. I want her to be there and I know I can't avoid her, but I know exactly what it'll feel like to see her again— like I'm missing a layer of skin. I don't know how to walk around like normal all day when I can run into her at any time.

But for today, at least, I don't have to deal with that. My ego-maniac English teacher makes jokes at various students' expense, and Keelor hunts me down in the hall and wants to know how I am. I can tell he doesn't get it, but at least he's trying. Keelor wants me back on the ice as soon as possible, but he's trying not to push it. Everybody's being so good and concerned and I'm glad, for sure, but underneath that there's another part of me that nothing even touches.

Ms. Navarro has the radio on during art class, like always, and it relaxes me a little even though it's jazz. Nathan talks to me in a mellow voice through the whole thing and that relaxes me too.

"So what happened to the journalism student from New Year's Eve?" I whisper. "You ever going to see him again?"

"Naw." Nathan stops sketching and looks up at me. "Not really my type."

Here we are again. I'm clumsy at this, not like him, but he needs to know that I'm going to try. Seriously, I mean it. "You know there will be somebody, though," I say under my breath. "It's just this stupid small town."

"Maybe." Nathan's eyes are suspicious.

"For sure," I tell him.

"You know." His tone turns breezy. "If I didn't know better, I'd think you were trying to tell me something."

"Shut up." I roll my eyes at him. "You know what I'm saying. Don't be an asshole."

"I know. Thanks for the approval rating." Nathan grins and shakes his head. "You're so uptight, Severson. What're you gonna do in university when the gay city boys start hitting on you?"

I give him a suitably dirty reply and Nathan busts his gut laughing. I laugh too. I laugh so hard that it hurts and I bend over clutching my sides. Ms. Navarro glances in our direction and I straighten up, this goofy grin stretched across my face.

I wish I could spend all day in art class, but the bell doesn't care. After it rings, Nathan and I file into the hallway, which is swarming with skaters, posers, stoners, brains, and jocks. Everybody's got someone to be and a group of people to be it with, but sometimes I'm not in the mood for it, you know. Sometimes it all feels foreign and phony. Like a big waste.

The difference is today I'm just glad I've got somewhere to be and I look over at Nathan, ex-jock and present everything, and say, "You want to watch the game at my house on Saturday?" The Leafs are playing the Boston Bruins and Nathan still watches the games. You can be an ex-hockey player, but I don't know if it's possible to be an ex-fan.

"You asking Keelor too?" He stops in the middle of the hallway.

Like I said before, Nathan always knows. "Like old times," I tell him. Not that I think it'll change anything between the three of us, but I guess I need it—even if it's just for a few hours.

"Sounds good, but I'm still grounded," Nathan says, arching his eyebrows. "Why don't you guys come by my place instead? Sound cool?"

It could be. I could even be looking forward to it except that it's a day closer to Monday and there's not a person in the world who can help me pull that day off.

Mom drives me over to Sports 2 Go on Saturday morning. My driving test is nine days away, but I'm exhausted. I slept for seven hours, but I could climb back in bed and do another seven no problem. A coma's exactly what I need right now, but what I have is Mom in the driver's seat, telling me that we'll have a lot more money if she gets this job. She's so psyched about the thing that we get to the mall in record time. I'm worried that she might spontaneously combust before Monday if she doesn't calm down.

My manager, Brian, is kicking around the store when I get there. A rack of fifty-percent-off outerwear that nobody wants has been shoved to the back of the store; otherwise there's no sign of the post-Christmas-sale madness. Grayson hovers around the whole morning, describing his weekend in elaborate detail. Personally, I have trouble believing that anyone who shoots off his mouth that much gets laid more than twice a year, but I stop just short of telling him that he's full of shit.

Sometime after two Grayson sidles back up to me and points, as discreetly as a guy like Grayson can, towards a girl strolling through the door. "The tall ones are the hottest," he says definitively. He bites his lip and groans.

I turn and take a long look. This isn't something new from Grayson, but sometimes he happens to be right. Turns out this is one of those times. Keelor's cousin Jillian is gliding towards us, wearing three-inch-tall shoes and black pants slung just below her waist and smiling right at me.

"Blond too," Grayson says. "You think it's natural?"

I think I came close to finding out. I smile back at her and start walking. We meet in the middle of the store, where I feel Grayson burning a hole in the back of my T-shirt.

"My uncle's driving me back tomorrow," she says. "Owen said you worked here so . . ." She shrugs like it's not a big deal. "I had some stuff to pick up and I thought I could say goodbye at the same time."

"It's good to see you," I tell her. Maybe it's not a big deal, but it's something. She has to be four inches taller than me in those shoes. I feel like a dwarf or a ten-year-old kid staring up at her and I just have to ask, "How tall are you anyway?"

"People always ask that," Jillian says with a laugh.

"And what do you tell them?"

"Five eleven and a half," she tells me, standing even straighter. "Without the shoes."

"It looks good." My stomach dips as soon as I say that. I shouldn't be this glad to see her.

"Yeah, you too." She grazes my shoulder and studies my face. "Your eyes kill me." She says it like she's fooling around. I am a midget, after all. I'm also bad news.

"Uh-huh," I say doubtfully. I toss a glance at Grayson and motion to the door. He's recovered enough to nod back and I tell Jillian I can take a quick break.

We take a seat by the fountain and she says, "So how are you? Did you see your girlfriend?"

"Yeah, I did. She's doing okay."

"I'm glad." The look on Jillian's face makes it clear she really means it. "You were pretty worried."

The word doesn't begin to cover it. I explain about breaking the news to my mom and my upcoming trip to Toronto to spend a few days with my dad.

"It sounds like you're working some stuff out," she says.

"I guess." I nudge her arm. "What about you? How's your mom doing?"

"I'm okay." Jillian nods and stretches her legs out in front of her. "I talked to her yesterday and she sounded all right, but it's not like it's ever really over, you know?" She shifts her attention to the water falling behind us. "I don't know if it's something I can trust in the long run."

"I guess no one ever knows that about anything."

"I guess." Jillian's lips spring into a smile. "How come every time we get together it turns deep?"

"Maybe we're just deep people." I smile back. "So are you gonna give me your IM or what?"

"Seriously?"

"Yeah, why not?" Unless I'm so much bad news that she'd never consider typing two words to me. "You can let me know how it's going back in Windsor."

Jillian tells me her IM address, but my brain is crawling along on half power and I know I'll never remember it. I jog into Sports 2 Go for a pen and piece of scrap paper and jot down my IM and e-mail addresses. Back at the fountain, I watch Jillian print out hers. She tears the paper in half and hands me the bottom part.

"Sorry I laid that stuff on you the other day," I say, sliding the paper into my pocket. "I've been pretty messed up lately."

"Don't worry about it. It was a mutual thing." Jillian hunches over, smiles, and folds her arms across her knees. "You see—deep."

"Well, the casual sex thing didn't work out," I tease.

"Hey." She rolls her eyes, but she's still smiling. "Reality check. I was never going to have sex with you." She sits up straight and glances over at Sports 2 Go. "Anyway, I guess I should let you get back to work."

We stand up together and I tell her I'll IM her next week. It sounds like a line, but I mean it. I hardly know her, but I'd like to find out more and IM is about my speed right now. With some distance between us maybe we can actually be friends. It's a nice thought and I'm standing there wondering if it's okay to hug her goodbye again when she leans down and kisses me fast on the lips.

"You'll be okay," she says.

She turns and I watch her stride off—all six feet plus of her, blond ringlets trailing down her back over her T-shirt. It's weird, she doesn't remind me of Kate Hudson anymore. The fact is, up close the only thing they have in common is blond good looks. Jillian is definitely the kind of girl all the guys chase, even though she doesn't act like it, but I'm better off out of the running. Everything's okay with us and I mean to keep it that way.

I walk back into Sports 2 Go and Grayson cuts me off at the new cargo pants display. "She your girl?" he asks, voice bursting with approval.

"She's just a friend."

"Now that," he says, earnestly shaking his head, "is a shameful waste."

Depends on how you look at it, but I don't drop an explanation on Grayson.

Nathan picks me up at the end of my shift. Keelor's already in the car and it's such a flashback to be in the car with the two of them that I shiver under my skin as I climb into the backseat. We swing by Taco Bell on the way over to Nathan's and pick up burritos, nachos, and quesadillas—your basic heartburn combo. The only thing missing is cold beer and the more the three of us talk about that the worse the craving gets. By the time we get to Nathan's house, we sound like your standard beer commercial and Nathan's dad actually smiles as the three of us charge through the front door.

"Unbelievable," Nathan whispers as we park ourselves in the living room. "We've barely said three words to each other since New Year's, but give him a whiff of testosterone and bingo, instant Mr. Congeniality."

"Is he watching the game with us?" Keelor asks.

"Without a doubt," Nathan says. "You think I could keep him away? It's probably the only reason he let you guys come over."

Sure enough, Nathan's dad joins us in the living room at game time. He looks more relaxed than I've seen him in months, like a man who has a handle on things. Familiar territory can do that to a person. I should know. I'm so glad to be sitting there with Nathan and Keelor that I don't even mind about Nathan's dad crashing the game.

It's an absolutely spectacular game too. The Leafs have four players out with injuries, but they battle hard. Chiaramonte gets off to a slow start, pissing himself off so much with his uninspired performance that he smashes his stick against the boards in disgust. That earns him an unsportsmanlike conduct penalty, but well-directed anger can work wonders and once he's back on the ice, he pulls himself together and scores two quick goals. Shane Vanderbreggen drives the puck into the Boston net too. Suddenly they're an unstoppable force out there. Lightning on ice. It's awesome to watch and when Leafs goalie Mulcahy finally lets one in during the third period, they hit back with another goal straightaway.

In the end they level the Bruins 5–2 and I soak up the victory and feel Keelor and Nathan soaking it up next to me. We've lived moments like this one so many times before, but it still seems fresh. The weirdest thing is that Nathan's dad is probably the only person in the room that gets exactly how I'm feeling right now. Nathan and Keelor, they've already let go.

Things are what they are, I guess, and these guys are my best friends, no matter what they think of each other. Together they actually manage to make me stop thinking about everything for most of the night.

twenty-two

SUNDAY IS HARD and slow. I do homework and think about Monday. Sasha will be at school every day from now on to remind me. It's like a sick joke. *Look at what you lost. Look at what you did. Now go to English and listen to Mr. Diebel rag on everyone who doesn't have a PhD understanding of* The Old Man and the Sea.

Mom, agonizing over her Monday morning interview, is nearly as tense as I am and Holland points out that we're both acting so whacked that she may have to become a teen runaway. I think she'd run about as far as Diego's house, but that's another story and her business (as she repeatedly reminds me).

By that night I'm wound up so tight that I have to finish *The Old Man and the Sea* twice because the words don't stick. I fall asleep with my earphones on sometime after two and wake up at three minutes after six. It's way early, but I'm wide awake so I start getting ready. Real slow. Like everything has to be perfect. I wipe the salt stains off my shoes and spend twenty minutes in the shower. Mom's up early too and we have toast and orange juice in the kitchen together. Her interview isn't until ten-thirty and she offers Holland and me a ride to school.

It's snowing heavy and the roads are slippery so everyone's late. I stand at my locker, my body jumping under my skin like something's about to happen. I figure I'll wait—get it over with first thing—but nothing happens. Kids are taking advantage of the weather and loitering in the hallway and I go upstairs and check out Sasha's locker. She's not there and I don't know what class she has first period. I go back to my locker and grab my physics textbook. My eyes are ready for anything and I glance at everyone I pass as I head for class. I can't do this and I can't not. There's no choice, just me blinking away like a freak and waiting.

That's my morning and Sasha must have a different period for lunch because I don't see her, Lindsay, or Yasmin in the cafeteria. Or maybe she's avoiding me, even though we said we wouldn't do that. There's no way to know, but my throat swells up like that's the answer and I almost bail early, but Keelor pulls me into the conversation and keeps me there until the bell rings.

I have Visual Arts next and part of me relaxes, despite everything. The radio, Ms. Navarro, and Nathan—it's the atmosphere I need right now and I'm swinging through the hall trying to keep that in my head when I see Sasha. Lindsay and Yasmin are standing on either side of her, making her invincible, and I stop and stare. Sasha hasn't seen me yet; her head's bent and Yasmin's whispering something into her ear. Suddenly her head whips up and her dark eyes meet mine straight on. The hair on the back of my neck stands up. My stomach somersaults. I'm terrified of this girl with the tiny hands and all the feelings underneath that surge to the surface too—in a race to see which of them is strongest.

Sasha bends her head and says something I can't hear. Yasmin and Lindsay march past me and Sasha stops directly in front of me. "Hi," she says soberly. "How are you?"

"Okay," I lie, then shake my head, giving myself away. "I don't know." Five skater guys are sauntering up the hall towards us with their boards in their hands and Sasha grabs my sleeve and guides me over to the row of lockers lining the hall. "What about you?" I ask. "You look good." Actually, I'm too freaked to judge, but as soon as I say it, I take a closer look and find it's true. Her hair's shining, she's wearing mascara, and she smells like vanilla. You'd never know anything happened to her.

"I'm all right." She's speaking so quietly that I have to lower my head to hear her. "Better than when you saw me last week. It's just weird to be back."

"I know." It's weird to have her standing next to me, looking like her old self. I have no idea how we're going to do this and I look into her eyes and say, "I'm glad you're back." I lean against the locker, trapping the pain behind my eyes. "I thought maybe you were gonna avoid me."

"No," she says. "I was never going to do that."

"It happened before," I remind her.

"We both did that before." She clears her voice and blinks up at me. "Anyway, I'm not, but I should get to chemistry."

"Yeah, I should get to art, but . . ." I reach out and squeeze her arm. "Welcome back." *How can that be it? What's left for tomorrow?* But it's too much to ask and maybe she doesn't know any better than I do. All I can do is take it day by day like my dad said. It seems impossible, but there's nothing else.

"Thanks," she says. Her eyes are still on mine and she takes a step closer and folds her arms tight around me. It's the thing I miss most and I throw my arms around her and breathe into her hair. Almost everything about it feels right, but it hurts at the same time and then I know Sasha's right—it could never work between us now, we'd just remind each other of everything that happened and everything that didn't. Things are what they are and I hold on to her and let the feelings rip into me, every last one of them.

I have no idea what will happen tomorrow, but it won't be this and that keeps me holding on longer. She's waiting for me to stop. I know it the same way I know everything about her. And so I let go and watch her take a step back. She looks the way I feel. Maybe we won't be able to talk much for a while, but I hope I'm wrong about that.

"I'll see you later, Nick," she says, her eyes trained on mine.

"See you," I say.

She walks away and I stand hunched over with one shoulder against the locker and my arms knotted in front of me. I need to catch my breath and I'm trying, sucking oxygen deep into my lungs and watching people hurry past, when someone thumps me on the back. It's Nathan, announcing that we're already late for class. I pry myself away from the locker and follow him into the crowd.

acknowledgments

Eternal thanks to my tireless first reader and sounding board, my husband, Paddy, for his unwavering faith.

Over the last few years I've spent numerous hours on Verla Kay's Blue Board and am grateful to Verla and my fellow Blue Boarders for creating such a wonderfully supportive and informative online writing community.

Special thanks to my agent, Stephanie Thwaites, for believing in this book with me and steering the ship.

Many thanks also to Kirsten Wolf, who secured the perfect home for my novel.

My editor Shana Corey's painstaking work has shaped *I Know It's Over* into the kind of book I always hoped it would be—I can't thank her enough.

Finally, thanks to my brother, Casey, for sharing his knowledge of Canada's favorite sport.

C. K. KELLY MARTIN lives in the Greater Toronto area with her husband. This is her first novel. You can visit her Web site and blog at www.ckkellymartin.com.